"Devon? Is t

The question was barely more than a whisper. "Is it really you?"

He closed his eyes for a moment against the stirring of desire deep inside him caused, as always, by the sound of her voice. She was sitting on the floor, her back to the wall. She held a sleeping child in her arms—a little girl. A boy, tall and sturdy, lay beside her, his arms wrapped around her waist.

He reached out and pulled aside the musty blanket that covered her. "It's me, Kath."

She looked up at him with eyes the same shade of blue as an autumn sky, the sky of his dreams. And he saw tears. Kathleen, *his* Kathleen, never cried.

"You shouldn't be here, Devon," she said. "It's too dangerous."

"I came to take you home to Tyler, Kath."

"I'm not leaving without the children." Her voice was low and steady, filled with urgency and absolute commitment. This was the Kathleen he knew—stubborn, combative, honest to a fault. Reaching out to touch his cheek, she gave him a fleeting caress that was over in a heartbeat and whispered, "Go without me."

Marisa Carroll is acknowledged as the author of this work.

ISBN 0-373-82560-9

MISSION: CHILDREN

Copyright © 1996 by Harlequin Books S.A.

MARISA CARROLL

Mission: Children

It was like living in a movie, but
would there be a happy ending?

Harlequin Books

TORONTO • NEW YORK • LONDON
AMSTERDAM • PARIS • SYDNEY • HAMBURG
STOCKHOLM • ATHENS • TOKYO • MILAN
MADRID • WARSAW • BUDAPEST • AUCKLAND

WELCOME TO A
HOMETOWN REUNION

Twelve books set in Tyler.
Twelve unique stories. Together they form a
colorful patchwork of triumphs and trials—
the fabric of America's favorite hometown.

Around the quilting circle...

"It's so romantic. Like something out of a novel," Tessie Finkelbaum pronounced as she surveyed the white-on-white bridal quilt that Martha Bauer had chosen for her granddaughter Kathleen Kelsey Addison's wedding gift. The quilting circle had been working on the intricate medallion pattern for two weeks and it was almost done.

"Imagine Kathleen going off all by herself to rescue that little boy and girl," Annabelle Scanlon chimed in. "Then coming back from that awful place married. And to Devon Addison of all people!" Annabelle was in high gear this snowy afternoon.

Bea Ferguson had to get her two cents' worth in. "It must have been love at first sight," she said with a sigh.

Martha Bauer didn't say anything, just settled her spectacles on her nose before picking up a spool of white thread and threading her needle. She wished her granddaughter every happiness. Each and every stitch in the elaborate quilt was evidence of how much she cared, but she was worried all the same. She really didn't see how the marriage stood a chance. Not when Kathleen had married a man for the sake of another woman's children, out of duty, not love.... But she surely wasn't going to say so in front of this bunch of old gossips.

CHAPTER ONE

THUNDER RUMBLED in the distance. Kathleen Kelsey shifted restlessly on the hard, straight-backed chair, trying to get comfortable. She'd been dreaming again. Dreaming of home, of family and of Tyler. She rubbed the back of her neck, attempting to ease the tension that tightened her nerves and sent shards of pain through her arms and shoulders.

Home. It seemed so very far away. It was autumn now. In Tyler apples would be ripening on the trees. Farmers would be busy in the fields and kids would be playing football in the vacant lot near her parents' house. There would be bonfires and hayrides, and trick-or-treating up and down the oak-lined streets of the small Wisconsin town where she'd been born and raised. The days would be short and golden, the nights long and frosty.

But here in the village of Triglav, in what had once been Yugoslavia, there were no hayrides or trick-or-treaters or long Sunday afternoon walks through the fallen leaves. Here there was war and terror and death, and people forced underground to live their lives like moles.

And she, Kathleen Anna Theresa Kelsey, was right in the middle of it.

When was the last time she'd sat in the sun or eaten a tree-ripened apple? Or eaten anything at all that was fresh and good and not from a can hastily heated over a camp stove? Almost too long to remember. She glanced toward the window of the room where she kept her vigil, to find it piled high with sandbags, curtains drawn against the night. Fragile protection from the death and destruction outside, which roamed at will.

Thunder roared again and Kathleen stifled a cry. She'd never been afraid of thunder in her life, but in the past three weeks her life had changed. Changed so radically she knew it would never be the same again. For the thunder that shattered the October night wasn't really thunder at all, it was the sound of mortar fire coming from the hills above the town.

Kathleen froze, listening to the eerie whine of a projectile that passed overhead, shuddered as the impact of its explosion rattled the walls and sent the burned-out light bulb above her head swinging on its naked wire.

"That one was close."

Kathleen stood, stretching tired muscles. She moved to the high bed in the center of the room, peering down at its occupant in the feeble glow of the single candle on the bedside stand. "I didn't think you were awake."

"Only the dead can sleep through this. And I am not yet dead."

Kathleen bit her lip, then made herself smile as she leaned closer to the pale, wasted figure on the bed. "Are you in pain?"

"I am all right." The deeply etched lines that bracketed Rujana Drakulic's mouth and furrowed her high forehead told a different story, but Kathleen didn't contradict her. It wouldn't do any good. There was no medicine to give her friend, no morphine or even aspirin to ease the pain of her wounds.

"Would you like some water?" Another mortar shell, this one outgoing, passed overhead. It was a response from the guns of the defenders of the beleaguered village, and the roar of it nearly drowned out her words. Kathleen tensed for a moment, then tried to relax. "It's fresh. I brought it up myself an hour ago when I went to check on the children."

"Yes, water. Please." Rujana tried to lift her head but she was too weak. Kathleen slipped her hand behind the hard, thin pillow and propped up her friend's skeletal shoulders. Rujana drank thirstily, then lay back, exhausted by the effort. It took her a long time to catch her breath. She was growing weaker by the hour.

Her friend was dying and there was nothing she could do about it. Kathleen fought back tears and a wave of panic so intense it threatened to buckle her knees. *What would become of the children when Rujana died?*

"How are the children? Are they sleeping?" Rujana asked when she could speak again. It was as if she had read Kathleen's mind.

Kathleen fought down her panic, forced it from her thoughts and her voice. "They're sound asleep. I left them with Ana."

Ana was an old woman, or perhaps not so old as she was worn-out with suffering and war. She had lost her husband and son and daughter-in-law in the shelling in Sarajevo years before and had come home to Triglav, the place where she was born. Like Kathleen, and Rujana's children, Andrej and Marta, Ana had taken shelter in the basement of the hospital, the largest, strongest building in town.

"Is it very late?" Rujana asked in a small voice. "I would like to see them. Andrej must practice his English. I would like to listen to him read." Rujana's hand moved restlessly on the sheet. Kathleen covered the thin fingers with her own.

She avoided looking at the window again. The cubicle she shared with the children was in the basement. Sometimes the temptation to pull the sandbags away from Rujana's second-floor window and stare out at the sunshine or the moonlight, no matter the consequences, was almost too great to resist. "Andrej is asleep. It's very late. In a few hours it will be dawn."

Rujana turned her head to the window, and Kathleen knew they once more shared the same thought. "What day is this?" The English words came slowly, haltingly.

"Tuesday," Kathleen told her.

"Market day." Rujana's voice was barely more than a whisper. "I always loved market day. Remember when you came to visit that first year that Josef and I were married, and I was carrying Andrej in my belly?"

"Yes," Kathleen said, pulling her chair close to the side of the bed. Rujana spoke more and more of the past as she grew weaker, closer to death. "I remember that year. We went skiing in the mountains and sailing on the Adriatic. It was my first trip to Yugoslavia, and I thought it was the most beautiful country I had ever seen."

She had been studying in Paris on a scholarship when she first met Rujana and Josef Drakulic. They were students also, newly married and expecting their first child. It had been a happy year for Kathleen. A year of seeing new and wonderful places, meeting new and interesting people. She had never dreamed then that her facility with languages and her familiarity with European customs and life-styles would eventually lead to a job as Edward Wocheck's assistant at DEVCHECK. Then it had only seemed like the once-in-a-lifetime chance to live and study in Paris for a girl from small-town Wisconsin. It had also been the beginning of a friendship with Rujana and Josef that neither distance nor war could come between.

Certainly war had been the last thing on their minds that long-ago summer. Yugoslavia had been basking in the glory of having recently hosted the Olympics. The economy was good, the borders open for its citizens to travel to Vienna and Trieste to buy jeans and boom boxes and television sets. Now it was a shambles, a battleground where neighbor fought neighbor and no one seemed to know how to make the killing stop.

"Do you remember when you and Devon came to visit us in Paris?" Rujana spoke as though once more reading her thoughts. Kathleen reached up to smooth a strand of hair from her friend's forehead.

"It seems so long ago." She had been working for Edward Wocheck for only six months when she made that second fateful visit to Paris. The travel and the rarified atmosphere of DEVCHECK's corporate headquarters had still been new and exciting. As had been her whirlwind love affair with Edward's stepson, Devon Addison. But the darkness of civil war had fallen over Central Europe, and Josef and Rujana, who were expecting their second child, had already been exiled from the country they loved so well. That summer in Paris they had tried to cover their unhappiness with laughter and the company of good friends, but the sadness they felt, and that Kathleen felt for them, was always with them, below the surface, ignored but never forgotten.

"They were good times." Kathleen smiled as she remembered the evenings she and Devon had spent in her friends' apartment, arguing over such diverse subjects as the relative merits of Japanese and American cars, and the philosophical implications of the *Star Trek* transporter beam. And when her guard was down and she couldn't shield her thoughts, Kathleen also remembered the sultry Paris nights she had spent in Devon's arms.

"Good times," Rujana echoed. "But they seem so far away now. So long ago."

Only four years. But so much had changed since those days, and none of it for the good. Kathleen had realized very shortly after those enchanted summer evenings that Devon Addison, the Prince Charming of every girl's dreams, was really just an ordinary man with feet of clay, with a life-style and a value system far removed from her own. So she had returned to Tyler without him. By Christmas she had convinced herself she was over him and, thankfully, with no one the wiser.

There was life after Devon Addison, and she intended to live it to the fullest. It was awkward at first, running into him at Timberlake Lodge and at Addison Hotel's corporate offices in London, but she had made herself treat him as no more than a friend and co-worker who just happened to be her boss's stepson. And Devon, to give him credit, was enough of a gentleman not to step over the line she'd drawn.

While Kathleen learned the ins and outs of Edward Wocheck's financial empire and mended her bruised and battered heart, the sporadic fighting in Yugoslavia erupted into full-blown war. By Christmas of the next year Rujana's husband, Josef, with the laughing eyes and ready smile, was dead. Now unbelievably, horribly, as the war went on and on, Rujana was dying, too, and there was no one left alive to care for her children.

No one but Kathleen.

A nurse appeared in the doorway, carrying a tray with another lighted candle. The hospital had a generator, but electricity was used only in the operating suite and the emergency room. The rest of the building was in darkness day and night, with only candlelight for the exhausted staff to work by.

"I have medication," the nurse said in French. Kathleen did not speak the local Slavic dialect, but most of the nurses and doctors spoke at least some English, or French or German.

"For the pain? What is it?" Kathleen was skeptical, and she was afraid it came through in her voice. To treat their patients, the medical staff at the hospital had been forced to resort to unconventional remedies and folk medicines, the efficacy of which was often in doubt.

"Morphine," the nurse whispered.

Kathleen breathed a sigh of relief. "Good. But how?"

"A shipment just came in, thank God," the nurse explained. "It will last for a few days, perhaps a little more." She was a young woman, but her eyes were old. She was haggard looking from overwork and loss of sleep, but her smile was beautiful and reassuring as she bent toward Rujana and spoke in hushed tones in her native tongue. "She will sleep now," she said once more in French as she straightened after giving the injection.

"Thank you," Kathleen said. "Was it a United Nations convoy that brought the medications?" Perhaps she could get to the commander, beg his help in finding a way to transport the children to safety.

The nurse shook her head, her hand on Rujana's wrist, monitoring her pulse. "No. It was a private shipment. I do not know how they got through, with the shelling so strong." Two more shells had passed overhead as they spoke, but the targets tonight seemed to be on the other side of town, and they paid them little attention. It was unbelievable the things that one got used to living in a war zone. The hospital so far had been off-limits, but Kathleen wondered how long that fragile truce would remain in effect.

"Will you stay with her until she falls asleep?" the nurse asked. "I have other injections to give."

"Yes." Kathleen nodded. "I'll stay."

"Good. I will check back as soon as I can." She patted Rujana's hand once more and left the room as quietly as she had entered.

"Kathleen?" Her friend's voice was a mere thread of sound.

"Yes, Ru."

"Are you still here?"

"I'm here." She squeezed the thin fingers gently between her own.

"Where did the morphine come from? Was it the U.N.? Was it the Red Cross?"

"I don't know," Kathleen murmured soothingly. "I'll find out as soon as you fall asleep."

"Yes." Rujana's breathing slowed, grew even more shallow. "See if you can learn who has come. Maybe . . . maybe this time we can get the children out."

"Yes, Ru." Kathleen wiped a damp cloth across her friend's forehead. "Maybe this time." Rujana's eyes were closed. Kathleen was glad her friend couldn't see her face. If what the nurse said was true, and it was not the United Nations that had broken through to bring the medical supplies, there was no way, no safe way, to get the children out of Triglav, away from the killing. Kathleen had tried. Lord, how she had tried.

When she first arrived in the village at the end of September, there had still been telephone service to the outside world. She had spent hour after frustrating hour attempting to get medical help for her friend and to find someone, anyone, who could assist her in getting travel papers for Rujana and her children.

She had met with dead ends and bureaucratic foot-dragging everywhere she turned. Ten days later, exhausted and desperate she had even attempted to call Devon Addison's mother, Lady Holmes, in London and beg for her help, only to be told her ladyship was vacationing on the Hawaiian island of Kauai, and that her staff did not know where to reach Mr. Devon at that moment. Two days later a new government offensive began and all phone service to the beleaguered village had been cut off. Kathleen had never heard from Nicole Holmes, or anyone else. She had been on her own ever since, and she had never felt so helpless in her life.

"I'm tired," Rujana whispered. She had been silent so long Kathleen had thought she'd fallen asleep, lulled into unconsciousness by the drug's hypnotic power.

"Shh, you need to rest."

Rujana's head moved on the pillow. "I'm afraid if I sleep I will not wake, and I cannot die until I know you and my children are safe."

Kathleen's throat tightened and she blinked away her tears. "Sleep, Ru," she whispered. "Sleep. I promise you I'll keep them safe."

DEVON ADDISON was beginning to wonder if he'd descended into the bowels of hell. All around him men in dirty khaki uniforms sat slumped with their backs against the wall, their heads cradled on bent knees, or else lay curled in the fetal position, so tired or so ill that they seemed oblivious to the noise and confusion. It was dark and cold and the building smelled of blood and fear, too little disinfectant and too many unwashed bodies.

Although Devon was dead tired and nearly falling asleep on his feet, he kept walking, following the woman with the lantern, who was lighting the way. She was a Polish nun, her lined face ageless within the frame of her white coif. She spoke some French, enough for him to make himself understood, and she was taking him to Kathleen.

He watched the wavering shadows made by the nun's skirts as she wove her way among the recumbent bodies, stopping to touch a forehead here, give a reassuring word there. Their progress was slow, and he grew more anxious by the minute. The last flight of stairs they'd descended had taken them into the basement. Devon's stomach clenched and the short hairs at the base of his skull stood on end. This place was a tomb, a death trap, and Kathleen had been living here for almost three weeks. The Triglav village hospital was neither large nor well-built. It would take only one accurately placed mortar round to bring it down around their ears. Devon had to find Kathleen and get her out of here, get her back across the border to safety.

"Here, monsieur," the nun announced, stopping in the doorway of a large open area that might once have been a cafeteria or a small auditorium. Cubicles had been formed around the room by blankets hanging from wires strung across the low ceiling. She pointed to one on the left wall. "The American woman is over there."

"Thank you, Sister."

She nodded. "I must go now. The fighting is heavy tonight. There are many new casualties to be treated."

"Sister, if there's anything I can do..." He wasn't certain what that would be. His medical skills consisted of what he could remember of a Red Cross first-aid course he'd taken in college, and not much more.

She smiled and shook her head. "You have done enough already, *monsieur*. God be with you."

"Thank you, for everything, Sister."

The open space at the center of the cubicles was lit by a kerosene lamp. A camp stove was set up on the table beside it. The smell of cooked cabbage and lamp oil temporarily overpowered the other smells swirling around him. He pulled a flashlight from the pocket of his jacket and walked toward the cubicle the nun had indicated was Kathleen's.

"Kath?" He could hear the restless sounds of people sleeping on either side. There was nothing solid to knock on, no way to announce his presence other than to pull back the blanket and walk in. He reached out his hand, then hesitated. They had parted in anger in London three weeks before, when she had told him of her plans to come to Triglav and he'd tried to talk her out of making the trip until he could assess the situation. He wasn't certain what his welcome would be. "Kathleen?" He raised his voice slightly.

"Devon? Is that you?" The question was barely more than a whisper. "Is it really you?"

He closed his eyes for a moment against the stirring of desire deep inside him that the sound of her low, slightly husky voice always produced. But he ignored the longing, as he'd learned to do long ago, letting nothing of what he was feeling show on his face as he reached out and pulled the musty-smelling blanket aside. "It's me, Kath."

"Oh God, Devon. How did you get here?"

The only illumination in the small cubicle came from a guttering candle in a holder on the wall. Its light was minimal, the effect of the small, enclosed space and the dark shadows disturbingly claustrophobic. Kathleen was sitting on the floor, her back to the wall, just like the exhausted men in the corridor. He could barely see her face, but he heard the catch in her voice, caught the sudden gleam of tears in her eyes. Kathleen, his Kathleen, never cried. Devon stepped through the blanket curtain and hunkered down in front of her. "Kath, are you all right?"

She held a sleeping child in her arms—a little girl who he knew from photographs had red-gold hair and Rujana's nose and stubborn chin. *Marta.* She had been an infant when he'd seen her last. A boy, tall and sturdy, lay beside her, his head cradled on a pillow, his arm wrapped around Kathleen's waist. *Andrej,* his father's pride and joy. The boy had been little more than a toddler the summer Devon had spent time with the family, but he remembered very clearly how much Josef Drakulic had loved his son, and the dreams he'd dreamed for his future.

"I'm fine." She spoke softly to keep from waking the children, but her breathing had quickened and a thread of hope and excitement wove through her voice. "Did you come with the convoy that brought the drugs and medicines?"

"I don't know of any convoy."

"Oh." She made no attempt to hide her disappointment at the news. "I had hoped . . . Then how did you get here?"

"I walked. At least I walked the last fifteen miles. They wouldn't let me bring the car any closer." It had taken two nights of hiking over rough terrain, hiding in bushes and abandoned and burned-out buildings during the day to avoid government patrols, but he kept those facts to himself.

Marta whimpered in her sleep and snuggled into Kathleen's shoulder. Kathleen stroked her hand over the little girl's hair, bent her head and crooned softly under her breath. Devon had a sudden, almost overpowering urge to reach out and run his fingers through the dark silk of her hair, assuring himself that she was real and unharmed. But he stayed very quiet, the blanket settling back behind him, wrapping them in deeper shadows and an illusion of privacy. Kathleen raised her eyes, eyes the same shade of blue as an autumn twilight sky, the stuff of dreams, his dreams. "You shouldn't be here, Devon. It's too dangerous."

"I came to take you home, Kath," he said quietly.

CHAPTER TWO

HER HEAD CAME UP and a spark of dark fire gleamed in her sapphire eyes. "I'm not leaving, Devon. Not while Rujana is still living. Not without the children."

"Kathleen, you can't stay here." He kept his voice low and steady for fear of waking the little ones. Except for recently in London, he hadn't argued with Kathleen Kelsey for a long time. They were "just friends" now; they never discussed anything more important than the weather or football scores. That was the way she wanted it. And because his instinct for self-preservation was deep-rooted and strong, so did he.

"I won't leave without Rujana and the children." Kathleen's voice, too, was low and steady, but filled with urgency, with absolute commitment. "But you have to go now. The same way you came. I won't be responsible for what might happen to you if you stay."

If he hadn't been so damned tired and so damned scared he would have smiled. This was the Kathleen he knew—stubborn, combative, honest to a fault. "Quit playing mother hen. I can take care of myself, Kath."

She smiled, too, just a little, but she blinked back tears. "Oh Devon, your mother will kill me when she finds out you came after us."

They didn't have time to discuss his mother. "The government is launching a new offensive. I have a friend at the embassy in Vienna. They're monitoring the situation."

Devon paused to let the words sink in. "There isn't much time left, Kath. If we don't leave soon we'll all be trapped."

"Then go. I didn't ask you to come." She listened to herself say the words and shook her head. She reached out to touch his cheek, a fleeting caress that was over in a heartbeat. "I'm sorry, Devon. I didn't mean that. I don't know why I said it. I'm glad you're here, truly I am."

"It's all right, Kath. I know you didn't mean it."

"All the same, it's true. You shouldn't have come. If something happens to you, your mother will never forgive me."

"I'll handle my mother. The important thing now is getting all of us out of this death trap."

"Not Rujana." Once more Kathleen's blue eyes filled with unshed tears. "She's dying, Devon," she whispered, as though fearing the sleeping children might overhear.

"I know. Sister Marie told me." This time he was the one to offer the comfort of his touch, smoothing back a flyaway curl of dark, silky hair from her cheek. She stiffened slightly, almost imperceptibly, at the fleeting contact, and he dropped his hand. "I came as quickly as I could. It took awhile to make the arrangements. And then at the last minute this damned new offensive threw all my plans into a cocked hat."

"I can't leave Rujana, Devon." Her voice broke. "Not yet. I can't. She has no one left and I won't let her die alone."

Devon was going to tell her she might have to do just that if there was to be any chance of leaving Triglav before the government troops began their final push, but just as he opened his mouth Andrej stirred and sat up, looking frightened.

The little boy rubbed his eyes and whispered something into Kathleen's ear. Devon didn't speak the local dialect, but it wasn't hard to decipher what Rujana's son was asking her. "I'm Devon Addison," he said in English. "I'm a friend of Kathleen's. And of your mother."

Andrej looked at Kathleen for guidance. She smiled and nodded. "Did you know my father?" he asked in English.

"Yes," Devon said. "I knew him."

"Are you here to take us to America?" He spoke with a definite Midwestern accent that he'd obviously picked up from Kathleen.

"Yes," he replied, carefully screening any doubt from his voice.

"My mother, too?"

Devon didn't have an answer for that one. He looked at Kathleen.

"Andrej, your mother is very ill," Kathleen said gently. "Too ill to travel."

"She is dying," Andrej whispered, tears sliding down his cheeks. "Just like my father."

"Shh, baby," Kathleen crooned, handing Devon the sleeping Marta so that she could gather Andrej into her arms. Devon took the little girl, holding her against his shoulder, awkwardly patting her back as he silently cursed the power-hungry men who had started this war, and the bloody arrogance that kept them fighting.

"I want to see my mama."

"Of course. We'll go right now. But she might be sleeping. The nurse gave her a shot to make the pain go away." Kathleen was silent momentarily, then she lifted her eyes to his face. "It was you, wasn't it? You brought the medicines."

"As much as I could carry. I wish it had been more."

What little color there was in her cheeks drained away. "Devon, do you know what they would have done to you if you'd been caught?"

"They didn't catch me." No use following that decidedly unattractive line of thought. He stood up, breaking eye contact. With his movement Marta stirred in her sleep, then opened her eyes—wide, frightened eyes, just as Andrej's had been. She stared at him, her thin, fragile body stiff with apprehension, but not a sound escaped her lips.

She was so small, almost weightless in his arms. His friends, Jeff and Cece Baron, had twin daughters about the same age, but Annie and Belle were tall, sturdy children with enough energy and imagination to drive most adults into exhaustion within half an hour.

"Hello, Marta," he whispered, wanting to allay the fear in her eyes, but not knowing how. "I'm Devon."

"She doesn't speak," Kathleen said, rising to her feet with Andrej still clinging to her waist. "She hasn't spoken a word since her mother was hurt."

"How did it happen?"

Kathleen smoothed Marta's tangled, red-gold curls from her cheeks. "Rujana was going to get water. She had to take the children with her because there was no one to watch them. A sniper started firing into the crowd. Rujana was hit in the lower back. She's been growing weaker ever since." She didn't want to say *she's been dying* in front of Andrej.

"If we got her out of here, to Paris or London? To specialists."

Kathleen closed her eyes. "I tried, Devon." Her voice was clogged with tears. "I tried, God help me, I tried. But it's too late."

"I know, Kath. I'm sorry I wasn't there when you called. I came as soon as I could." He wanted to reach out and pull her close, soothe her pain as she had soothed Andrej moments before, but his arms were full and he was all too aware she wouldn't appreciate the physical contact, not from him, not ever again.

"Mama," Andrej demanded, breaking the silence that had settled between them like the heavy blanket sealing the cubicle. "I want Mama."

"We'll go to her right now," Kathleen said, in control of her emotions once more. "Devon, will you come?"

"Of course. She's my friend, too, Kath."

"I'm sorry. It will give Rujana comfort to know you're here to help me with the children." She pulled the musty blanket aside and they stepped out into the relative openness of the communal area. "This way," Kathleen said, holding Andrej by the hand as she headed toward the stairs.

Marta had relaxed slightly in his arms, but she still stared at him like a solemn little owl. He smiled, and she laid her head on his shoulder, hiding her face, as they picked their way past the exhausted and sleeping soldiers lining the hallway.

It will give Rujana comfort to know you're here to help me with the children.

He didn't know what it was about those words that had hit him so hard. It was why he'd defied his mother and the entire board of Addison Hotels to come to Triglav, wasn't it? To get Kathleen and Rujana and her children to safety? But before he'd walked into that tiny cubicle, seen how worn and scared Kathleen was behind her brave mask, held this tiny, warm scrap of humanity in his arms, it hadn't been real. It had been just him against the bad guys. It hadn't been a matter of anyone's life or death but his own. Now it was real. Very, very real. But for the life of him he still didn't have a clue how he was going to get them out of this hellhole without getting them all killed.

THE NUN, SISTER MARIE, was outside Rujana's room. She saw them coming down the short, dark hallway and met them near the top of the stairs. Kathleen's stomach tightened. Something was wrong. There was too much light and movement inside Rujana's room.

"Sister, what is it?" she asked in her fluent but formal French.

"Rujana has taken a turn for the worse," the nun said quietly, smiling at the children to hide the sad news of what she had to tell. "There is very little time left. It is good you have brought the children to see her. Father Paul is with her. She has received the sacraments and she is ready to go forth to meet God and the saints."

Kathleen was Catholic, as were Rujana and the children, but she did not have Sister Marie's rock-solid faith; hers was not so strong and accepting. She wanted to scream and cry and beg God not to take her friend's life. She stood rooted to the spot, her hand wrapped so tightly around Andrej's fingers that he squirmed.

"Mama," he said, looking from Kathleen to the nun. "I want my mother."

"Come, child," Sister Marie said, switching to the local dialect. "Your mother is almost ready to go to heaven, but she wants to see you and say goodbye."

Andrej nodded silently and followed the nun into his mother's room.

"Oh God, Devon, I can't do this." Kathleen's voice broke.

"Yes, you can, Kath. You can do whatever you have to. You always have. You always will."

She turned to look at him. His dark gold hair was mussed and dulled with dust, and there were dark circles of exhaustion beneath his eyes, gray eyes the color of a rainy twilight, eyes so compelling that she used to find herself drowning in their fathomless depths. "Not watch my friend die. I'm not strong enough for that. I can't—"

He handed her Rujana's child. "Marta wants to see her mother," he said. For a moment she almost hated him, but then she realized that he knew her well enough to know that sympathy would only send her over the edge.

"Yes, m'lord."

"Kathleen."

She tried to smile. "I'm sorry, Devon. Bad timing. Bad joke." She had used to tease him about his aristocratic forebears. Then the teasing had stopped. When their idyllic time together in Paris ended and they returned to the real world, the differences in their background had become insurmountable. So she had broken off the affair. She had insisted they go their separate ways.

He owed her nothing, but he had risked his life to come to her—and the children. His fine-cut, aristocratic features were lost in shadow, but her eyes found his. "Thank you for coming, Devon. Thank you for being here when I needed you." She turned and walked into the room before he could respond.

Rujana was propped up in the bed—to help her breathe, Kathleen suspected. Her face was paper white, her lips gray from lack of oxygen. Andrej stood beside her bed, holding her hand, Sister Marie behind him. Father Paul, the parish priest, spoke English and greeted Kathleen softly in that language.

"It is only a matter of hours now," he said. "The nurse has made her comfortable and she is ready to go to God."

"I am not ready," Rujana said faintly. "But I have no choice. Marta, my sweetling. Let me hold her."

Kathleen set the silent child down on the bed. Rujana lifted her free hand. Marta snuggled against her. "Kathleen, you are my salvation," she said, fighting back tears. "Promise me you will take care of my children."

Kathleen leaned forward and kissed Rujana's cold cheek. "I already love them as if they were my own."

"You will take them to America with you?"

Kathleen glanced at Father Paul. "I'm trying, Rujana. But—"

"Rujana." The tall, lean priest bent low over the bed. "The government is nearly at a standstill. Most of the legislators have fled the country. It is very difficult to get anything done."

"There must be some way." Rujana's voice rose slightly. Sister Marie reached out and took Marta from her arms. Rujana clung to her child for a heartrending moment, then let her go, her desire to provide for her children's future overriding even the need to hold her baby one last time.

"I admit it might be possible if Kathleen were married. There are provisions for taking orphaned children out of the country, but only if they are going to be adopted. And only by a married couple. The republic does not allow for single-parent adoptions." He shrugged apologetically. "It is not done."

Rujana's eyes fixed on Devon. "God has sent you today, Devon, my friend," she said. Her voice was even weaker than it had been a few moments before. She fought for breath.

"What do you want me to do, Ru?" His voice was gentle, soothing. He stepped forward and took Rujana's hand. He was so close that Kathleen could feel the heat of his body, and she longed to lean into his strength and his warmth. But she held herself rigid beside the bed. If he touched her at all, made any move to comfort her, she would break down and sob her heart out, and she couldn't allow that to happen. Not in front of the children. Not while Rujana still lived, still held on to the hope that Kathleen could save her children.

"Marry Kathleen," Rujana said. Her voice was weak, but the words were clear.

The room began to spin in slow circles around Kathleen as the impact of her friend's words hit her brain, then her heart. *Marry Devon Addison?* At one time that would have made her a happy woman, but not anymore. Not for a long, long time.

The muscles in Devon's arm tightened, accenting tendons and muscles below the rolled-up sleeve of his shirt. "Rujana, I..." Kathleen could feel the words hit him just as hard as they had hit her.

"Marry her and take my children to America."

"No, Rujana." Kathleen spoke without conscious thought, a cry from the depths of her soul. "That's impossible. I can't marry Devon."

"You must." The dying woman was becoming very agitated. She pushed herself up from the pillows, reaching out with a clawlike hand to grasp Kathleen's wrist. "You must do this for me. You must do this for my children."

"I... don't love Devon," Kathleen said helplessly.

"No love? I remember—" A fit of coughing cut off her words, left her gasping for breath. Andrej was crying softly, clutching his mother's arm. Marta buried her face in Sister Marie's neck, her small body shaking.

"I can't marry Devon, Rujana..." Kathleen swallowed against the tightness in her throat, blinked back the sting of tears in her eyes.

"You must." The words were a gasp of pain, a plea for help. Rujana's sunken eyes bored into Kathleen's very soul. "You must."

"Just rest, Ru," she whispered, easing her friend back against the pillows. "We'll find a way to get the children away safely. We'll talk about this later, when you're stronger."

"Later I will be dead," she said flatly. "There is no other way. Marry Devon. Promise me, Kathleen. Promise me, Devon."

"Rujana, my daughter." The priest leaned forward, his hands on Andrej's shoulders. The little boy was watching his mother's face. He didn't seem to be taking in the conversation going on around him. "I cannot sanction this marriage—"

Rujana's voice held a note of desperation. "Kathleen is Catholic, Father. She will care for them, raise them in the faith. Please, Father, do this for my children's sake."

The priest's English seemed to be inadequate for what he wanted to say. He spread his hands, looking from one to the other of them.

"I..." Kathleen's mind was spinning. She couldn't seem to catch on to a coherent thought.

"I agree to the marriage if Kathleen does."

Kathleen spun around. Devon's face was a mask, his gray eyes, the color of thunderclouds in a summer sky, were shuttered, his thoughts impossible to read.

"Devon?"

"We have no choice, Kath," he said quietly, reasonably.

"I don't want to be married to you," she blurted out.

His lips twisted in a travesty of a smile. "I seem to remember you telling me that once before. Kath, I don't see any other way out of this mess. If Father Paul agrees to marry us we might be able to get exit visas for the kids. We can certainly get them into the States a lot easier if we have some kind of proof that we're their legal guardians." His gaze flickered to Rujana's pinched face and sunken eyes. "If you will agree, I'll marry you for the children's sake."

It made sense, but her heart was in turmoil. "Father?"

"What he says is true. I do not like this plan. But also for the children's sake I will do as Rujana asks." He held up his hand. "I do not know if the church will sanction such a union. But remember," he said sternly, "in the eyes of God you will be man and wife."

The next few minutes passed with the unreality of a dream. Later, whenever Kathleen tried to recall her marriage, she could remember nothing but the feel of Rujana's fingers, cold and fragile, around her wrist, and on the other side Devon's strong, warm hand enfolding hers.

Father Paul intoned the wedding vows, a familiar ritual, familiar words in an unfamiliar language that only added to the dreamlike quality of what was taking place. Kathleen responded when she heard her name, and Devon did likewise. The priest hesitated when he asked for the ring, and Devon lifted his hand to indicate that he had none. "I'm sorry, Kath," he said, bending his head to catch her eye. "I don't have a ring."

"It's all right." She didn't know what else to say. He squeezed her hand a little tighter, looking as confused and uncomprehending as she felt herself.

The priest shrugged and went on, speaking the final blessing. "You are now man and wife," Father Paul pronounced, making the sign of the cross. "May God smile on your union."

Kathleen smiled for Rujana's sake, and for Andrej, who was staring at her with big, dark eyes. But she couldn't look at Devon, her husband, and in her heart of hearts, she cried.

CHAPTER THREE

DEVON DROPPED to the balls of his feet and studied the face of the sleeping woman before him. His wife, Kathleen Anna Theresa Kelsey. No, now he supposed it was Kathleen Addison. A name he'd bet money she'd never use without putting up one hell of a fuss.

God, he was married to Kathleen. At least in the eyes of the parish priest, and by the consent of the government of the prefecture of Triglav. Devon doubted the marriage would be considered legal anywhere else on earth, as his mother would most certainly point out.

Married. Kathleen was his wife. At one point in his life, the idea had held a certain attraction. A home and family of his own. Children, lots of them, with Kathleen's sparkling blue eyes and dark curly hair. But that was a long time and a lot of hard feelings ago.

What did she think of this whole fantastic situation? he wondered. She was Catholic, and though she never made an issue of it, he knew her religion was important to her. How did she feel now that she was bound to him by the tenets of her faith and the laws of this tiny, beleaguered country? What did it feel like to find yourself married to a man you had once described as a better-educated, slicker-talking replica of his robber-baron ancestors?

Married. Man and wife. Did it make her blood race and her thoughts turn back to the heated passion of their long-finished romance? Did it turn her heart cold with de-

spair? Or did it just scare the hell out of her, the way it did him?

He reached out and touched her shoulder. "Kath, wake up," he said softly, then a bit more loudly when she didn't respond to his touch. He gave her a little shake. "Kath, it's time to go." He never called her Kathleen. Only when they were arguing—or when they were making love. He hadn't forgotten that, either—not one moment of the time they'd spent in bed together. Maybe if he could, he would have been able to get her out of his system a lot quicker than he had.

"What? Devon?" She blinked against the glow of candlelight and rubbed the back of her hand across her eyes like a little girl. "What time is it?" she asked, her voice more husky than usual, but pitched low so as not to disturb the children sleeping close by her side.

"It's almost midnight. We have to go."

She sat up, fully alert. "The papers. Do you have all the documents?"

"Father Paul brought them to me an hour ago."

"You should have wakened me then. We should have left right away." She rose to her knees. Her eyes, those glorious sapphire eyes, were nearly on a level with his own. She was a tall woman, only a few inches shorter than his six feet, thin but not skinny, with curves in all the right places. Breasts that just filled his hands, hips that were lush and . . . Thoughts like that were definitely off-limits.

Devon raised his hand, palm up. "We had to wait for the moon to rise, Kath. I don't know the countryside well enough to find my way back in the dark to where I hid the car."

"Oh...of course. You're right. I—I just want to get out of here."

She looked worn to the bone, the way he felt. It had been a rough thirty-six hours. Kathleen had been alone with Rujana when she died, only a few hours after she had witnessed their marriage, but he had been the one to accompany their friend's plain, wooden casket to the graveyard in the small hours of the morning, stumbling over tree roots and shattered headstones. Like everything else in Triglav these days, even the task of burying the dead must be carried out under the cover of darkness to avoid the snipers. He had been the only mourner to stand beside her grave in the moonlight and say goodbye, because it would have been too dangerous to expose the children to the journey through the rubble-filled streets.

Now he had no choice. The fighting was coming closer every hour. Father Paul had told him the short-wave radio reports indicated that government troops would probably have the town sealed off within twenty-four hours. They had to leave very soon or they might never get out.

"It's time to wake the children."

"Poor little things. They're exhausted."

"They'll bounce back once we get them to Vienna. Kids are tough."

Kathleen shook her head, stroking Marta's none-too-clean hair. "They have to be to survive what they've been through. Devon, did you get any sleep at all today?"

"A little," he lied. "While I was cooling my heels at the prefect's office."

"How much did it cost you to get the adoption papers?"

"Don't worry, Kath. I can afford it, remember?" He was too tired to filter all the old bitterness out of his voice.

"I'll pay you back."

"Don't bother, Kathleen."

She bit her lip but didn't respond. "You're sure they're all in order?" she asked instead. "We don't have a second chance to get them right."

He patted his jacket pocket. "They're all here. Everything we need. The children's birth certificates." He hesitated a moment to swallow a sudden lump of emotion that had lodged itself in his throat. "Rujana and Josef's death certificates. Our marriage license, and the adoption papers signed by the prefect himself."

Kathleen propped the tips of her fingers together in front of her lips, her eyes closed as she struggled to control her emotions. "Thank you, Devon. From the bottom of my heart." She leaned forward and gave him a kiss on the cheek. Devon drew back in surprise. It was the first time she'd kissed him in four years. Before he could respond, she dropped back to sit on her heels. "Now we can get the children out of Triglav. We can take them home."

"We're not out of the woods yet, Kath." He hadn't meant to sound so gruff.

She blinked and sobered instantly. "I know. But we'll make it now. I'm sure we will."

Half an hour later they were on their way. Father Paul had arranged for them to ride about half the distance to Devon's rented car in an ambulance evacuating wounded soldiers to a safe zone in the hills. They were packed into the vehicle like sardines, but Devon was still uncomfortably aware that he had taken the place of a fighting man who might die or be captured because he had relinquished his seat.

Kathleen had given Father Paul all the money she had left—small compensation for all he had done. It would buy drugs and food on the black market, if he could get the stuff through enemy lines. She and Devon carried nothing with them but Devon's lightweight nylon backpack containing the precious packet of documents, a few photographs, Rujana's grandmother's garnet necklace and a pocket watch that had come to Josef from his father's family. It was all that was left of the dreams of a long and happy life together that Rujana and Josef had cherished for themselves and their children.

There were still approximately five hours left before dawn when the ambulance pulled into the nominal cover provided by a grove of pines and let them off in the silvery darkness of a moon-bright night. Devon knew they were taking a chance that an alert gunner would spot them making their way through the low scrubby hills toward the border, but there was no other way out of the tiny, dying country.

Silently Kathleen took the small backpack and secured it over her shoulder. Devon hoisted Marta onto his back while Kathleen whispered of piggyback rides and cowboys and Indians. When the little girl was settled, Kathleen took Andrej's hand and they started to walk, not too fast, but a steady pace that Devon hoped wouldn't tire the little boy too quickly. They had a long way to go to the car—if it was still where he'd left it. And they had to be within sight of the border before the sun rose or they would be sitting ducks on the road.

"I DON'T HAVE a thing you can wear, I'm afraid."

Kathleen turned from the fairy-tale view of Vienna's fabled Inner City to face Devon's mother. "I'd be very surprised if you did," she responded, forcing a smile to her lips. "I'm six inches taller and thirty pounds heavier than you are."

"Not thirty pounds, Kathleen dear," Nicole said sweetly, smoothing an imaginary wrinkle from the leg of her tailored white slacks. With them she wore a matching flame-colored silk shell and collarless jacket that set off the burnished gold of her hair and made her look at least ten years younger than she really was—which was fifty-six. Kathleen knew because she was privy to that information at DEVCHECK and Addison Hotels. And once, four years ago, it had been very important for her to know everything she could about Devon Addison and his mother. Now, it was important again, but for vastly different reasons. "I've put on weight shamelessly since the divorce."

"It doesn't show." If Devon's mother had gained weight since the last time Kathleen had seen her it certainly wasn't apparent. Nicole Addison Wocheck Donatelli Holmes was small and slight with a dancer's lithe grace and a deceptive air of fragility, and would look that way until the day she died.

"Yes, it does." She patted her slim hips coyly. "But my dressmaker can work miracles. You should try her sometime."

"Thank you for offering." Kathleen was so tired she could barely stand, and she wasn't up to trading barbed comments with the older woman. The moment Kathleen crossed the threshold of the palatial hotel suite, a world removed, a universe removed from the way she'd been living the past month, a lot of her old insecurities had come rushing back. She felt almost as overwhelmed as she had the first time she'd become aware of the opulence and grandeur that the Addison fortune could command, and how far removed it was from Tyler, Wisconsin, and the life she'd always known.

Nicole giggled, a light, chiming sound with only the slightest hint of sharpness around the edges. Enough sharpness to bring Kathleen out of her thoughts and put her on guard. "That came out all wrong, didn't it? I didn't mean to imply that you needed to camouflage any part of your figure.''

"Of course not, Lady Holmes." Nicole's third marriage had ended well before Kathleen left for Triglav. Devon's mother might have parted ways with her husband, an English baronet, but Kathleen suspected she had no intention of divorcing herself from the courtesy title. Nicole adored being called Lady Holmes.

"Although I must admit you fill out that ensemble admirably." She stood and walked over to the white marble fireplace, picking up a poker to stir the embers of the fire. It was a gray, rainy fall night in Vienna and the added warmth in the huge, high-ceilinged sitting room was welcome. "Still, I doubt if you want Devon to return unexpectedly and find you in my negligee."

Kathleen couldn't stop herself from smoothing her hand over the heavy silken fabric. "You're right, I wouldn't want him to see me this way." She met Nicole's critical, gray-green eyes with equanimity, willing herself not to blush. She knew her look was cool and detached, unconcerned. Her expression and the tone of her voice were a perfect match. They ought to be; she'd practiced them often enough in the mirror. It was a great defense mechanism, one she'd perfected early on in her dealings with DEVCHECK officials and Addison Hotels personnel. But inside she was still just Kathleen Kelsey from Tyler, and when she was around Nicole Holmes, she never forgot that.

By the time the little refugee party had traveled all of the night before through dangerous countryside, pressing on to Vienna for most of the day, Kathleen's clothes, none too clean to begin with, were beyond respectability. Nicole had hustled them off to the hotel laundry and produced a negligee and robe of heavy embroidered silk, with long flowing sleeves and a skirt that was meant to sweep the ground in regal folds. Nicole had designed it herself and it suited her flamboyant personality perfectly.

But on Kathleen the sleeves ended above her wrists, the skirt hung several inches above her ankles, and if she took a very deep breath she couldn't be responsible for the consequences to the expensive fabric or what remained of her dignity. The color was one of her best, though—a deep emerald green—and at least she was clean and well-fed and the children were sleeping safely in their beds. For that she would forgive anything, even Nicole's cattiness.

She hadn't liked being left behind in the hotel with *dear Lord, her mother-in-law,* but she'd had no choice with nothing to wear. Devon had borrowed a pair of slacks and a shirt from the assistant manager of the hotel and that was the end of it. Kathleen and the children hadn't been that lucky.

"Will you join me in a cup of espresso?" Nicole asked, gracious once more now that she had reminded Kathleen of her proper place.

"No, thank you." Kathleen returned her gaze to the window, mesmerized by the expanse of unbarred, unobstructed glass. Beyond and below lay Vienna. A magical place. She'd only been here once before, then only for a day and a night, with Edward on a whirlwind inspection tour of his European properties. There were far worse places to be in exile while she and Devon dealt with the bureaucratic technicalities and outfitted the children for their trip to America. She would insist on moving the children to a more modest suite as soon as possible, though. She wasn't about to spend any more time than necessary under Nicole's thumb.

"It's getting late. I wish Devon would give up this scheme of trying to see the ambassador tonight and start

fresh in the morning. I'm worried about him. He was under so much stress from the baksheesh scandal with the
Bangkok property before this even happened. There are
people in the organization who would like to see him fail,
you know. People who want Edward back as CEO, even
though it was my ex-husband's idea to step down in
Devon's favor."

"Yes. I know." But Devon could handle any opposi-
tion the old guard at Addison could muster. Nicole knew
that as well as Kathleen did. She was just trying to make
Kathleen feel guilty, and she was damned close to suc-
ceeding.

"And then, out of the blue, rushing off to that godfor-
saken place to rescue you and those children. When I think
of what he's been through in the past week. Well, I try not
to."

Kathleen heard the delicate chime of china against china
as Nicole returned her cup to its saucer with more force
than necessary. But she didn't turn around. She did not
have to imagine what he'd been through. She knew, and
she would be forever grateful. Devon had quite literally
saved her life, and the children's. She would never have
found her way to the border on the twisting narrow back
roads that Devon had driven with such ease. She shuddered to think what the hostile, narrow-eyed border guard
they encountered just before dawn would have demanded
of her as a bribe to allow them to cross safely into neutral
territory.

"I should have gone with him to see the ambassador,"
she murmured.

"And leave me here alone?" The slight emphasis on the
word *alone* was to remind Kathleen that Nicole had left
London so hastily that she had left her personal secretary
and her butler, the ubiquitous Wellman, behind. "With

two children who don't know me from Eve and who don't speak a word of English?'' The velvet gloves were off. ''I refuse to be relegated to the role of nanny while you and my son run all over Vienna, trying to get exit papers for the urchins.''

Kathleen bit her lip and swallowed a sharp reply. Their appearance at dawn with two exhausted and crying children had been a shock. But the news of their hasty marriage, no matter how compelling the reason for it, had set the seal on Nicole's bad temper. Kathleen Kelsey from Tyler, Wisconsin, was the last woman in the world Nicole Holmes had intended for Devon's bride.

Definitely, first thing in the morning, she would ask to be moved to a suite of her own.

There was a knock at the door. ''Good,'' Nicole said sharply, opening the door with a flourish to reveal two bellmen struggling with armloads of clothing and boxes of shoes. ''I took the liberty of having them send up a few selections from the boutique in the lobby. The children really must have new clothes before you can even take them shopping for more. And—well, so must you, my dear.''

Kathleen ground her teeth. Nicole was right, of course, but that didn't make it any easier to accept her patronizing. ''Thank you, Lady Holmes.''

Nicole's carefully made-up face stiffened for a moment before she smiled again, coolly, politely. ''Don't you think it's time you started calling me Nicole? After all, we are . . . family.'' Again the pause was slight but deliberate.

''Thank you, Nicole.''

''I can't imagine being a mother-in-law,'' the older woman said, directing the bellmen to place the clothes on one of the suite's matching Louis XIV sofas. ''No matter how temporary the condition is likely to be.''

VOICES, A PHONE ringing. Ordinary sounds, but they registered with alarm in Kathleen's sleeping brain. It was late; she knew that without opening her eyes. They all should be asleep, but what was she doing curled uncomfortably on the unwelcoming curves of the antique sofa?

One of the voices, deep and masculine, penetrated the fog of her exhaustion. Devon. He'd returned from the embassy. She opened her eyes and sat up, fighting off a wave of dizzy fatigue. "What time is it?" she asked, attempting to smooth her hair, which was coming loose from its pins.

"Good, you're awake." Devon advanced across the room, carrying a cup of coffee. She took it gratefully. It was strong and hot and just what she needed to banish the cobwebs of sleep from her brain.

"Is it very late?" She had given her wristwatch to the young nurse who had helped take care of Rujana. It had been destroyed when her apartment building was shelled.

"It's almost one." Devon sat down beside her. He looked tired, worn to the bone, and Kathleen caught herself just before she reached out to brush a heavy wave of dark gold hair off his forehead. She took a too-hasty swallow of coffee instead and burned her tongue.

"How long have you been back?" Kathleen curled her bare feet beneath her and scooted farther into the corner of the sofa. Thankfully one of the slacks and sweater sets that the bellman had brought up from the boutique had been her size. She might be barefoot and sleep tousled, but at least she wasn't sitting next to this familiar stranger, *her husband,* dressed in nothing but Nicole's extravagant robe and negligee.

"About an hour. Mother bullied the kitchens into sending up something to eat. I was going to wake you then but she said to let you sleep, that the kids had been little monsters to get settled and you needed the rest.''

Kathleen bristled. "The kids were not monsters. They were just confused and upset. They've never seen any-place like this in their lives." She indicated the palatial surroundings. "Strange people. Strange food." And so much of it. Rich and varied. She wanted to taste every-thing she saw, everything she smelled. And she had only been in Triglav for a few weeks. She couldn't imagine what the children must think of such bounty.

Devon held up his hand to stem the flow of words. "Hey, I'm not criticizing. Neither is my mother."

"Of course not." Kathleen forced herself to smile. "I'm tired, that's all. And so are you, from the looks of you."

He rubbed his hand across his beard-darkened face. "That bad, huh?"

She leaned forward and covered his hand with hers. "You look like a man who saved all our lives. Thank you, Devon."

He turned his hand over and captured hers within its strong grasp. His thumb traced over her palm in a gentle, sensual caress that was disturbingly erotic. It felt so right, so wonderfully right that Kathleen's breath caught in her throat. She raised her eyes and saw the same surprise, the same heat in Devon's gray gaze.

"I don't want any thanks, Kath. I want you to be happy."

They were skating too close to the edge of the old unre-solved feelings between them. She dragged her eyes from his and pulled her hand away, deliberately pretending to misunderstand. "Telling me you have all the necessary paperwork to take the children home to Tyler will make me the happiest woman in the world."

He stared down at his still-open palm for a moment without responding. When he raised his eyes to hers again they were darker than before, shuttered, his thoughts unreadable. "Everything is in order. Even if I did have to pull rank on the ambassador and threaten to withdraw Addison Hotels's pledge of a substantial contribution to the old man's daughter's congressional campaign to get to see him."

"Devon? A bribe?"

He laughed, genuinely amused. "Not a bribe. Don't remind me of the Bangkok mess. I'm going to have to deal with that too soon as it is. It was a legitimate campaign contribution. I happen to think she's a damned qualified candidate in her district, which just happens to include two Addison properties, but the ambassador didn't have to know that."

Kathleen blushed. "I'm sorry. I didn't mean to imply you were doing anything illegal. I'm getting punchy from lack of sleep."

"Don't ever feel you have to apologize to me for speaking your mind, Kath."

"Devon..." Her thoughts were a shambles. Her palm still tingled from his touch.

"All the necessary documents will be delivered before noon tomorrow. I thought we could spend a couple of days here. Get the kids outfitted, give them a little time to adjust and rest up before you return to Tyler."

"Yes, I've been thinking the same thing." Kathleen was anxious to get home, but she and Devon did need time alone together. They had to make some kind of plans for the future. She had no idea how long it would take to finalize the children's adoption, how long they would have to remain man and wife. They needed to set up guidelines... She curled her fingers around her still tingling palm. And boundaries.

"What's the matter, Kath? Are you homesick?" he asked, his voice a low rumble in the quiet room so far above the late-night comings-and-goings on the streets of the Inner City.

Tyler. A much safer topic than their marriage, and with the added advantage of being the truth. "Yes, I am, a little. But I'm glad we'll have some time together. We—we have a lot of things we need to settle between us. Devon, I want you to know I won't make any demands—"

He leaned over, put his finger to her lips. "You're right, Kath. We do need time together. We do have things to settle between us if we're going to make this arrangement work for all of us. But not tonight. We're both too tired and we've been through too much in the past seventy-two hours. Let's take this marriage one day at a time."

The chandelier in the center of the room suddenly flashed on, showering them both with shards of cold, bright light. Nicole appeared in the doorway of her bedroom. "Good. You're both still awake."

"What is it, Mother?" Devon asked, rising from the couch in one strong, graceful motion. Kathleen swung her feet to the floor but remained seated because, to her chagrin, her left foot was asleep.

Nicole glided into the room, the skirts of her satin damask gown sweeping the floor. "I've just been on the telephone," she said breathlessly, her critical gaze taking in Kathleen's careless hairstyle and bare feet with disapproval—and more than a little satisfaction, Kathleen couldn't help noticing. "I've been speaking with a friend in New York."

"At this hour?"

Nicole glided closer, smiling indulgently at her tall son. "It's the shank of the evening in New York."

"You're right, Mother. I forgot. But what was so important in the conversation that you have to repeat it to us tonight?"

"I was speaking to Henry."

"Henry Burlington? The U.N. attaché?" Devon's jaw tightened, his eyes narrowed. Kathleen felt her own pulse accelerate with alarm as she watched his reaction. "What's up, Mother?"

"It's about Triglav." Nicole steepled her fingers and closed her gray-green eyes for effect before raising them once more to her son's face. "The government forces have attacked all along the border. They don't expect the defenders to hold out more than twenty-four hours. Kathleen must get the children to America as soon as possible, or all you have done will be in vain. If the government falls, your guardianship papers will be null and void. The children will be classified as refugees. Under no circumstances will they be allowed to leave Vienna."

CHAPTER FOUR

KATHLEEN WAS SEATED at her desk in her small, functional office in the new wing of Timberlake lodge. Beyond the window the last of the oak leaves clung tenaciously to the wind-tossed branches of the trees that lined the narrow service road leading to the kitchen and laundry. If she leaned forward a few inches she could see a tiny portion of the whitecapped, slate-colored waters of the lake. The prospect was cold and uninviting. It was raining again, but it didn't matter. All that mattered was that she was free to look out the window whenever she wished.

Kathleen swiveled her chair away from the depressing view and faced the daunting amount of work awaiting her on her desk. But she couldn't seem to make much headway on the backlog of phone calls and corporate reports that were piled up in front of her. Each time she tried to concentrate on her work her thoughts wandered to the children and all the things she still needed to do for them.

There were physicals and eye exams, dental visits, immunizations to update, not to mention the legalities of dealing with children's services and the immigration people. Amanda Trask had agreed to handle the paperwork, and Paul Chambers, Tyler's pediatrician, had promised to do his best to find a therapist for Marta. But since they weren't certain how much English she understood, the prospects for finding someone qualified anytime soon were not bright. The same situation existed with hiring a tutor for Andrej until he was acclimatized enough, and confident enough in English, to begin attending Tyler Elementary. For now, Paul believed, and Kathleen agreed, it was more important for the two children to be together, for them to feel safe and secure, in their new life and new country, than anything else.

Kathleen glanced at the clock above her desk. Almost eleven a.m. She was tempted to turn on the radio and listen to the news. The fall of Triglav was imminent. The defenders had held out for almost ten days, confounding all the experts, but the result was still inevitable. And when the tiny prefecture dissolved into the morass of violence that was all that remained of most of Yugoslavia, what would the children's status be? Amanda hadn't seemed too sure that the adoption papers would be considered legal and binding here. As for the marriage certificate... Amanda had just thrown up her hands and told Kathleen not to worry, she'd start looking into it. Even though she knew that Amanda was the kind of lawyer who wanted all the *t*'s crossed and the *i*'s dotted, Kathleen couldn't help but worry. It was all she seemed able to do these days.

And then there was the problem of where she and the children were going to live. She couldn't continue to live at her parents' house, already filled to the rafters with boarders, and with Glenna's family while they waited to move into their new home. Her parents would be aghast when they learned she was contemplating moving out as soon as possible. But the children needed a place of their own, space of their own where they could all three put down new, strong roots together.

Kathleen shook her head and rubbed her hand across her tired eyes. She didn't regret for a moment the promise she had made to Rujana. But she hadn't anticipated how overwhelming the reality of instant motherhood would become. She opened a file folder and stared at the flow charts and related data inside as if they were hieroglyphs from some ancient, lost civilization. She dropped her head in her hands.

"Kathleen, what are you doing here?" Edward Wocheck was standing in the doorway that separated their offices. She hadn't heard him knock or open the door.

"I thought it was time I come back to work," she said, straightening in her chair.

"You've only been back from Triglav a little more than a week." He was watching her very closely. *Now even Edward Wocheck was doing it, treating her as if she might shatter at a cross word, go to pieces without warning.*

Kathleen pasted a smile on her face. "Ten days of R and R with my mother in charge is about all I could stand." Anna Kelsey had been hovering over her and the children night and day since they'd landed at O'Hare, fussing and fretting, cooking and baking and clucking like a mother hen.

"Where are the children?"

"At TylerTots," she explained. "Mom's spoiling them to death at home. We ... Glenna and I ... We thought it would be a good way for them to start meeting other children."

"You look tired," he pronounced, taking two steps across the room and leaning both palms flat on her desk. He was a tall man, handsome and distinguished, with dark hair just beginning to gray, although he was in his midfifties, her father's age.

There was no use denying the obvious. "I am tired. The kids haven't been sleeping well. And they refuse to sleep anywhere but in my bedroom. It's natural," she hurried to explain. "They need the reassurance of having me close by.

Paul Chambers told me not to worry about it. Not right now..." She saw Edward glance at the pile of folders on her desk. Kathleen stiffened, suddenly defensive. "I'll be caught up on this stuff by the end of the week."

Edward raised assessing green eyes to hers. "Kathleen, you and those kids have been through a hell of a rough time—"

She was a Kelsey. Kelseys didn't break down, didn't have hysterics. They persevered, they overcame. They did not admit defeat, or even doubts about what they'd set out to do. They certainly didn't break down in tears in front of their employer. "I'm fine," she insisted. She knew there were dark circles under her eyes and her naturally pale skin had an ivory cast that wasn't flattering.

"I'm sorry, Kathleen. I have to differ with you. You look worn to the bone. I don't expect you to deal with this backlog in four days. I don't expect you to be at your desk at all right now. Especially not when you're trying to adjust to instant motherhood. And marriage to my stepson."

"Devon and I aren't—"

Edward held up his hand. "I know all the details. I've heard them from both you and Devon. I know you had good and sufficient reason for what you did. I wouldn't have expected less from Devon under the circumstances. But the fact remains you are married to each other." He smiled, a charming, masculine smile that, privately, Kathleen found almost irresistible. "And that fact alone must be a major shock to your system."

Kathleen held up her ringless hand, fingers spread. "He saved our lives, Edward. I truly believe that, and I'll be grateful to him for his help for the rest of my life. But I— I don't feel married. And I'm sure Devon doesn't, either."

Edward's smile disappeared. "Alyssa says it's romantic. But I imagine it's unsettling."

"To say the least." Kathleen folded her hands in front of her, hoping Edward didn't notice the fine tremors. He didn't know that she had once been Devon's lover and that that fact made their awkward situation even more uncomfortable for her.

"Did you know that he's returned to London from Bangkok?" Edward asked.

"We spoke last night." Addison Hotels was building a new 200-million-dollar luxury hotel in the Thai capital, the Addison Bangkok Lotus, and while Kathleen had been stranded in Triglav it had hit a major, perhaps crippling, snag. One of the primary Thai contractors was caught up in the latest palace bribery scandal. Devon, with Edward's complete agreement, had ordered the man fired, but work was at a standstill. Devon had left Vienna the same day she and the children had, but he had flown to Bangkok, not Tyler, to get the project back on schedule.

"How soon is he planning to return to Tyler?"

"As soon as possible." How odd it seemed that Devon's stepfather should be asking her what his plans were, as if she were really his wife. She tried to ignore the funny little pain around her heart that not knowing caused. She shouldn't feel this way, couldn't feel this way. Devon wasn't the right man for her. He never would be.

"I was considering flying out there myself," Edward informed her.

"You were? You never said anything to me. I . . . I don't know how I'll be able to get away. Not with the children to look after." She realized what she'd said. "I didn't mean that exactly. Naturally, if you have some business you want me to do away from Tyler—"

Edward held up his hand to silence her disjointed flow of words. "I know exactly what you mean. And we're not going to Bangkok or anywhere else. Not now. And not for the foreseeable future. Devon's the CEO of Addison Hotels now. I'm merely the president, a figurehead, if you will."

He and Kathleen both knew that he was far more than a mere figurehead, but it was true. Devon was now CEO of the huge conglomerate. Edward had stepped down from the position shortly after Devon's grandfather, Arthur Addison, died. Her husband had claimed his legacy. *The Boy Wonder of the hotel industry. The acknowledged head of a billion-dollar corporation.* Edward was still speaking. She tried to pull her scattered thoughts into order and pay attention to what he was saying.

"I promised Lyssa I'd stay home in Tyler until after the holidays. I want to be here for her until the F and M is up and running full speed again."

"Of course." Kathleen hoped her relief didn't show. It had been one of the many problems that had contributed to her sleepless nights. She simply couldn't leave the children to travel on Edward's business. Not now, not so soon.

"And you are to take as much time as you need for you and the children to get settled in." He was watching her very closely. "You are okay, aren't you, Kathleen?"

"I'm fine." *She was fine. She did not hear echoes of gunfire, and the screams of injured men and the sobs of heartbroken women.* She did not.

"Good, then that's settled."

Kathleen managed a smile. "You did that on purpose, didn't you."

"Did what on purpose?"

"Made a point of coming in here to tell me not to worry about any business trips until after the first of the year."

He grinned, the Eddie Wocheck grin that she'd seen often smiling back at her from the pages of her parents' Tyler High yearbooks. "Yes," he said.

Tears burned behind her eyes and she blinked them away. "Thank you, Edward. I don't know how I would have coped..."

He leaned forward, serious once more. "Kathleen, you are a valuable business associate, not to mention a friend. I just want you to know that Alyssa and I are behind you one hundred percent. Take all the time you need to get adjusted to your new life."

Kathleen's stomach tightened. *New life.* She couldn't let him know how scared she was about becoming a mother, about making it all work, keeping it all together. She didn't dare start talking about it or the fear might get out and start wrapping its tentacles around her heart and soul, and then she could never make it go away. "Thank you, Edward," she said stiffly, wincing at the strained sound of her own voice. "I appreciate your concern, but I'll be able to do it all. I know I will."

Edward's thick eyebrows pulled together in a quick frown. "I never doubted that for an instant. But remember you have friends and family. And we're all here to help."

"You don't know how—" The phone by his left hand beeped. Kathleen gave an apologetic shrug. "Excuse me. I'd better take that. Only Mom and Glenna know I'm here so it must be important." She lifted the receiver, grateful for the interruption so that she could get her emotions back under control.

"Kathleen Kelsey," she said into the receiver.

"Kath? It's Glenna."

"Glenna? What's wrong? Are the children okay?"

"Physically they're fine," her sister assured her. "But emotionally..." She hesitated.

"Glenna, what's wrong?"

"I'm sorry, Kath. It's Marta. She's very, very upset. The first- and second-graders from Tyler Elementary came by today to show the children their Halloween costumes. Two or three of the boys came dressed as hunters and soldiers, in camouflage, with their faces painted. It upset Marta terribly. She won't stop crying. I think you should come and get her. I feel terrible. It never occurred to me..."

Kathleen's hand tightened on the receiver. She could barely stop herself from slamming down the phone and running out of the office to her car. *Poor Marta. How frightened she must be.* "Don't beat yourself up over it, Glen," she said, forcing calm into her voice. "I'll be right there." Of course it wouldn't have occurred to Glenna that the sight of little boys playing at being soldiers would terrify Marta. Why should it? Why should any mother anywhere have to worry that her child would be traumatized by the sight of a uniform?

"What's wrong, Kathleen?" Edward was watching her even more closely than before.

She replaced the receiver carefully, avoiding his eyes until she had herself in hand again. "I'm sorry, Edward. I have to go. Marta has had a fright. Glenna thinks I should be with her."

"What will you do with the children after that?"

"Why, I don't know. Take them home, I guess."

"Why don't you bring them back here for the afternoon? They can try out the new playroom. It doesn't get much use during the week. We can have lunch together with Dad in the family suite. Seeing the children will be good for him."

"Has he been ill?" Kathleen hadn't seen Phil Wocheck since she'd returned to Tyler.

Edward frowned. "Not ill. But... not himself."

Kathleen didn't like the sound of that but she was too distracted by her own concerns to pursue the topic at the moment. "Tell Sheila I'll check with her about the scheduling of the first group of Santa trainees and what meeting rooms they'll need as soon as I can make time." A temporary-employee service had contracted with the hotel for meeting space to train department-store Santas for the entire month of November. "I'll be back as quickly as I can," she assured her boss, grabbing for her purse and jacket.

"Kathleen." Edward's tone of command halted her headlong rush for the door. "I meant what I said about staying away from this office. It's an order, not a suggestion. Sheila can cope with the Santa trainees on her own."

"Yes, sir."

"And one more piece of advice. Marta and Andrej are being well taken care of. You won't do them any good blowing into TylerTots looking like the devil himself is on your heels."

Kathleen took a deep breath. "You're right. I'm not very good at this mother thing yet."

"You will be," Edward said with a smile.

Kathleen tried to keep that positive thought uppermost in her mind as she arrived at Tyler Fellowship Sanctuary, where TylerTots day care was located. Angela Murphy, the center's director, led her to a quiet corner removed from the noise and activity of the ongoing Halloween party.

"Here's Kathleen, sweetie," Glenna crooned as Kathleen approached. Her sister, who like all the Kelseys had dark hair and blue eyes, looked up from the rocking chair where she sat cradling the little girl. Andrej sat cross-legged on the floor beside them, arms folded across his chest. He looked fiercely protective.

"How is she?" Kathleen asked nervously.

"She's feeling better, aren't you, honey?"

Marta sat up, red-eyed and white-faced. Her sobs had faded away to hiccuping sniffles. She held out her arms and Kathleen sank to her knees, pulling her into her embrace.

"I'm here, baby. It's all right." The spasm of emotion that gripped her heart was physically painful. She nestled her cheek against Marta's red-gold curls and closed her eyes. "No one's going to hurt you. Not ever again."

"My sister hates it here," Andrej pronounced.

Kathleen reached out and patted him on the arm. "She doesn't hate it here."

He nodded forcefully. "Yes. And I, too."

"It's all right, Andrej. Marta's all right. She was just frightened by the boys, that's all," Glenna assured him. "Do you really hate it here?"

"I do not like it much." He looked thoughtful, choosing his words carefully. "I wanted to hit them for making fright for Marta. But I know better. They are more little than me. That is wrong."

Kathleen fought new tears. "Yes, Andrej," she said. "Hurting those little boys for frightening Marta would be wrong. They meant no harm."

"Miss Glenna says in America soldiers and police are not to be afraid of."

Kathleen looked over at her sister, who shrugged. "I didn't know what else to say."

"She's right," Kathleen assured him. "In America policemen and soldiers take care of little children and protect them from harm."

Andrej nodded. "Like John Wayne," he said.

The response was so unexpected that both Glenna and Kathleen laughed aloud. "John Wayne?" Glenna repeated, still smiling but looking puzzled, as well.

Andrej nodded emphatically. "Yes. U.S. Cavalry. Horses. Cowboys. Indians. I like John Wayne movies. I see them on German TV. Before." The light faded from his eyes for a moment. "Before the war."

Marta was still holding on to Kathleen like a limpet, but she was no longer crying, just watching her brother with big dark eyes. She was a sensitive child, and Kathleen knew Andrej's distress would transfer itself to his sister if she didn't do something to distract them both.

"Would you like to come back to Timberlake with me for the afternoon?" Was that the right thing to do? She glanced at her sister for support. Glenna nodded. She was three years older than Kathleen, divorced and recently remarried. She was a wonderful mother to her own children and to all her charges at TylerTots. Mothering came naturally to her, or so it seemed to Kathleen. So why couldn't she make even a simple a decision about Marta and Andrej's welfare without second-guessing her every thought?

"Could we?" Andrej asked. "I am tired of being with babies."

Marta looked up at her, questioning.

"Would you like to see my desk? Where I work, and then play in the new playroom?" she asked, wondering how much of what she said registered with the little girl. She looked at Andrej and he translated her words in a burst of excited chatter. Marta nodded vigorously.

"I think that's a great idea," Glenna said, but still a tiny frown replaced her smile.

"What? Don't you think that's a good choice, taking them with me for the rest of the day?" Kathleen asked.

"No," Glenna responded. "I think that's a good idea."

"Then why are you frowning?" Kathleen demanded.

"Because *you* don't look as if you think it's a good idea."

"That's because I haven't the foggiest notion whether it is or not." Kathleen gave her a lopsided grin. "I'm flying blind here."

"You're doing great," Glenna assured her, but her tone was a little too hearty, a little too cheerful. Kathleen was beginning to feel like a bug under a microscope. Her family watched her like a hawk, worrying over her and the children. She knew they wanted her to tell them about Triglav. She knew they would be sympathetic, even more supportive, if that was possible. But she wasn't ready to talk about those terrible days and nights. Perhaps she never would be.

"Sure we are. That's why Marta's crying her eyes out."

"Hey. You guys have only been a family for ten days. There are bound to be rough patches like this to get past." Glenna brushed her fingertips over Marta's silky curls.

Kathleen's insecurities bubbled closer to the surface. "I'm all the mother these kids have got." She tried not to sound frightened by her own words, but she wasn't certain she'd succeeded.

Glenna's voice gentled. "Don't underestimate yourself, Kath."

"I'm trying not to."

"And don't be afraid to ask for help."

"I know you're always here for me."

"Of course I am," Glenna said, giving Andrej a little push toward the stairs. "That's what sisters are for. But I didn't mean me. Or the rest of the family, for that matter. I meant Devon. He's your husband, after all."

CHAPTER FIVE

AN HOUR LATER Kathleen was wishing for all the help she could get, even if it meant coping with her absent husband's unsettling presence again. She sat at the table in the dining area of the Wochecks' private suite at Timberlake Lodge, watching Marta bang her spoon noisily against her plate while Andrej complained loudly, in both English and his native tongue, that he wasn't going to eat steamed carrots no matter how good Kathleen said they were for him.

"Edward, I'm sorry. They're usually so well behaved." She reached across the table to cover Marta's spoon-wielding hand with her own. What if the little girl didn't stop? Should Kathleen scold her, or just take the spoon away? Or let her go on disrupting the meal until she got it out of her system? She nudged a dish of applesauce closer to Marta's plate, hoping to distract her. Thankfully, when she lifted her hand Marta started eating the fruit instead of continuing what she'd been doing. Kathleen breathed a silent sigh of relief.

Her employer waved off the stammered apology. "No problem. I can't see Annie or Belle eating steamed carrots without making some kind of fuss. And Margaret Alyssa..." He shuddered and left the sentence unfinished. "Andrej." Edward didn't raise his voice, but the boy stopped complaining and fell silent instantly.

"Yes, sir."

"Steamed carrots are not my favorite vegetable, either. But with the addition of a little melted butter and salt they're tolerable."

"What is going on out here? There is enough noise to wake the dead," an imperious old voice complained. Phil Wocheck, Edward's father, wheeled himself out of his bedroom, scowling at Kathleen and the children from beneath bushy white eyebrows. His complexion, usually so ruddy, was pasty-looking, his thin white hair standing up in tufts all over his head like dandelion fluff. He looked small and very frail within the confines of the metal wheelchair, his shirt was buttoned crookedly and his sweater hung from his bony shoulders in scarecrow fashion. Kathleen was shocked by his appearance but tried not to let the reaction register on her face.

"Mr. Wocheck, it's good to see you again."

"Well, Kathleen, you have acquired a family in your absence. And a husband, too, if the gossip the maids pass on to me is correct."

"Yes," she said. "These are my children, Marta and Andrej Drakulic."

"Umm." Phil scowled at the little ones. "Noisy kids."

"Dad, I'm glad you decided to join us," Edward said, glancing quickly in Kathleen's direction, gauging her reaction to his father's altered appearance. "Better hurry and start eating. Your food's getting cold."

"I'm not hungry," Phil insisted, gliding closer to the table where a place had been set for him. His wheelchair was equipped with an electric motor that he generally disdained using, preferring instead to get around under his own power. But not today, it seemed. He scowled at the silver cover but made no attempt to remove it. "Eating is too much trouble."

Edward rose and walked toward the old man as though to forestall his leaving the room. "How about a cup of coffee, then? Or one of those vitamin-supplement drinks Jeff Baron prescribed?"

Phil curled his lip. "Infant pap," he growled, but he allowed Edward to push his chair closer to the table. Kathleen caught herself frowning. *Vitamin-supplement drinks?* Phil's appetite was excellent. Or it had been before she left for Triglav.

Edward returned to his seat as the old man lifted the cover from his plate, then dropped it again with enough force to cause the china to ring. "Steamed carrots. I hate steamed carrots."

Andrej nodded. "I want pizza," he announced in English. Marta looked up at Kathleen and smiled.

Kathleen was outnumbered, but felt she had to take a stand. "You must eat your vegetables to grow strong and healthy. If you finish your lunch we'll have pizza for dinner."

Andrej looked as if he were considering the compromise.

Inspiration hit Kathleen. "And we can't go to the new playroom until we finish lunch."

"I will finish other food," Andrej conceded. "But not the carrots."

"Steamed carrots," Phil muttered, the remnants of his rich Polish accent still evident in his speech. "Pah. Worse than infant pap."

"Yes." Sensing reinforcements, Andrej folded his arms across his chest and rattled off a sentence in his native tongue. "No carrots," he added in English, looking mutinous.

Kathleen stared back in horror. It was the first time he'd attempted to defy her authority. A part of her was relieved to see the little boy assert himself, but the rest of her was scared to death that she would botch her first real mothering crisis and never get back on solid ground with either of the children. Maybe she could use one of her mother's favorite tactics: the old try - two - bites - and - then - if - you - don't - like - it - you - don't - have - to - eat - the - rest routine. "Andrej—"

"What did you say?" Phil demanded of the boy, interrupting Kathleen without ceremony. "Speak again."

"Pizza?" Andrej looked puzzled.

The old man barked a guttural command.

Andrej repeated his earlier sentence, but in a far more docile tone than before. His dark eyes were as big as saucers when Phil answered haltingly in the same language.

Andrej replied with passionate intensity, gesturing disdainfully at the cooling vegetables on his plate.

"Dad, what's going on?" Edward demanded.

"I will tell you later." Phil held up a restraining hand, silencing his son. He spoke again to Andrej, then removed the cover from his plate and picked up his fork with gnarled, trembling hands. "I will eat them if you do," he told the boy in English. "When you are done we will ask Kathleen's permission to go to the new activities room my son has had built. There are not many children here at this time of year. It is not being used enough to pay for itself."

"Are there video games?" Andrej asked excitedly.

Phil snorted. "Yes. But there are other things, as well. Swings and slides and tumbling mats."

Andrej puffed out his chest. "I was the best gymnast in my school."

"Good." The old man took two bites of carrots and then put down his fork and looked pointedly in Andrej's direction. "Hurry. They are even worse tasting when they are cold."

The boy hesitated, nodded and picked up his fork. He speared a bite of carrot and put it in his mouth. Phil made a sound of approval and began to eat again himself.

Marta watched them both as the vegetables disappeared, then wiggled off her seat. Before Kathleen could stop her she raced around the table to stand beside Phil's wheelchair. Still silent, but with eyes shining with excitement, she lifted her hand to his mouth, placing her small fingers against his lips.

Phil took her hand in his. "What do you want, *malushka?*" The endearment was Polish. Kathleen had heard Phil use it with Margaret Alyssa and the twins several times.

Marta shook her head vehemently, glancing at her brother for support, then placing her fingers against Phil's lips once more.

"She wants him to talk again. Like we do at home," Andrej said. Tears sparkled in his dark eyes. "Like Mother. And Father."

Phil backed his wheelchair away from the table and patted his bony knees. "Come, little one. Sit on my lap." Although he spoke to Marta in her native tongue, Kathleen understood intuitively the meaning of the unfamiliar words.

"How do you come to know their language?" she asked as the little girl settled against his chest, looking up at him with dark, questioning eyes.

"My grandmother came from the mountains around Triglav. She always spoke the old tongue. I am surprised I have remembered this much over all these years." He gave a rusty chuckle, his glance straying to the wall of glass behind them and the whitecap-covered lake beyond. But Kathleen suspected that what Phil was really seeing was even more remote, in both time and place. "Almost a lifetime has gone past and still I recall her voice. Perhaps I am not as senile as I feared."

A concerned frown passed over Edward's features, but it was gone, Kathleen noticed, when his father turned his gaze back to the present and the small group that surrounded him.

"You never told me about your grandmother—my great-grandmother," Edward said, leaning close but not touching the old man. Kathleen knew, because her mother had told her, that Edward and Phil's relationship had never been an easy one. Indeed, for many years Edward had stayed away from Tyler and all the hurtful memories the town held for him. It wasn't until the discovery of Margaret Ingalls's long-buried body, and the life-altering events that discovery had set in motion, that the two men were able to work past their differences and forge a new and strengthened bond between them.

Phil was silent a moment, his hands stroking Marta's shoulders. "I know. I should have talked of her. Of the old country. But they were all gone, dead in the war, and it hurt too much."

Edward laid his hand on the old man's knee. "It's not too late," he said quietly.

Phil straightened in his chair, looked at the little girl in his lap and then at his son. "No," he said. "While there is breath in the body it is never too late."

"I'd like to hear about your grandmother. And all the others."

"For many years you never wanted to hear about the past." Phil's tone was guarded.

"I was wrong," Edward said bluntly. "We should never ignore our roots."

"Very good," Phil said, his voice stronger. "Soon we will have that talk. But not now. Now I have promised my new friends that we will go and play. Will you join us, Kathleen?''

"I'd like to, but I have a great deal of work to do."

"She'll join you in a few minutes, Dad," Edward responded in a tone that said the matter was settled. "Andrej, can you push my father's wheelchair for him?"

"Of course." Andrej's face went red with pleasure. "I am very strong. I can push the chair even with my sister, too."

"Pah." Phil scowled up at Edward, who had risen from his chair. "I can do it myself."

"That's not what you've been telling me for the past six weeks."

"Today I am stronger. We will argue no more. Kathleen, come."

"Give me five minutes with her, Dad."

"Five minutes. No more. This way, Andrej."

The boy spoke excitedly, but Phil answered, sternly. "Speak English. We are in America now."

"Yes, sir." Kathleen heard the disappointment in Andrej's voice. She opened her mouth to urge Phil to change his mind, but the old man forestalled her.

"We will also talk in the old way, sometimes," he decreed to Andrej. "You will be my teacher. I will learn my grandmother's language again."

Edward opened one of the big double doors that led to the private hallway beyond. Andrej maneuvered his charges safely through. "Show the way," he said.

Phil waved expansively in the direction of the main lobby and the new wing beyond. "We go this way. Hurry."

Marta leaned past Phil's arm and waved back at Kathleen. There was a shy, sweet smile on her face and she looked excited and happy.

"Damn, if I didn't know better I'd swear those two kids were professional miracle workers," Edward said, watching the small procession out of sight. "Dad's been shut up in his room for over a month. I've been worried sick about him. Jeff Baron and George Phelps both swore there was nothing wrong with him. I mean, nothing serious. Just his arthritis and mild depression, Jeff said. He prescribed some medication, but Dad wouldn't take it."

"Did you tell Jeff that?"

"Of course. Jeff said not to force him to take it. He's keeping a close eye on him. But Dad's past eighty...." Edward ran his hand through his hair. "Well, I was afraid."

"That it was more serious?"

"Yes. But today he's like his old self again. Kathleen, what do you say to letting the kids stay here at Timberlake? At least until Andrej is ready to join his classmates at Tyler Elementary."

"Edward, I have no idea how long that will take. I... I have to find a tutor who speaks their dialect and that's not going to be easy."

"It may not be as hard as you think."

"You mean your father could do it?"

"Not exactly. I don't mean Dad should tutor Andrej. But I know he could help by translating. An hour or two a day of stimulating mental activity is just what the doctor ordered. Literally. Call Jeff and ask him if you don't believe me."

"Of course I believe you. It's just that..." Kathleen's head was in a whirl. Having the children close by at the lodge would take a load off her mind.

"I'm not asking you to move in permanently."

"Move in?" Kathleen looked around her at the large, casually elegant room with its comfortable, overstuffed sofa and chairs, the baby grand piano, massive fieldstone fireplace and French doors looking out across the grounds to the lake.

"Yes. Move in. Here in the suite. It's the perfect place. There are two empty bedrooms. We can put Andrej in Devon's room next to Dad's, and a bed in the dressing room for Marta. You can leave the door between the master bedroom and the dressing room open so she won't be afraid."

"But your father. The noise. The disruption of his routine . . ."

"It will do him good. He's been acting more like himself this past hour than he has for weeks."

"I—I don't know."

"Don't get on your Kelsey high horse," Edward said with a grin.

Kathleen smiled back. She couldn't help herself. Like Devon, Edward Wocheck's charm could sweep a woman off her feet if she wasn't careful. Still, his offer would solve at least one of her problems. It was tempting. Very tempting. The answer to her prayers.

"I'm doing this for myself as well as for you," Edward continued, sensing her hesitation. "You saw what Dad was acting like before he made contact with the children. I've been worried sick about him for more than a month."

"But what will he think of them moving in here, invading his territory?" What would her parents think about her moving out so abruptly? What would Devon think? *Devon.* A new wave of panic hit her in midthought. "What about Devon? Where will he sleep?" The words were spoken before she could bridle her tongue.

Edward's green eyes narrowed slightly. "That shouldn't be a problem."

"It is," Kathleen said, her heart beating too fast, her breath coming too quickly at the thought of sharing a bedroom with the man she had married. "I—I mean . . ."

"I know what you mean, Kath," Edward said, his voice gruff but gentle. "You don't have to explain yourself. What *I* meant is that Timberlake is a hotel. There are more than enough beds and bedrooms to go around."

"DEVON!" His mother's tinkling voice drifted into the high-ceilinged room before she did. "What do you think of my costume? It's an exact copy of a ball gown that Madame de Pompadour wore at Versailles."

Nicole twirled in a circle, her heavily embroidered, gold damask skirts draped over side hoops of immense proportions whispering across the parquet floor. She looked as if she'd stepped out of a page from the past. Diamonds sparkled at her throat and on her wrists and winked from the towering powdered wig that covered her own much shorter blond hair.

She beamed at Devon from above a scandalously low-cut neckline, smiling to highlight the dark beauty spot at the corner of her mouth. "What do you think?"

"I think you'll catch pneumonia if you intend traipsing around London on a night like this, dressed in that," he said dryly.

Nicole giggled, fluffing the lace of her décolletage, and opened the ostrich-feather fan she carried in her gloved hand. "You're probably right. The neckline is quite risqué, isn't it?" she said, sweeping across the room to admire herself in the Chippendale mirror above the Adam fireplace.

Nicole's private suite at the Addison Mayfair Hotel was as opulent and extravagantly decorated as all her other residences. The sitting room was filled with delicate French furniture and Chinese porcelains. Her bedroom was a symphony of cream and gold.

Devon's own bedroom was done in mahogany and linenfold oak, with a Jacobean bed the size of a football field and a bathroom of pink marble, with gold fixtures, a sunken tub and a mirrored ceiling. The place gave him nightmares. But until the past few weeks he'd never noticed how much he hated it. *How much Kathleen would hate it.* Until the past few weeks, he'd never thought very much at all about where he lived. Where he would spend the future. Certainly not about a home of his own. But he did now. All the time. And the home he dreamed of was not a mansion, not a showplace. It was truly a home, large and sun-bright, comfortable, well lived in, filled with children's noise, and toys, and laughter, and Kathleen's warm, welcoming smile.

"I swear this corset is an absolute torture device," Nicole said, shrugging her slender, bare shoulders. "I can barely breathe. But of course, without it the effect would be totally ruined." She giggled again and snapped the fan shut with a flick of her wrist. She gave herself one last admiring glance, and glided to a halt in front of his desk.

Devon signed the missive he'd been reading and slipped it into an envelope before his mother could ask what he was doing, and then object long and volubly when he told her. He'd drafted a codicil to his will providing for Kathleen and the children in the case of his death—an insurance policy of sorts. Enough to raise and educate Andrej and Marta, but not enough to cause his mother to take it into her head to oppose the will. And not so much that Kathleen would refuse to take the money on principle. He grinned. Not an easy figure to arrive at.

"What are you smiling about?"

"I'm smiling because I think you are going to be the belle of the ball tonight."

"Of course I am. But every belle needs an escort." She pouted and fluttered the fan coquettishly. "You're not dressed."

"I'm not going with you to the Wycliffes' party." They'd had this argument before, yesterday when he'd arrived back in London from Bangkok. And this morning when the costumes had been delivered from the dressmaker.

"But you have to come. It's the earl of Wycliffe's Halloween Ball. It's the premier event of the autumn Season," Nicole said, her voice rising a note or two, a sudden frown marring her perfect features. "Everyone who is anyone will be there. Rumor has it that Princess Di will attend. Your costume is all laid out in your bedroom."

Silk knee breeches and a powdered wig. Forty-eight hours ago he'd been one-on-one with the Thai economics minister trying his damnedest to save a 200-million-dollar project. A week before that he'd been running for his life from an invading army. Now his mother wanted him to dress up like...one of Cinderella's footmen and attend a Halloween ball. If he weren't so damned tired, and so damned worried about Kathleen and the kids he'd think it was funny. But it wasn't, it wasn't a damned bit funny.

"I'm sorry, Mother. I have to get back to Tyler. I've booked a seat on a nine o'clock flight out of Heathrow." The urgency to return to Tyler had been growing stronger with each passing day. The youngsters' situation was a tenuous one. When he talked to Kathleen, she pretended not to be worried, to be satisfied to let Amanda Trask deal with all the legal technicalities. But Devon knew her too well to be fooled by her apparent nonchalance.

His mother was still pouting prettily. She held out her hands. "Please, Devon—"

He was too tired to play her little games. He cut her off abruptly. "I don't suppose you heard the evening news. Triglav's fallen. The government's been dissolved."

"Was there ever any doubt that would happen?"

"No," he admitted. "Poor bastards. They held out longer than anyone expected." He thought of the overworked nurses and doctors, of Sister Marie and of the exhausted, hollow-eyed soldiers sleeping in the corridors of the hospital, and wondered what had happened to all of them.

"It's over and done with." Suddenly serious, her expression contrite, Nicole laid her gloved hand on his arm. "There's nothing more you can do."

He covered her small hand with his. "I know that, Mom. It's Kathleen and the kids I'm worried about now."

CHAPTER SIX

KATHLEEN CLICKED OFF the remote and turned off the television. There was nothing there she wanted to see. Shivering, she hugged her knees to her chest and pulled the edges of the homey, handwoven cotton throw around her shoulders. Although the family suite at Timberlake Lodge was warm and well-insulated, the November wind howled around the edges of the old building, evoking unsettling memories.

It was very late, but Kathleen couldn't sleep. In two days' time her world had turned upside down yet again. She looked at the boxes and bags piled around the edges of the room. She hadn't realized there was so much paraphernalia involved with raising children. Clothes, underwear, shoes, new winter coats, toys, books . . . there was even a small television with video recorder for her bedroom so that Marta could watch "Sesame Street" as she fell asleep and be comforted by its familiar characters, even though for her they spoke an unfamiliar language.

Andrej, it turned out, was a very fussy housekeeper. After Devon's possessions—surprisingly modest for so rich a man, Kathleen had noticed—had been removed from the small bedroom adjoining Phil's, the boy had begun moving his new treasures into drawers and closets, arranging everything with almost military precision.

Marta and Kathleen had watched in awe, then hurried off to their own rooms, inspired to do the same. But first

Marta, and then Kathleen, had been distracted by Disney's *Beauty and the Beast* video. The result being that when Marta at last fell asleep, tucked in her new little bed with its pink gingham coverlet and lace-trimmed pillowcase, bought the day before at Gates' Department Store, very little had been accomplished.

By ten o'clock, with both the children and Phil in their rooms, the suite was quiet. Kathleen had taken a quick shower and changed into sweats and an old Tyler High T-shirt, determined to bring some order to the chaos. But once more she had been distracted by the television. The late-night news shows were analyzing the effect that the defeat of the small Balkan prefecture of Triglav would have on the peace process in the region. Kathleen had watched the battle footage in horror and regret, refusing to let the tears that burned behind her eyelids fall, for fear Andrej or Marta would waken and see her crying—for all they had lost.

She wondered what Devon had thought when he heard the news. It was morning in London, the business day about to begin. She could call him, ask his advice on what to tell the children about the loss of Triglav. A little? A lot? Nothing at all? It would be good to hear the sound of his voice, even though they were separated by oceans and continents and time zones. It was quieter here, less hectic, and she longed to speak to him without the myriad distractions of a busy household going on around them, without others listening in.

A key turned in the lock, and the main door to the suite swung open. A man's tall form was outlined by the faint light from the hallway. Kathleen looked up, startled but not afraid. "Who's there?" she asked, rising to her feet, the throw still wrapped around her shoulders.

"Kath?"

"Devon? What are you doing here?" She blinked to make sure she wasn't dreaming. Devon was still there, striding into the room, a carry-on suit bag slung over one shoulder.

He shut the door quietly, then rested the suit bag against the back of the sofa before shrugging out of his trench coat. "I might ask you the same question," he said, coming toward her. In the faint glow of the dying fire on the stone hearth that dominated one wall of the suite, she could see the stubble of beard on his cheeks, and the way fatigue had carved deep lines from nose to chin. It was morning in London, she reminded herself again. He'd probably been awake at least twenty-four hours.

"I...we..." She gathered her composure and held on to it as tightly as she did the cotton throw. "The children and I are living here now. At Edward's invitation. It all happened very suddenly, but it's been a lifesaver. Mom and Dad's house is full to the rafters. I meant to tell you when we next spoke on the phone." Her words were tripping over themselves. She shut her mouth with a snap, determined not to say anything more until she could control her prattling tongue.

"This is Edward's hotel," Devon said gently, his voice rough-edged from the cold. "He can invite whomever he wants to live here without my say-so." He bent to pick up a small log. "Do you mind?" he asked, before placing the wood on the coals. "It's colder than the devil out there. The heater in the rental car was on the blink."

"Of course not. Have you eaten?" she asked automatically.

"They served breakfast on the plane."

"Airline food." Kathleen made a face, then looked up and caught him watching her in the bright new flames flickering to life, his eyes the same dark gray as a winter sky.

"It wasn't too bad. For airline food, that is." He grinned, a tired, lopsided grin that tugged at Kathleen's heartstrings. She had to get a grip on her emotions. She couldn't let his unexpected arrival throw her this way. With a sigh, she sank back onto the sofa again. She was very tired. It was very late. He'd surprised her by showing up when she was vulnerable and in need of someone to talk to, that was all. She could handle this sudden proximity. She had no other choice.

"Andrej has moved into your bedroom," Kathleen said quickly, too quickly. She took a deep breath. She was being ridiculous. Surely she could say the word *bedroom* around the man without her heart starting to pound against her rib cage, without blushing like a...a bride. "I'm sorry. We didn't expect you back so soon. I can't believe you got the Bangkok venture back on line so quickly."

He shrugged out of his suit coat, tossing it carelessly over the back of the couch. The fine wool garment came to rest just inches from her shoulder. She could feel the warmth of his body still lingering in the weave of the fabric, could catch the faint scent of his woodsy after-shave in the air currents that stirred around it. "It won't be completely resolved until we find a new contractor that we can trust. I put Liam Hardesty on the project."

"Your new vice president? But you only hired him three months ago." Kathleen let the cotton throw slip from her shoulders as she leaned forward, keeping her voice low so as not to disturb Phil or the children.

"He might as well get his feet wet on the Bangkok deal."

"Is he up to speed?" This was firm ground. This was business. She and Devon had always been on the same wavelength when it came to their work. It was their private dealings with each other that had gone so disastrously awry.

Devon tilted his head, watched her carefully, appraisingly, for a long moment. "Yes, Madame Executive Assistant," he said finally. "I think he is. And if he isn't, he'll come up to speed in a hurry. That's what I'm paying him a quarter of a million dollars a year to do."

"But is he familiar with the complexities of doing business in Southeast Asia? I..." The words froze in her throat. Devon wasn't wearing a tie. The collar of his white shirt was open at the throat, and the soft, fine linen strained across his broad shoulders, stretched taut over the hard, flat planes of his stomach. Kathleen watched, fascinated in spite of herself, as he unfastened the cuffs and rolled the sleeves to just below the elbow. It was a purely masculine ritual, one she'd seen her father and brother perform hundreds of time, but this time was different. This time it was Devon.

Her husband.

Any interest in Addison Hotels' new vice president taking on the problems with the Bangkok acquisition, indeed, coherent thought of any kind was suddenly beyond her capabilities. *Her husband.* His hands were gilded by the fire, the cords and tendons sharply outlined by the flames. Even though she didn't want to, tried not to, she remembered the warmth of those strong, supple hands on her skin, felt again the heavy weight of his body covering hers, and for a blinding moment, she experienced in memory the pleasure his lovemaking had brought her.

"Kathleen?"

The sound of her name sliced through the maelstrom of images and sensations. She spoke automatically, trying to secure the dangling ends of her thoughts. "Of course Liam

Hardesty will deal with the Bangkok mess. He's highly qualified. Edward showed me his résumé.''

"That's not what I asked you," Devon said. She hadn't been listening to a word he was saying for the past minute or two. He wondered where her thoughts had taken her. Certainly she was no longer interested in the bribery scandal that had brought the Bangkok project to within a hairbreadth of disaster. He sat down on the couch beside her, only the minimal barrier of his suit coat between them.

"It wasn't? I—I'm sorry..." She stammered to a halt. A flush spread over her neck and throat. She turned her face away, looked into the fire. Her silky dark hair fell forward and hid her profile, the curve of her cheek and the clean line of her jaw. "I...my thoughts must have wandered for a moment."

"We can discuss the Addison Bangkok tomorrow. In fact, I'd like to have your input. And Edward's." With the width of a desk between them they were always in sync. "I asked you how the children were doing. How they took the news of Triglav's defeat." He longed to reach out and tuck the ebony veil of hair behind her ear, but he kept his hands to himself.

"I...I haven't told them."

"Why not, Kath?"

"I...I didn't feel it would do any good. And I was afraid it might do harm?" There was a rising inflection in her voice, as if she was posing a question. He saw the ghost of old terror flare briefly in the blue depths of her eyes. He saw the unconscious tightening of the muscles in her jaw and shoulders as she pushed those terrors away. He knew, because he had asked Edward to watch over her, that she refused to talk of the time she'd been in Triglav in any but the most superficial terms. She was willing and eager to discuss the children and their ordeal, solicit advice from the people she loved and trusted. But she would not talk about herself to anyone, even him. Especially him.

"Are you asking my opinion?"

"I'm sorry, Devon. I didn't mean to put you on the spot. I'm going to have to handle these situations. I'm going to have to quit second-guessing myself. I'm their mother now."

He couldn't stop himself. He reached out and rested his hand lightly on her knee. "Kathleen, they're my kids, too. My name's on the adoption papers the same as yours. Exactly the same, Kathleen Anna Theresa Kelsey Addison."

She stiffened immediately and he took his hand away. *Damn.* He'd gone one step too far again, pushed a little too hard at her defenses. He folded his fingers into a fist. The heat of her skin had radiated through the thin cotton fabric of her running pants, burning his skin, sending shards of sensation along his nerve endings all the way from his head to his feet.

"That's why you came home so suddenly, isn't it? Because you were worried about Andrej and Marta."

"Yes," he said. It was close enough to the truth. "Things are bound to get more complicated now that they're refugees from a country that no longer exists."

She caught her lower lip between her teeth. Her eyes were troubled when she finally looked at him. "I know. I've done nothing but worry since I heard the news. But, Devon, you don't have to feel bound by what happened in Triglav."

"Dammit, Kathleen. At least give me a chance to do the right thing here." He stood up. Anger at her stubborn independence flared inside him like the flames of the rejuvenated fire, and died away just as quickly. She was determined to hold him at arm's length, and there was nothing he could do about it.

"You've already done far more than that." She didn't rise from her seat but held out her hand. A small hand, he noticed as he had so often before—soft and supple, but possessed of hidden strength, like Kathleen herself. For a brief instant his mind flashed back to their summer in Paris, to the feel of those small, strong hands in his hair, on his skin, her lips following the same path her fingers had taken, caressing him, encompassing him, reducing him to a quivering, almost mindless composition of flesh and bones.

"I'm a part of this whether you want me to be or not," he said, his voice tight with the effort to lock his memories away. "I made a promise to Rujana just as you did."

"Rujana. Yes." Her voice softened, gentled. "Devon, please forgive me." Kathleen was standing now, still a few feet away. "I'm sorry. I shouldn't have said those things. I—I'm scared, that's all. It's all so complicated, especially now that Triglav's fallen. What—" Her voice broke momentarily. "What if the authorities try to take the children away from us?"

Devon covered the distance between them in the space of a heartbeat, realizing as he did so that she wasn't wearing a bra. Her breasts rose and fell against the thin cotton of her T-shirt, but he forced himself not to look, not to touch, not to react. He took both her hands in his, brought them close to his chest. "Don't worry, Kathleen. I know you think I don't count for much in the greater scheme of things." She opened her mouth as if to protest, but he went right on talking. "Still, I am your husband. At least for the time being. And being Mrs. Devon Addison *does* count for something in this world, thank God. It's going to make it easier to deal with all the pettifogging bureaucrats that will be coming out of the woodwork at us. It will open doors that it would take you months to hammer down on your own."

"I'm not sure..." Her softly arched eyebrows pulled together in a frown he knew all too well. *Money. Filthy lucre. He had it, sinful amounts of it. It was temptation and damnation if you didn't use it right. And Kathleen's Catholic, Midwestern, middle-class upbringing told her most everyone in his position didn't use it right.*

"Kathleen, don't look at me that way."

"What way?"

"The look that tars me with Grandfather Addison's brush, that keeps searching my face for signs that I'm following in my mother's jet-setting footsteps or about to run off to join my father leading safaris in the African bush."

That was another mistake he'd made that summer. Devon had felt so at home in Tyler that he'd forgotten what a shock his life-style would be to Kathleen. He'd brought her to London and dropped her smack into the middle of his mother's crowd of titled divorcées and pseudo-aristocratic hangers-on. He should have realized the sophistication Kathleen had acquired working for Edward was newly minted, a thin glittering shell. Inside she was still Kathleen Kelsey, from a small town in the Midwest, and the infidelities, the shallow self-indulgence of his friends' lives were alien and distasteful to her. She'd taken one long look around her and had headed back to Tyler on the first available plane.

"I don't think that way of you, Devon."

He shook his head. "You have in the past."

"That was a long time ago," she said defensively. She tugged gently at his imprisoning hands, wanting to be free. He could feel her remembering, too, and as she did, he could sense her strengthening barriers, reinforcing old prejudices.

Devon resisted, tightening his grip incrementally so that she had no choice but to hear him out. "For once let me make good use of what I've been given, Kathleen. Believe in me."

"I can't ask this of you, Devon. I can't ask you to give up a year or more of your life in a sham marriage... It's so complicated. I—I never thought when I promised Rujana...." Tears sparkled in her blue, blue eyes. "Devon, please. Let me go."

He forced himself to loosen his grip, forced himself to take a step back, give her space. "We may have a marriage in name only," he said gruffly. "But we both want what's right for the kids. I promise you, Kathleen, for as long as we're married I will never give you reason to regret being my wife. And I promise you this as well. I will be the best father I can possibly be to Marta and Andrej. I can't offer you more than that."

She didn't come closer, just reached out and touched her finger to his cheek. "Thank you, Devon. I'll never ask for anything more."

KATHLEEN STRETCHED and rolled over. Two pairs of bright brown eyes were watching her from the side of the bed.

"Good morning," Andrej said formally. Marta smiled and patted her cheek.

"Good morning, you two," Kathleen replied, giving the little girl's cheek an answering caress. Both children had spent the night in their own rooms, although she had left the door open between her room and Marta's. There had been no nightmares, no crying out at unfamiliar noises, or shadows on the wall.

Marta was smiling. She smiled more often now. Surely that was a good sign. Phil had agreed to act as translator for Andrej's tutor and for a therapist if one could be found for Marta. But the old man was of the opinion that time and love would heal the little girl's terrors more quickly than dealing with another stranger, and Kathleen was inclined to agree with him.

She sat up and glanced at the bedside clock. She'd overslept by more than an hour and a half. She hadn't expected to go to sleep at all when she'd finally left Devon, who had decided to bed down on the couch in the living room. His proximity and her anxiety over the children's being away from her should have kept her awake for the rest of the night. But she'd slept soundly, deeply and dreamlessly. "Goodness, look at the time. Shoo, you two. I have to get dressed, pronto."

"Pronto?" Andrej digested the strange word.

"It's a Spanish word. It means quickly."

Marta tugged on her brother's shirtsleeve. She pointed in the direction of the living room.

"Devon is sleeping on the couch," Andrej announced.

"I know. He arrived very late last night."

"We can't wake him."

"Let him sleep. He was very tired. It's a long flight from London to Tyler."

"Phil wants his breakfast." Andrej screwed up his face in his effort to get the unfamiliar words just right. "He says not look good for room service to find husband sleep on couch."

Kathleen felt a blush begin to rise to her cheeks even though there was no reason for it. The whole situation would be as uncomfortable and awkward for Devon as it was for her. She thought of asking Andrej to suggest that Phil have breakfast in the restaurant, but realized the message would be difficult for the boy to convey. "I'll talk to Phil myself." She swung her legs over the edge of the bed. "Andrej, would you bring me my robe, please?" When he did, she slipped the sapphire velvet garment on over her cotton nightgown and belted it around her waist. The robe, a gift from Patrick and Pam the first Christmas they were married, was old and beginning to show some wear, but it was comfortable and familiar, and Kathleen needed that reassurance to deal with her husband.

Phil Wocheck, with the support of his walker, was standing behind the high-backed, overstuffed sofa, staring down at the younger man. He looked up when she entered the living room with the children. "He's still asleep," he announced in a none-too-quiet voice.

Kathleen was surprised and pleased to see the elderly man using the walker and not sitting in his wheelchair, but she kept that observation to herself. "Shh, don't wake him." She looked down at her sleeping husband and her breath caught in her throat for one heart-stopping moment. She had used to love to watch him sleep. Even dead to the world he was one of the most handsome men she had ever seen. The stubble of beard on his chin was heavier than it had been a few hours before. His dark blond hair fell over his forehead in a thick wave. He looked neither boyish nor abandoned, but slept with the same quiet efficiency that he brought to everything he did.

Devon's clear gray eyes opened and he stared up at her. That was something else she had forgotten. That he came awake instantly, alert and oriented to his surroundings, unlike her. She hated waking up. She took as long about it as she could. "Good morning, Kathleen," he said, as though they were alone in the room, alone in the universe.

"Good—good morning, Devon," she stammered, frowning as she tried not to remember those other long-ago mornings when wrapped in his arms, he had awakened her inch by inch with his kisses.

He pushed himself up on one elbow and raked his hand, fingers splayed, through his hair.

"It looks like I overslept."

"So did I. I'm sorry we woke you. You need the rest." The words almost stuck in her throat. Except for last night, they hadn't spoken face-to-face in almost two weeks. She'd forgotten how devastating the sight of him could be.

"I'm fine. I caught a couple of hours' sleep on the plane." His voice sounded strange, a little strained, or so she imagined.

"I want my breakfast," Phil demanded once more.

"Breakfast," Andrej seconded, leaning over the couch. Marta smiled, nodding shyly.

"Do you think she understands?" Devon asked, smiling back.

"I hope so." Kathleen motioned the little girl toward the dining area. "I think so. Paul Chambers says children her age pick up foreign languages so much more quickly than adults. But she still doesn't speak."

"Give her time. She's been through a hell of a lot for a four-year-old." Devon sat up. He dropped his head in his hands. "Wow, I feel like I've been run over by a truck."

"Jet lag. You'll feel better when you've eaten. I'll order from room service," Kathleen offered.

"I want oatmeal with brown sugar and a boiled egg," Phil announced. He was already seated at the table.

"Pancakes," Andrej ordered. "Maple syrup." It was his favorite American breakfast food.

Marta tugged on her brother's sleeve.

"For Marta, too. With lots of syrup," Andrej translated.

"Your wish is my command," Kathleen said. Laughing at the three expectant faces, she bent to pick up the house phone. "What would you like, Devon?" She turned, still laughing.

He was watching her, his interest focused on the swelling curve of her breasts just visible above the open neckline of her robe. His hand balled into a fist on his knee. He lifted his eyes and their gazes collided, locked. Dark fires smoldered in the misty gray depths of his eyes. Kathleen shivered, wanting to hug her arms tightly around her to ward off the allure of his spellbinding gaze. "I thought you might remember what I like for breakfast," he said, so quietly the others couldn't hear.

"Devon, please." Once again she was too aware of her sleep-tousled appearance, too aware of her nakedness beneath the robe and thin cotton nightgown, of her bare feet and the way her hair curled wildly about her shoulders. Far too aware of his body, hard and strong and totally, uncompromisingly male, only inches from hers.

Her nipples tightened and heat rushed to her belly. She knew exactly what he was thinking. This was how she had always looked, how she had always felt when they had awakened after he had made love to her all through the silvery Paris night and into the long, lazy summer mornings. Days and nights when they had needed neither food nor drink, but only each other. It would be so easy to let herself fall into that same pattern again. *So easy to fall in love with him all over again.*

"Devon," she said, hearing the panic in her voice and unable to filter it out. "Don't do this to us."

He blinked and looked down at his fist. Slowly, deliberately, he relaxed his grip. When he looked at her again his eyes didn't smolder with the embers of remembered passion, didn't burn with the heat of new love. They were unreadable, hard and brilliant as diamonds reflecting a winter sky. "What do I want for breakfast?" he asked, as though the moment just past had never happened.

"Yes, breakfast." The two words were all she could manage. She took a step backward, away from the dizzying, dangerous combination of heat and ice.

"Coffee." He stood and headed for Phil's bathroom. "Just coffee. Hot and black and lots of it," he said over his shoulder, not looking back.

CHAPTER SEVEN

"C'MON KIDS, this way. There's someone here I want to talk to," Devon said, hoisting Marta into his arms. She had been picking golden fallen leaves from along the pathway and now had a sizable bouquet. She'd kept tugging on his hand as they walked, stopping him to add another specimen to her collection, holding each one up for his inspection as he oohed and aahed. Now the little girl shifted in his arms and waved at a bright red cardinal sitting on a tree branch. "Look, Andrej," Devon said, pointing out the bird to the boy.

Andrej studied the cardinal. "Red bird," he said succinctly. He clapped his gloved hands together, but the bird didn't fly. He waved his Chicago Bears cap in the air, but the cardinal just fluffed his wings.

"A cardinal," Devon informed him.

"Cardinal," Andrej repeated dutifully.

"Pretty red bird," Devon said, hoping to elicit some response from Marta. She tilted her head and looked at him with bright, intelligent eyes, much like the bird on the tree branch. Devon held his breath, wishing, hoping she would respond but she remained silent. He swallowed his impatience and his disappointment. "Red bird," he said once more for emphasis, trying his best to follow the advice Paul Chambers had given Kathleen. *Go slow, let her set the pace. When she's ready, when she's healed, she'll let you know.* It didn't matter at all which language she spoke, only that she did.

In the meantime he'd just muddle on as best he could, reading to Marta from picture books, discussing dinosaurs with Andrej, watching *Barney* and *Sesame Street* and *Jurassic Park* on video while Kathleen eased herself back into her office routine. At bedtime, he helped tuck both kids in before going off to his own Spartan room in the employees' wing. Each morning since he'd arrived Devon had also stuck around for Andrej's English lessons with Phil, but as of Friday his services in that department would no longer be required.

Kathleen had interviewed a special-education major from the university, Julie Weber, the day before. Devon had been closeted with Edward discussing the progress Liam Hardesty was making on the Bangkok project at the time, but Kathleen had been enthusiastic about the young woman, and Phil had given his approval by pronouncing her intelligent and not too "yackity." She would be coming three hours a day to tutor the children starting the following Monday.

"What's in there?" Andrej demanded, interrupting Devon's thoughts. The boy had spied a long, low building ahead of them.

"That's what I want you to see. Come on." Devon really hadn't expected to enjoy himself this much when he suggested they skip the last half hour of English lessons before lunch and go for a walk. The bright, late-morning sunlight glinting off the ice-blue waters of the lake had been irresistible. Even Phil had agreed it was an uncommonly fine day, more like late September than November, and had emerged from the suite to sit on the terrace, wrapped in a heavy wool sweater with a blanket over his knees.

Marta settled happily into the crook of Devon's elbow and wrapped her arms around his neck, tickling him with the wet leaves, but he didn't complain. She felt too good, too right in his arms, and he didn't want to do anything to spoil the tenuous rapport. Wiggling into a more comfortable position, the little girl gave him a hug, and his heart lurched. He hugged her back. He'd never been around kids much in his adult life, but he was finding that it was easy to get addicted to this kind of unquestioning acceptance and trust.

Damned easy.

Devon stopped in front of the large metal building that housed his grandfather Addison's collection of classic cars. The structure was the newest addition to Timberlake Lodge, although it was one the guests never saw. It sat at the end of the service road behind the hotel, protected by an elaborate security system and an armed guard at night. The cars inside were worth a small fortune, and Devon didn't know what the hell to do with them.

He punched in the pass code on the keypad outside a door in the side of the building and entered. Michael Kenton was bent over the engine of a sleek, sky-blue Bugatti Type 57-S racing car. He straightened as Devon appeared with Marta in his arms and Andrej at his heels.

"I heard you were back in Tyler," Michael said. He lifted a grease-stained hand holding an oily rag in lieu of a handshake. "Welcome home."

"Good to be back." Devon returned the salute with his free hand. They both did think of Tyler as home, although neither of them had been born or raised there. "What's up with the Bugatti?" He hoped nothing serious. No two of the classic race cars designed by Ettore Bugatti in the twenties and thirties were built alike. All replacement parts had to be specially made, so keeping one in running condition could be a full-time job.

"She's fine," Michael assured him. "Just a routine maintenance check."

"Hope you weren't planning on firing up the engine." Devon indicated the silent, bright-eyed child in his arms with a nod of his head. "I'm not sure how Marta would react to the noise." While sleek and fast on the road, the Bugatti had an engine so loud it sounded as if all the hounds of hell had been let loose in the building.

"Not today," Michael assured him with a smile in Marta's direction. He lowered the cowl over the engine and fastened it down with two leather straps while Andrej watched with round, fascinated eyes. "Do you want to sit in the cockpit?" Michael asked.

"Sit in? Yes, please." The boy looked at Devon for permission.

"Go ahead," he said with a grin. His grandfather Addison had never once allowed him such a pleasure. The cars had been sacrosanct, inviolate, hidden away on his Yorkshire estate. They were still hidden away, but far from sacrosanct.

"I will drive in Grand Prix," Andrej said, already lost in a fantasy of speed and racing glory. As Michael boosted him up into the car, the youngster fairly beamed with pride and excitement. He grabbed the steering wheel with both hands and began making engine noises in his throat that were almost as loud as the genuine article.

"They're all roadworthy if you want to take one out," Michael said, looking over the two rows of restored and refurbished classics, ranging from the Bugatti to a 1917 Pierce Arrow touring car, a Bentley, a Rolls-Royce Silver Ghost and a half dozen of Detroit's finest models.

"No thanks," Devon said, conscious as always of fitting in with the natives. He knew how quickly his tenuous acceptance as one of them could congeal into certainty that he really was nothing but an English-bred, Harvard-educated rich boy playing at being just a regular Joe. Driving a 1930 Duesenberg up to the front door of Gates Department Store to buy a pair of socks would do it as quickly as anything.

He didn't have to explain further to Michael Kenton. Even though they came from vastly different backgrounds, they were both outsiders working to make a place for themselves in the small, close-knit community.

But Kenton had by far the harder time of it. An ex-convict, a stranger in town, he had been the prime suspect when Ingalls Farm and Machinery had burned the year before. Even though he had been technically cleared of the arson suspicion early on, and later had married Sarah Fleming, the minister of Tyler Fellowship, a few townspeople still remained wary of his presence among them. Devon wasn't one of them. He could only be thankful that a man with Michael Kenton's knowledge and experience with vintage cars was available to take charge of his grandfather's collection.

Being outsiders working to make a place for themselves wasn't the only thing they had in common. They had both been born without a name. Devon because his mother had not cared to marry the French playboy who got her pregnant, and because she wanted her son to carry on the Addison name. And Michael Kenton because his mother had been a teenager seduced by Ronald Baron, a philanderer married to Judson Ingalls's daughter, Alyssa.

"Great day for a drive," Michael prompted. "Probably one of the last nice days we'll have." Despite the warm sunshine outside, winter was nipping at Tyler's heels.

"I know. And the Caddy's tempting." Devon eyed the robin's-egg-blue 1959 El Dorado Biarritz convertible with appreciation. "She's a beauty, isn't she?"

"Tail fins and all," Michael agreed. He smiled again, but there was a rueful twist to his lips. "It's a car even some of Tyler's most hidebound citizens could appreciate."

Devon gave his friend a sharp look, knowing Kenton had discerned the path of his thoughts. He hoped Michael couldn't visualize what else he'd been thinking as he gazed at the convertible. Crystal clear and perfect, the image of Kathleen sitting beside him in the front seat of the Caddy—her hair blowing in the wind, her hand on his knee as they raced along the deserted back roads near the lake— had popped unbidden into his brain. "I'd better pass," he said reluctantly. "It's pretty cold for the kids to be riding in a ragtop."

"You're taking the kids with you?" Michael asked, closing his toolbox.

"We're heading out to Barney's Farm Market," Devon revealed.

"Probably should pass on the Caddy," Michael said. "One of them might catch cold or get an earache."

"Yeah," Devon said with a reluctant grin. "I thought of that myself. We'll take the Bronco."

"Listen to us." Michael shook his head. "We sound like two old hens clucking over their chicks." Michael and Sarah were expecting their first child at Christmastime, so it didn't surprise Devon that the other man would consider the children's welfare first. His friend had had months to get used to the idea of being a father. But it surprised the hell out of Devon that his own thoughts had followed the exact same path. After all, he'd only been a full-time father for two days.

"Amazing," Devon said, and he meant it.

Michael glanced at his watch. "It's almost noon. I'd better be calling it a morning. I want to get back to the parsonage and make sure Sarah gets a nap after lunch."

"Is anything wrong?"

Michael shrugged. "No," he said, but the denial wasn't convincing. "Just tired, I guess. She works too hard, does too much. She doesn't want anyone to think the baby coming's slowing her down."

Devon nodded, picturing Kathleen doing the same thing. But only for a moment. Thinking of Kathleen carrying a baby, his baby, was definitely off-limits.

"Why don't you call her and have her drive out? We'll all have lunch together here."

Michael held up his grease-stained hands. "I'm not exactly dressed for the tea-and-crumpets routine."

"Who said anything about tea and crumpets?" Devon said with a grin. "Steak hoagies for us, burgers for the kids. Soup and salad for the ladies."

"Ladies?" Michael quirked a dark eyebrow.

"I hoped to talk Kathleen into joining us."

Michael shook his head. "Thanks for the invitation, buddy, but no. I saw Jeff's car in the parking lot when I went up to the lodge to use the phone awhile ago."

"He probably dropped in to check on Phil."

"Probably." Michael slammed the lid on his toolbox with just a little more force than necessary.

Devon had two good friends in Tyler. One of them was standing before him; the other was Michael's half brother, Jeff Baron. The trouble was the two men weren't on speaking terms, and probably never would be, if Jeff couldn't come to terms with Ronald Baron having fathered another son. Once, a few months before, Devon had attempted to act as intermediary between the two brothers. The meeting had been a disaster, with Jeff stalking out of the room without saying a word to Michael, and Devon hadn't had the nerve to try again. For now he walked a tightrope between the stubborn siblings and bided his time, hoping sooner or later the two of them would come to their senses and realize that blood was thicker than water.

"I'm hungry," Andrej announced, having brought his pretend car trip to a halt. "Lunch." He repeated the word in his native tongue and Marta began to squirm in Devon's arms. He set her feet on the floor.

"You'd better get those two something to eat or they'll take off your arm," Michael advised with a grin.

"I guess you're right." Marta was tugging Devon in the direction of the door. Andrej grabbed his other hand and added his weight to his sister's. "Give me a call when you and Sarah have a free night."

"Does that mean you're going to be staying around town for a while?"

Devon thought about the unstable situation with the Addison Bangkok property. He thought about his commitments to DEVCHECK and to his mother's social calendar, then looked down at his insistent captors and grinned. "You damned well better believe it does."

PHIL, TIRED AFTER being "poked and prodded" by Jeff Baron, decided not to join them for lunch, so Devon and the children went in search of Kathleen on their own. Marta and Andrej stayed close to his side, smiling shyly but delightedly at the half dozen department-store Santas and Mrs. Santas, in full regalia, gathered in the lobby as they headed for the business offices behind the main desk. But Kathleen wasn't in her office. She wasn't conferring with Sheila Wagner, Timberlake's manager, or anyone else that he could see. The young room-clerk trainee on duty thought she might be checking on the setup for the Santas' afternoon sessions, so Devon headed in that direction.

That lead was a dead end, too. They finally found Kathleen sitting at a table in the restaurant. But she wasn't alone. Devon narrowed his eyes, not quite certain who the man with her could be. He was too broad-shouldered, his hair too short and brown to be Jeff Baron. It wasn't Edward or any other member of Timberlake's staff that he recognized. A quick stab of something he'd rather not put a name to jabbed at his gut.

Devon didn't like the way the guy was leaning across the narrow table, his hand on the tablecloth just inches from Kathleen's, talking low, making *his wife* laugh the way she used to laugh with him. Except, of course, she had every right in the world to be laughing like that, talking like that. Theirs wasn't a real marriage; it was a necessity. A convenience. Wasn't that what they used to call them a hundred years or more ago? A marriage of convenience. In their case not a union for power or wealth, or dynastic ambitions, but for the children's sake.

"C'mon, kids. Let's join Kathleen," he said, not realizing how harshly he had spoken until he caught Andrej looking up at him in alarm.

"She is not alone," the boy replied.

"It's okay."

Devon raised his hand in greeting to three or four people he recognized as the little party crossed the room. Kathleen looked over her companion's shoulder as they approached. For a moment he thought her smile altered as she recognized them, grew softer, more thoughtful. But he blinked, and found she was laughing as brightly as before. "Devon. Kids. Are lessons over so soon?" She glanced at her watch. "Good heavens, it's almost noon."

"Lessons are over and we're hungry." The guy must be a real spellbinder for Kathleen to lose track of time in a restaurant crowded with noontime customers. "We thought you'd want to join us for lunch. We're going on a picnic."

"A picnic? It's November."

"It's a great day." He stared pointedly at her companion.

"Devon, you remember Josh Rader," Kathleen said hastily. "And these are my...our children, Andrej and Marta." The guy grinned at the kids and half rose from his chair and held out his hand. "Edward has just promoted Josh to manager at the Aspen Creek property. We're celebrating with a cup of coffee."

"Of course, I remember. We met in Chicago last spring. How are you, Josh?" Devon held out his hand, training from years of forced etiquette classes overriding his instinctive dislike of Josh Rader's handsome, grinning face.

"Couldn't be better." Josh rose to his full height in deference when he realized who Devon was. They were the same height, and about the same build. The other man's handshake was hard and firm, his smile full of strong, white teeth. He worked out, Devon guessed—lifted weights, probably ran. He was in good shape, and it looked as if he worked just as hard on his tan. Quite a specimen. Devon swallowed an ungentlemanly sneer. He was going to need a toupee, though. And soon.

"Congratulations on the Aspen Creek job." Like Timberlake Lodge, the property in the foothills of the Rockies had once been a privately owned hunting preserve. It was Edward's newest acquisition and had the potential to be a real moneymaker. Josh Rader might look like a snake-oil salesman, but Devon remembered reading the man's résumé and it was impressive.

That wasn't why he felt like belting the guy. The reason for his dislike was a lot more basic, more primitive than that. It had to do with the other tidbit of information Edward Wocheck had let drop when they were discussing Josh Rader's future on that dreary March day. It was because he was dating Kathleen.

And because she had never said a word to Devon about it, then or later.

And nothing about the man coming to Tyler today.

"Thanks. I'm looking forward to it," he was saying expansively. "The Aspen's quite a challenge. Just the way Timberlake must have been a few years ago." He looked around the slowly filling dining room. "Doing well now, though. 'Course, the old man's taken a special interest in the place."

"The old man takes a special interest in all the Addison properties," Devon reminded him. "And now, if you'll excuse us, I'd like to have lunch with my family." He saw Kathleen's eyes narrow at the slight emphasis he placed on the last word, but pretended not to.

"Certainly." Josh shot Kathleen a questioning look. "Are we still on for tonight?"

"Of course." Her lips curved in a smile, but her eyes were the dark, frosty blue of a December midnight sky when she turned to Devon. "Josh has asked me out tonight. We're going to the Heidelberg for dinner."

"Checking out the competition." Josh's expression didn't change, but Devon had the impression he wasn't really talking about the area's only other upscale restaurant. He wondered exactly what Kathleen had told the man about their marriage, about Triglav. Rader hadn't offered his congratulations. Kathleen must have made it clear she didn't want any.

Devon raised an eyebrow but didn't say anything more. He was reminding himself that he didn't have any right to keep Kathleen from seeing Josh Rader; she was his wife in name only. But the strength of his antagonism toward the other man, a gut reaction he couldn't control, surprised and silenced him.

Josh took his silence as a dismissal. He excused himself and walked out of the restaurant.

Kathleen turned on Devon, her voice low and restrained, her eyes sparkling with anger. "Whatever got into you? Josh is a valued employee and a friend. You treated him like—like a servant."

Devon winced. *Here we go again,* he thought. *Just like the bad old days. That damned lord-of-the-manor business. She made it sound as if he had some kind of disease, something catching.* "I know. I know. The high-and-mighty Lord Addison routine. You don't have to say it. I'm sorry," he said, meaning it. "His being here threw me, that's all. I—I forgot you were seeing him."

A hint of color rushed to her cheeks. "I'm not *seeing* him," she said, just a little too nonchalantly to be credible. "At least not the way you mean. But we have gone out together a few times, and I felt I owed him an explanation." She lifted her shoulders. "About us. About the kids, that's all."

"You already told him about our marriage?"

"Of course." She sighed. "We must be the talk of the whole DEVCHECK—Addison Hotels conglomerate. He already knew."

"I'm not surprised. News like that travels fast." Devon didn't like having this kind of discussion in a crowded dining room, but it seemed as if they were never alone together. "Look, let's get out of here. We came to invite you to go to Barney's Farm Market with us."

"Barney's?"

"Sure. They're still open, aren't they?"

She nodded dumbly.

"I thought we could buy the kids a hot dog and cider and doughnuts. Maybe a candy apple for dessert. That's the picnic. Then we could show them the horses and the farm animals."

"I—I thought I'd call my mother and meet her for a sandwich at Marge's."

"Oh." He looked down at Marta, who was following the conversation with her eyes. "Were you planning on taking the kids with you?"

"Well, no. Sheila Wagner said she'd keep an eye on them for an hour or so." She glanced at Andrej, who was intent on the progress of a department-store Santa wandering through the dining room, looking bewildered and lost. She lowered her voice. "Mom's been researching holiday customs with Elise Fairmont at the library. She wants to make sure the children aren't disappointed at Christmastime." The maître d' came to the lost Santa's rescue and pointed the way to the meeting rooms.

"They'll expect a present in their shoes on the eve of St. Nicholas Day," Devon said. "That's December fifth. St. Nicholas Day is December sixth."

"How did you know that?" Kathleen looked impressed.

"I asked."

"I see."

"Look, you go have lunch with Anna, and I'll take the kids to Barney's."

"No," she said, looking down at her ringless hands. Devon had seen her seal herself off like that from him before—four years ago, after she had told him there was no hope for them finding common ground in their lives, no way for them to go on without breaking each other's hearts. His gut tightened and he braced himself for the worst. "I'll go with you. Mom will understand. We've got things we have to discuss. And now is as good a time as any."

CHAPTER EIGHT

"YOU'VE GOT powdered sugar on your chin."

"Where?" Kathleen asked, running her tongue over her lips.

"Here." Devon pointed to a spot on his own square chin. "Shall I wipe it off for you?"

"No!" Kathleen said, too quickly, too forcefully. She didn't want him to touch her, not even casually. "No, thank you. I have a napkin." She dabbed at her mouth. "Did I get it?"

"All gone." He crumpled his own napkin and tossed it in an old wooden barrel that served as a trash container. The tension between them was as thick as the smoke rising from a distant pile of burning leaves, and she knew it was her fault. She was just too uncertain of her feelings, too confused by the conflicting emotions he aroused in her to allow him any intimacies.

"Where are the kids?" she asked, looking over her shoulder. She scooted around on the bench seat of a picnic table in the front of Barney's Farm Market and scanned the parking lot and yard of the big, white farmhouse. The snack area was surrounded by stacked pyramids of late-season pumpkins and squash, old-fashioned pushcarts piled high with multicolored Indian corn, bright orange bittersweet bouquets and grapevine wreaths.

"They're watching Jacob curry the horses." Devon hooked his thumb over his shoulder in the direction of the huge red barn that dominated the low hill behind them. "He came to get them while you were talking to Mrs. Beamish. He promised them a ride in the surrey when he's through."

"They'll like that. Did you mention to him that Marta doesn't speak?" Jacob Beamish was a former circus performer who had retired to Tyler ten years before. He owned saddle horses and had taught a lot of Tyler kids how to ride. For the past couple of years, in the fall, he and his wife had teamed up with the owner of Barney's to give hayrides and host riding parties in the woods that bordered the lakeshore. The autumn ritual had become popular with both residents and tourists alike.

"I didn't have to tell him, Kathleen. He knows." Devon scooped up the leftovers from Marta's and Andrej's sandwiches, threw the crumbs to the birds and dropped the rest into the barrel. "Most everyone in town knows the kids' story. The Tyler grapevine is very efficient. Especially with Grandma Bauer holding court at Worthington House."

Kathleen laughed, feeling charitable toward him once more. "I stand corrected." She forced herself to relax, to enjoy what was certainly one of the last nice afternoons they would have for many months. She had to stop being so overprotective of the children. They were safe here in Tyler. They were all safe.

Devon took a swallow from his foam cup of hot cider. "Do you want the last doughnut?"

She shook her head. "I couldn't eat another bite."

"I can." He finished off the doughnut and brushed the powdered sugar from his lips and hands. "How about one of Mrs. Barney's cinnamon candy apples?"

She shook her head. "Thanks, no."

Devon raised an eyebrow. "Such fortitude. What about some of the maple walnut fudge I saw you eyeing at the candy counter? I can't believe you have the willpower to say no to both of them. You, the owner of the world's most powerful sweet tooth.''

Kathleen stuck out her tongue. "A gentleman wouldn't point out a lady's weakness that way."

His gray eyes narrowed, held her pinned to her seat. "But a husband would."

"Devon—"

He stood up and offered his hand, forestalling her words. "C'mon. Let's take a walk back to the lake. We'll meet Jacob and the kids there and hitch a ride back in the surrey with them. How does that sound?"

She sighed and stood, bracing her hands against the table. It had always been difficult for her to deny him anything when he was in this mood—witty, tender, cajoling. But the things she had to say to him today were too important to leave unspoken. Mentally she stiffened her spine, and her resolve. "I have a ton of work still to do this afternoon, but that's an offer I can't resist. It sounds heavenly. I'll walk back to the lake with you, but I won't eat a piece of fudge or a cinnamon candy apple."

"How about a plain apple, my pretty?" he asked in a falsetto cackle as he pulled a bright red one from the pocket of his jacket.

"Don't tell me. Marta made you watch *Snow White* again last night, didn't she."

"Heigh-ho."

Kathleen held out her hand for the apple. "Devon, what am I going to do with you?"

He looked at her for a long, heart-stopping moment, then turned on his heel and led her down the rutted wagon path to the lake. "I don't know, Kathleen. What are you intending to do with me?"

She ignored the flutter of longing that coursed through her veins as he pushed a wave of heavy blond hair off his forehead. Ruthlessly she channeled her thoughts away from the long, strong legs keeping pace with hers and the heat of his sun-warmed body. She had to be in control today. She had to think with her brain, not with her hormones, with that squashed-down, longing, sensual part of her that craved the touch and taste and scent of this man like a drug. What they had to discuss was too important, too volatile for her to allow herself to be distracted by his sexuality. "For starters, I need to ask you to keep the children while I have dinner with Josh tonight."

"Ah. You need a baby-sitter. Is that why you've forgone giving me a real dressing-down for treating Rader like—how did you put it? A servant?"

Kathleen broke off a tall stalk of dried grass and twirled it between her fingers. The autumn scents of burning leaves and ripe highbush cranberries swirled through the crisp air. A lone grasshopper, intent on some mysterious errand of great importance that must be accomplished before its winter sleep, hopped along the path ahead of them. "I'm the one who should apologize for that crack," she said at last. "But you were being just a little overbearing."

"Bad genes. Remember, my grandfather was a robber baron," he said, giving her that quizzical, lopsided smile that always made her weak in the knees.

She averted her gaze before it happened again. *Damn him.* He knew her too well. She had been hard on him in the restaurant, but as usual he had been able to push all her buttons without even trying. "I didn't mean to say you couldn't be a jackass when you put your mind to it." She bit her lip. This was going to be more difficult than she'd imagined. "It's just that I overreacted back at Timberlake."

"I see." He looked down at his shoes, but from the corner of her eye she saw that he was still smiling.

"You're not making this easy for me."

"Making what easy, Kath?"

"This apology. We aren't used to being married. We . . . I'm not used to being referred to as half of a couple. You caught me off guard."

"Is that what you meant when you said we had a lot of things to talk about?" He was no longer smiling. He was gazing ahead, his mouth a straight line, his profile like sculpted marble, the face of a medieval Norman knight she'd seen once on a tomb in an English country church—proud, handsome, aristocratic, impossible to read.

"Yes."

"I'm sorry *I* overreacted to Josh asking you out. I'd forgotten you two were seeing each other before . . . before Triglav." He was choosing his words as carefully as she was. They broke through the trees, and the lake was spread out before them, the slight breeze from the southwest rippling its placid waters, brown and yellow fallen leaves bobbing on the surface like elfin boats that had lost their crews.

Devon indicated a wooden bench on the shore near the wagon track, and they sat down to wait for Jacob and the children.

"I'm seeing Josh tonight to explain our situation," Kathleen said softly. "I owe him that much, and I don't like him having heard about it through the corporate grapevine."

"And after tonight do you intend to go out with him again?"

She turned her head, alerted by a slight roughness in his voice, an edge to his words. *Jealousy?* She thought not. She hoped not. Because if she let herself believe he cared, she would let herself start to dream again, to care again, too, and that way lay heartache and despair. She couldn't, wouldn't, suffer through that misery again. "I don't know. We saw each other quite frequently this summer. It's... difficult."

"I should buy you a ring," he said softly, almost as if he were talking to himself. He glanced at her hands. "A plain gold band. To show the Josh Raders of the world where to draw the line."

"No," she said too quickly, too forcefully. "No. I don't want a ring." She wasn't certain how she felt about Josh Rader. She enjoyed his company, his kisses, but that was all. She'd never allowed herself to go farther, never wanted to go farther in the relationship, either emotionally or physically, but instinctively she knew she didn't dare reveal that information to this man.

"You don't want to be taken for a married woman, you mean."

"Don't try to score a point off Josh Rader by making me wear your ring."

Devon continued to stare out across the lake, toward Tyler where the grain elevator, water tower and church steeples were visible above the barren treetops in the distance. "Forget I brought it up. Forget I even mentioned Josh Rader."

"I can't forget you asked," she said, pretending to watch a red-tailed hawk soar above the shoreline, but in actuality seeing little of the autumn landscape. "I can't forget you have the right to ask."

"Kathleen—"

She held up her hand. "Let me finish. I've thought about this, worried about it every night, and I can't find a solution."

"A solution to what?"

"To us. Devon, what are we going to do about our marriage?"

"Exactly what we've been doing. You stay in the suite. I stay in the employees' wing. We see the kids together, work out their problems together."

"But, Devon, you shouldn't have to be a part of this. Surely Amanda can find some way around all the legal technicalities so that I can adopt the children by myself. Single-parent adoptions are approved everywhere, every day."

He turned on her so fiercely that Kathleen shrank back in momentary alarm. He took her by the upper arms, his grip implacable but not painful, holding her so that she couldn't turn away. His gray eyes bored into hers. "Listen to me. We're staying married until there is no longer any question whatsoever about the children's legal status. Until all the papers are signed, sealed and delivered into our hands that say they are our children, now and forever. Ours, Kathleen. Not just yours."

She wanted to close her eyes against the power of that image: the four of them a family, complete and whole. An image so compelling it took her breath away. Compelling, but insubstantial. A dream, a fantasy—nothing more. "I don't want to be married to you, Devon," she said helplessly, all the sorrow and heartache of their long-ago affair boiling up inside her, the pain as new and fresh as if it had ended only yesterday, and not four years before.

"Why not?" he asked helplessly. "What in hell is so wrong with me that you can't stand the thought of staying married to me?"

"We're not married, Devon," she said, trying desperately to form her argument when all she could think about was the touch of his hands on her arms, the brush of his hard thigh against her knee. She had always thought she would marry a man like her father. Good. Strong. Capable. Uncomplicated. She would have the kind of marriage that Anna and Johnny had. She had never intended to fall in love with a man whose background and life-style were so far removed from her own. A man with whom she had nothing in common, a man whose world she neither wanted nor belonged in. "Not truly. Not the way it should be. We have a business arrangement. You described it so yourself. I sleep in the suite. You sleep in another wing of the hotel...."

"If not sleeping together is what's bothering you," he said, gentling his grip, sliding his hands down her sleeves to her hands, taking them between his own. "I don't think it would be a hardship for either of us to remedy that lack."

"No, it wouldn't be a problem. Sex was never a problem," she said, the words sifting between her lips before she could stop herself.

He raised his hands to frame her face. His thumbs brushed the corners of her mouth and her lips parted slightly. He looked perplexed, as off balance as she felt as he leaned closer, until they were only inches apart. His breath, warm and spicy, caressed her lips. He kissed her then, a brush-stroke kiss that set her lips to tingling and sent a sharp, sweet stab of desire coursing through her veins. He felt her involuntary response, and the kiss grew hungrier, more intense. Her lips parted as the pressure of his mouth increased on hers. His tongue slipped inside, and hers answered the dark caress. He tasted of sugar and apples and passion. Kathleen leaned closer, her breasts brushing his chest. The curl of desire inside her blossomed into need, harsh and acute.

Devon spoke, his breath like fire against her cheek. "No, sex was never a problem between us. It was a pleasure. A very great pleasure. Making love we were always in sync, always in harmony, Kathleen. We never fought while we were naked, while we were in bed in each other's arms. It was as if we were alone in the universe when we were together in the dark.''

Oh, God, he was good at this, weaving a spell with his words and his touch. She could almost believe. Almost. Kathleen put both hands on his chest and pushed him away. She leaned back, away from the temptation of his kiss. ''Unfortunately, the same couldn't be said for when we were fully clothed.'' She lurched off the bench and went to stand at the water's edge.

''We've been doing a pretty good job of it so far.''

Dammit, their kiss had nearly undone her, yet he sounded completely in control of himself. An aristocrat to his very toes. ''We've been together a total of five days,'' Kathleen reminded him, still with her back turned. ''We're living in separate wings of a hotel. We hardly even see each other.''

''We can find a house.'' He was standing, too—she could tell by the sound of his voice. Far out on the lake a loon called, a sad, lonely sound that spoke of approaching winter and the death of another year, because the striking, black-and-white birds only appeared on Tyler's lakes as they stopped to rest on their long migration south.

''No,'' Kathleen said. ''That wouldn't work. Devon Addison, heir to the Addison fortune, going to Rotary Club luncheons and heading up the recycling committee? Living on Sycamore Street in Tyler, Wisconsin? What a joke.''

He was beside her in a heartbeat. She didn't have time to react before he grabbed her arm and turned her to face him. ''What was that crack supposed to mean?''

"I was talking about myself, Devon. The joke's on me. Don't you see? I can't be what you want and need in a wife. I'm not glamorous enough or sophisticated enough to be Mrs. Devon Addison."

"The hell you aren't." He was very angry now. "I've seen you charm the pants off diplomats and millionaires in half the capitals of Europe."

She whirled back to the lake. A motorboat arrowed across the water, a die-hard fisherman out for one last afternoon of angling for perch and bass. "That wasn't really me," she said between clenched teeth. "That was Edward's executive assistant. She's not the same woman. She's not me."

She thought of the people Devon had introduced her to in London—his friends, his mother's friends. Men and women who changed life partners and sex partners as easily as they changed shoes. Mothers who sent their children, some barely older than Andrej, off to military school and boarding school so that raising them wouldn't interfere with their parties, their spa visits, their skiing vacations to Saint Moritz and Aspen.

Even though she'd learned to hide her shock and dismay when she met and mingled with those people as Edward's alter ego, she would never, even if she lived a thousand lifetimes, be that sophisticated, that blasé. But Devon didn't understand. To him it was as natural as a Knights of Columbus potluck supper in Tyler.

They were from two different worlds. Worlds that couldn't meet, only collide. She didn't want to fight with him. She didn't want to love him. She didn't want to feel strongly about him for any reason, good or bad. She reached out and touched his jacket very lightly. "I can't be that kind of woman. And you can't give me what I want."

"I can give you everything."

"Exactly." She shook her head, not trusting her voice. She could feel the heat of him through the cloth that separated her fingers from his skin. She could feel the slow, steady thud of his heartbeat reverberate along her nerve endings. His voice was low, his words rough with emotion. Tears pricked behind her eyelashes and threatened to fall. She blinked them back. "I'm still just Kathleen Kelsey from Tyler, Wisconsin. I can't be like your mother, like your titled friends. I don't want to be."

The sound of harness bells and wagon wheels came from the direction of the trees. Devon swiveled his head to look and a muscle jumped in the hard line of his jaw. He turned back to Kathleen. "I get the idea. You're never going to believe that just because those people are my mother's friends, and mine, that I would chose to live my life differently from theirs. Maybe I'm a fool to even attempt to break through that rock-hard, Midwestern sanctimoniousness of yours and try to convince you otherwise. But get this straight, Kathleen. I meant what I said about wanting those kids as badly as you do. I won't back out on my commitment to them. I gave Rujana my word."

The surrey came into view, pulled by two matched dapple mares. The red-painted wheels whirled along in a blur. Andrej waved from the high seat and Jacob touched his whip to his hat. Marta was seated between them, beaming.

Kathleen dashed the tears from her eyes and pasted a smile on her face. "Hi, kids," she called out in a bright, false voice. "Can we hitch a ride back to the barn with you, Jacob?"

"Sure," said the rotund, jolly man, flicking his whip above the horses' rumps. "Hop aboard." The horses moved at a quicker pace, eating up the distance between them.

They had only a moment or two more of privacy. "Please, Devon," Kathleen whispered desperately. "Don't fight me on this. We're only making each other miserable. Let me go. I won't change my mind. We can't keep up this sham marriage. It will destroy our friendship, maybe even our lives. Tomorrow, the first thing in the morning, I'm going to talk to Amanda and Father Hennesey. I'm going to start proceedings for an annulment, and if you care about what's best for us all, you won't try to stop me."

DEVON LOOKED OUT onto the square from the long, low windows of Amanda Trask's law office. The leaves were gone from the maples, although a few clung tenaciously to the highest branches of the big oaks. He had a good view of the comings and goings on Main Street. Business was brisk at the Hair Affair this Tuesday morning, he noted. And Nora Forrester was arranging a Thanksgiving display of pumpkins and Indian corn in the front window of Gates Department Store. A little farther down the street he saw the imposing, white-haired figure of Judson Ingalls holding the door of Marge's for the Lutheran minister, Pastor Schoff, to enter the diner. Devon glanced at his watch: ten-fifteen. Judson was an hour late for the daily gathering of coffee drinkers.

Devon wondered if there was some problem at the F and M. The plant had been up and running at full speed for only a few weeks. There were still some kinks in the new machinery, some slow-ups on the assembly line that needed to be ironed out before work could begin in earnest on the two new contracts Alyssa and her assistant, Nate Cummings, had just finished negotiating with one of the big tractor manufacturers. Although DEVCHECK still held stock in the company, Devon had nothing to do with the day-to-day operation of the plant. Still, he'd give Alyssa a call, see how things were going, as soon as they got this interview out of the way.

"All right." The child-services caseworker raised her head, drawing his attention back into the room. "I think I have all the particulars straight." She smiled, tiny laugh lines at the corners of her mouth and eyes creasing her coffee-brown skin. "You say the children have been in the States for about a month."

"A little more than three weeks," Amanda answered for them.

The caseworker, Mrs. Parker, swiveled her head in the lawyer's direction, still smiling. "And all the paperwork for the immigration and naturalization people has been filed?"

"Yes, of course," Kathleen said, tapping her fingers on the arm of her chair. "All the information is there in front of you."

Devon could feel the tension radiating from his wife. He didn't have to turn his head and look at her pale, drawn face to see how nervous and edgy she was. To tell the truth, so was he. It was four days since the scene at the lake. Kathleen had been withdrawn and silent the entire time, working late in her office, eating at her desk, spending time with the children when he was away from Timberlake on business of his own.

She'd gone out with Josh Rader twice, leaving Devon alone in the suite with Phil and the children. She'd seen Amanda once and gone to lunch with the Catholic priest, Father Hennesey, on Friday. Devon knew because she'd made a point of telling him. But she'd avoided being alone with him. To top it all off, she hadn't been prepared for the social worker to show up at this meeting with Amanda.

Actually, neither had he, but because Mrs. Parker was in Tyler making a home visit in another adoption case today, she had made arrangements with Amanda to meet with them all. Now what should have been a simple up-date with their friend and lawyer had become far more than routine.

"All right..." The woman's voice trailed off as she continued reading from her notes. The file in her lap was almost an inch thick. Devon wasn't surprised. They'd been filling out paperwork and filing affidavits since the first day he'd returned to Tyler. "I see from your financial re-port, Mr. Addison, that there will be no problem whatso-ever in your ability to support the children." She looked up, pinning him to his seat as she gazed over the lenses of her half-glasses. "And I see, as well, that you have made generous provisions for Andrej and Marta in case of your death."

Devon nodded. Kathleen turned her head, giving him a puzzled look. "What does she mean by that?"

"I changed my will to include the children," he said quietly, realizing he should have told her sooner. He raised his voice, speaking directly to the social worker once more. "Naturally, the codicil is only temporary. When the adoption is final I will make them my heirs."

"Devon, I can't—"

He looked Kathleen straight in the eye. "Can you think of any better way to make sure they're provided for in case something happens to the two of us?"

"No," Kathleen said. She managed a smile when she looked back to find the caseworker eyeing her with a slight frown between her brows.

"You do have the children's birth certificates and the natural parents' death certificates," the woman contin-ued. "But so far you haven't found anyone to translate them into English, is that correct?"

"That is correct. We hope to have a qualified translation by the end of the week," Amanda assured her. "Triglav was a very small part of Yugoslavia. The dialect was not widely spoken. And of course, with the renewed hostilities in the region..." She lifted her slender shoulders in a shrug.

"I see." Mrs. Parker ruffled a few more sheets of paper and looked up, still frowning. "The same thing seems to be the case with your marriage certificate."

Devon held his breath. Kathleen leaned forward in her chair. "Yes," she said. "We were married by a parish priest in Triglav."

"I see." Another notation went into her notebook.

Amanda Baron Trask stood up from her chair. She walked around the big walnut desk and rested one hip on the corner, running a short-nailed hand down her skirt to smooth the material over her knee. "May I inquire where this line of questioning is headed, Mrs. Parker?" she asked politely, but with a hint of steel underlying her friendly query.

The social worker tilted her head to bring the younger woman into focus. "This whole situation is highly unusual, Mrs. Trask. I don't have to tell you that. The children's official background has been almost totally obliterated. The documents you do have are in a language very few people can understand."

"We were in a war zone, Mrs. Parker," Kathleen said sharply. "We barely escaped with our lives."

"I understand that. But the lack of official documentation does complicate my job a great deal," she answered patiently.

"The children have been granted official refugee status," Amanda reminded her, tapping her own stack of manila file folders. "The paperwork for legal adoption in the state of Wisconsin is also in the pipeline."

"Surely it's all routine from here on out?" Kathleen said.

"Has Mrs. Trask informed you that we have located relatives of the children's father?"

"Relatives?" Kathleen's hands gripped the arms of the chair so tightly her knuckles showed white through the skin.

"I'm sorry, Kath. Devon," Amanda said. "Mrs. Parker informed me this morning that cousins of Josef had been found in Cleveland only yesterday."

"Rujana told me there were no living members of the family," Kathleen murmured. "We never even thought to look for any."

"It was a routine immigration check," Mrs. Parker explained. "We weren't expecting to find blood relatives. But we have. They've been notified. I've instructed them to contact Mrs. Trask if they wish to know more about the children."

"Devon?" Kathleen turned to him, her eyes stricken.

"Don't borrow trouble, Kath," he said, reaching out to cover her hand with his own. She didn't flinch away, but neither did she acknowledge the contact. *Damn! He hadn't expected this. Relatives. Cousins.* He shouldn't have taken Rujana at her word. He should have instigated a search for relatives on his own, then they wouldn't have been blindsided like this, learning that the kids had relatives—who might want them for their own.

Kathleen faced the social worker once more. "You had no right," she said in barely more than a whisper.

"Yes, I do. That's why I'm here. To represent the best interests of two children who are officially wards of the state of Wisconsin. I have the authority,'' Mrs. Parker returned quietly.

"What do you mean, Mrs. Parker?'' Devon asked, making sure his voice held not the slightest hint of antagonism. "Are you saying that my wife and I are not qualified to raise Andrej and Marta?''

"I'm saying no such thing. I'm only stating the obvious. This is a very difficult situation. Your petition for adoption will most likely be heard by Judge Weinberger.''

"Weinberger?'' The name was unfamiliar. Devon looked to Amanda for enlightenment.

The expression in her cobalt-blue Baron eyes was slightly grim. "Judge Weinberger is an extremely conservative jurist,'' she said carefully.

Mrs. Parker nodded. "While Mr. Addison's considerable wealth will assure the children an adequate lifestyle—''

"I think *adequate* is an understatement, Mrs. Parker,'' Amanda said dryly.

The woman looked flustered. "Yes, of course. A very affluent life-style, naturally.''

Devon groaned inwardly. Kathleen's shoulders looked even stiffer, her mouth more tightly drawn than ever. He wished to hell they wouldn't keep bringing up his money. He had the suspicion he could swear on a stack of Bibles that he shared the same values, the same work ethic they did and they would still look at him as if he were some exotic specimen in a zoo.

He wanted to get the subject back on track. He had a bad feeling about the mysterious judge. "We all know the children will be well provided for, Mrs. Parker. What about this Judge Weinberger? I've never heard of him.''

"He's the family court judge for Sugar Creek county," Amanda explained. "He's very conservative, as I've already mentioned. Very family oriented."

"Good," Kathleen blurted out. "He should be pleased as punch that we want to make Andrej and Marta our own."

"It's not that simple," Mrs. Parker said. She took off her half-glasses and leaned forward in her chair. "The judge is more than just conservative. He's...well, he's fanatical about family values."

"What do you mean?"

"He isn't going to be happy with the fact that you're living in a hotel."

"Kathleen and the children are living in the family suite at Timberlake Lodge, Mrs. Parker," Amanda interrupted, lifting a warning hand in Kathleen's direction. "They are personal guests of Mr. Edward Wocheck."

"Yes, but the judge will want to know how soon you intend to move the children to a home of your own. When you intend to start living together as a family."

"I...we—" Kathleen broke off helplessly.

"The children are very happy at Timberlake," Devon said, letting a little of the arrogance that Kathleen always accused him of possessing seep into his words. "Phil Wocheck, Mrs. Trask's step-grandfather—" he glanced at Amanda, who nodded encouragement "—speaks enough of their native language to communicate with both children."

"He's been a wonderful help to us," Kathleen said. She cleared her throat, crossed her legs and leaned back in her chair, transforming herself in the blink of an eye into a confident, no-nonsense businesswoman. He'd seen her this way before, when she had made up her mind to fight for what she wanted, to prevail over any obstacles thrown in her path. "I don't know what we would have done without him."

"If it's only a house you're worried about, Mrs. Parker," Devon said, "we'll start looking for one this afternoon."

"It's not only a house," Mrs. Parker said. "I'm afraid the judge may take issue with the circumstances of your marriage."

"What?"

"Are you certain your marriage is legal in the eyes of the state of Wisconsin?"

"Amanda?" There was an edge of panic in Kathleen's voice, so well-hidden Devon didn't think the other two occupants of Amanda's oak-paneled office detected it. But he did. And he knew the reason why.

"I told you the judge was ultraconservative," Amanda interjected. "Mrs. Parker's right. I was going to suggest this myself." She didn't look directly at either of them, but focused somewhere in between. "Just to be on the safe side, just to plug all the loopholes, I think you should get married again."

CHAPTER NINE

"KATH, YOU CAN'T MEAN you're going to be married in that old thing. Why, if I've seen you wear that suit once, I've seen it a dozen times."

"You've seen it a dozen times because it's a classic Chanel, Glenna," Kathleen said, holding on to her patience with both hands. "I think it's a very good choice." She surveyed her figure in the mirror attached to the closet door in the bedroom where she'd grown up.

"It's dark and somber. It looks too much like Aunt Kathleen's going to a funeral, doesn't it, sweetheart?" Glenna cooed to the infant in her arms. The baby gurgled back. "Listen. She agrees with me. Does this child have fashion sense or what?" She rubbed noses with the little one.

"She is a child to be reckoned with," Kathleen agreed. She and Glenna were baby-sitting for Johnanne Patrice Kelsey while Patrick and Pam were shopping with Anna for the perfect Thanksgiving turkey, their contribution to the huge Kelsey family celebration planned for three days' time—the day after Kathleen's second wedding.

The four older children, Glenna's two and Marta and Andrej, were watching a video in the den. Quarreling voices—Megan's and Jimmy's, from the sound of them—floated up the stairs. Glenna bounced off the bed and left the room, leaning over the banister to call for silence or they would suffer the consequences.

"However," Kathleen said, picking up the conversation when her sister had returned, "Johnanne is too small to recognize the importance of minimizing certain body traits. I bought this suit because it makes me look thinner." She surveyed her figure with a critical eye. She hadn't felt like eating much for weeks, but she hadn't lost a pound. "How is it that every female character in every book you read always loses weight when confronted with any sort of stressful situation, but it never seems to happen in real life?" she asked, turning this way and that.

"Because none of them are Irish-German." Glenna's reflection nodded wisely above the baby's fuzzy head. "We're genetically programmed to survive famine, pestilence and plague. Good breeding stock, Grandma Bauer calls us."

"Hippy," Kathleen said in disgust. "And you can talk. You inherited the Kelsey physique. You look like a seventeen-year-old."

"Thank you, baby sister," Glenna said, looking pleased. She laid Johnanne on the Irish Chain quilt that Martha Bauer had made for Kathleen when she graduated from Tyler High and began humming "Itsy-Bitsy Spider," walking her fingers up and down the baby's belly until she giggled with pleasure.

Kathleen turned her attention back to the mirror. The black suit with its simple jacket and straight skirt did look awfully severe. Just right for the DEVCHECK or Addison boardrooms, but totally out of place for a bride, even a reluctant one. Kathleen sighed. "What do you suggest I wear?"

"What about that white wool sheath you wore to the Ingallses' Christmas party two years ago?" Glenna replied, not looking up. "You could wear Mom's veil with it. It's in a box in a closet here someplace. I'll go look for it."

Not white, Kathleen's inner voice shrieked. *Not a veil.* "No!" she said, then lowered her voice. "I—I'm not sure that dress still fits," she lied. Real brides wore white, not women who proposed to a man in a lawyer's office to close a legal loophole.

"Okay." Glenna turned her attention back to the big walk-in closet where most of Kathleen's clothes were still stored. "How about that cream silk suit with the lilac shell?"

"It's even older than the white sheath." Old enough that Devon would remember she had worn it that summer in Paris, but she couldn't tell Glenna that. Besides, she'd run out of excuses, and patience, herself. "All right, if it fits I'll wear it." She dragged the skirt over her head, pulled on the shell and jacket, observing herself critically in the wavy old mirror. "What do you think?"

"It looks great," Glenna pronounced. "Now I'll know what kind of flowers to order. How about baby's breath and pale yellow spider mums?"

"I don't need flowers, Glenna."

Her sister brushed the objection aside. "Of course you do. Every bride needs a bouquet—I should know. Something to do with her hands. Besides, since you aren't going to even let us attend—"

"It's only going to take ten minutes. It's not worth driving all the way to Sugar Creek."

"Tell that to Mom."

Kathleen felt a surge of desperation and she didn't try to hide it. "Glenna. I—"

"I know." Glenna held up a placating hand. "I've heard all your excuses." She ticked them off on her fingers. "There isn't room for everyone in Ethan's chambers.

We're going to have a lovely party at Timberlake right after the ceremony. Ron and big-sister Laura are right there in Sugar Creek, so it's real convenient for them to be your witnesses—"

"Glenna, please."

"All right. Enough of the guilt-tripping. I understand, really. And so do Mom and Dad. I think. But I feel better getting it off my chest. And I will be ordering you a bouquet. And a boutonniere for Devon. Don't argue."

"Okay, I won't." Kathleen managed a smile. "Thank you. It will be nice to have flowers."

"Take off the suit and I'll drop it at the dry cleaners on my way to the florist."

"I'll have to have it back by noon tomorrow," Kathleen said, taking off the suit and handing it to Glenna. She pulled on her jeans and sweatshirt and reached for her brand-new niece. She kissed the soft brown curls on top of the baby's head, then wiggled her nose, eliciting one of Johnanne's adorable smiles. A bright, sharp shaft of sensation, half pleasure, half pain, knifed through her body. She would like to have a baby.

Devon's baby. Blond hair. Gray eyes. An arrogant, aristocratic nose...

Oh God, this was worse than before. Before she had never dreamed of having his baby. Her heart started hammering in her chest. Her hands were shaking. *A baby. Devon's baby.*

"What are you thinking about?" Glenna asked perceptively. "You're staring at that baby as if she'd grown horns."

"I was thinking I'd like to have a baby of my own someday," Kathleen said, before her brain could censor the words. "Good heavens. Why did I say that? I can't imagine what came over me." She laughed a little too loudly, a little too brightly.

"Seems natural to me," Glenna said, looking mischievous. "You are going to be married in two days' time."

"Glenna, don't." Kathleen handed the now fussy baby back to her sister. "I need to concentrate all my energy on Andrej and Marta. And you know why Devon and I are marrying again. It's a technicality. That's all." Her voice cracked on the last word. "I don't want to discuss this anymore."

"Okay. Forget I said anything. Anyway, don't you know God programmed women to want a baby as soon as they pick one up? Those big eyes, and tiny fingers and toes. I swear, I want to drag Lee up the stairs and start making one of our own every time I get my hands on her." She tickled the baby under her round, pink chin, and Johnanne obliged with a gurgling coo. "See what I mean?" She rolled her eyes in surrender.

"Glenna, are you telling me you and Lee are considering starting a family together?" Kathleen was thankful for the change of subject.

Her sister colored slightly. "Well, yes. I think we are. Soon. I've already gone off the pill."

Kathleen knelt to catch her sister and the baby in a quick hard hug. "Oh, Glenna, that's great. I'm so happy for you."

"Thanks." Glenna sniffed back an emotional tear.

"It's like a mini-baby boom in this town." Kathleen did her best to smile. She could handle this. She could talk about babies without thinking of having one—with Devon.

"Do you suppose it's something in the water?" Glenna asked facetiously. "First Pam and Patrick. Then Raine and Gabe Atwood—such a beautiful little girl. Another playmate for you, sweetheart," Glenna cooed to the baby.

"And Sarah Kenton. A Christmas baby for Sarah and Michael."

"And more customers for your video enterprise, Madame Entrepreneur."

"Of course. That goes without saying. But it's only a bonus. For a while there…well, I thought maybe Lee…" Glenna shifted Johnanne in her arms and stood up. "I was worried that the problems he had with his children would sour him on having more. But—"

"Things are going better with them now, aren't they?" Kathleen finished for her.

"Yes. When their mother decided to move to Florida on a whim this summer, and they both refused to go along, I think it knocked some sense into her head. And it opened the kids' eyes. They stopped blaming everything that went wrong in their lives on Lee. And Shelley's not quite so quick to blame him, either. They've got a long way to go yet. I'm not such a Pollyanna that I don't see that. But it's a start. A very good start."

"You're a great mother, Glenna. You deserve a whole houseful of little ones."

"Heavens no," Glenna said with a laugh, leading the way out of the room. "Not a whole houseful. One. Or two. That's enough."

Two children. That's enough, Kathleen told herself silently. *I don't need anything more.*

THE BAR AT TIMBERLAKE Lodge was almost deserted—not surprising for the Monday evening before Thanksgiving. By Wednesday night, though, the hotel would be nearly filled with couples and families who lived too far from friends and relatives to journey home for the long holiday weekend. There would be older couples with empty nests taking advantage of the inn's facilities to host small parties of their own, and as always a few loners with nowhere else to go, who would keep loneliness at bay by eating turkey and stuffing with all the trimmings in the firelit dining room. Happily, this year he wasn't going to be one of those lonely souls, Devon mused. This Thanksgiving he would be surrounded by friends and family, sharing the holiday feast with the Kelsey clan and the Ingallses' extended family.

All the Ingallses and Barons except Michael and Sarah Kenton.

"I said, who do you pick in Thursday's game?" Jeff Baron said, looking perplexed.

Devon wondered how many times his friend had repeated the question while his own thoughts had been elsewhere. "Who's playing?"

"The Packers and the Lions. I've got Green Bay by a touchdown in the hospital pool." For most of the inhabitants of Tyler there was no other football team but the Green Bay Packers. Unless, of course, you were a Chicago Bears fan.

"Sounds like a good pick." Devon nodded in agreement. "Detroit's had a bad year. Lots of injuries. How about another beer?"

"Thanks, no," Jeff replied. "I've got to be on duty at the clinic at seven tomorrow morning. Two's my limit when I have to get up that early."

Devon settled back in his chair and waved off the attentive waitress as she headed for their small corner table. "Thanks for coming out tonight to take a look at Phil," he said, as Jeff took a swallow of beer.

"Glad to do it. But next week why don't you try to get him to come into town, if the weather's good? He's acting more like his old self, but I'd like to see him get out a little more."

"I'll pass the suggestion on to Edward. You're sure Phil's not overdoing it, spending so much time with the kids?"

Jeff shook his head. "His blood pressure's down. His heart rate is excellent. His attitude..." He grinned. "Well, he's as outspoken and opinionated as he ever was. I'm pleased with his progress."

"Great. That's great. I'll call Edward as soon as I get back to my room." He'd share the good news with Kathleen, too, when she returned from the Kelseys'.

"Good God," Jeff Baron said, picking up his beer bottle and checking the level of the amber liquid through the dark glass. "This is only my second beer, but I could have sworn I just saw a small flock of Santa Clauses head through the lobby."

Devon grinned without turning around in his seat. "It is only your second beer. And you're not seeing things. Tonight's graduation night for our last batch of department-store Santas. A company that specializes in providing mall Santas has been holding training sessions here all month. I think this bunch is headed for a chain of stores in the Milwaukee area, if I read Sheila's memo correctly. Were they all Santas, though? There should be three or four Mrs. Santas, too."

Jeff nodded. "You're right. There goes one now. I'm sure glad I don't have Belle and Annie with me tonight. They'd be after them like a shot."

"They wouldn't be disappointed that they weren't the 'real' Santa?" Devon asked curiously, giving a fleeting thought to looking in on the Santa graduation when his friend left. He'd never believed in Santa, himself. His mother had always considered it too much of a bother to keep up the pretense, and his grandfather Addison never had time for Christmas, period.

Jeff gave him a pitying look. "You really are ignorant about kids," he said bluntly. "These are obviously 'Helper Santas.' They do all the legwork for the old guy so he can stay at the North Pole, in a workshop that's shielded from satellite detection devices," he added with a grin, "and concentrate all his energy working on the toys kids are asking him for."

"No kidding," Devon said, looking suitably impressed. "That's what Annie and Belle believe?"

"Pretty smart for four-year-olds, if I do say so myself," Jeff boasted. "Of course, I dreamed up the part about the satellite detecting devices. It was only a matter of time until they started asking stuff like that. I figured I'd get a head start."

"Good idea." Devon laughed. Maybe he didn't know much about telling kids about Santa, but he was a quick study. And anyway, Andrej and Marta were going to be learning about Christmas in the nineties right along with him.

"Annie and Belle would have demanded to tell each and every one of those Santas what they wanted for Christmas." Jeff laughed, too, and took another swallow of his beer. "Just in case one of them might leave something off the list when they tell the 'real' Santa at the North Pole. What do Andrej and Marta think of having Santas around all the time?"

"Andrej was impressed at first, but he's gotten used to them. Marta?" He shrugged.

"Don't force her, Devon," Jeff said, the smile gone from his face. "Paul Chambers and I are in agreement on this. Give her time."

"It's hard not to worry."

Jeff leaned back in his chair, the leather creaking as he readjusted his position, twirling the neck of the beer bottle between his fingers. "I know. The kid's been through plenty."

"A hell of a lot more than any kid should ever have to suffer." Devon took a pull on his beer, looking into the fire and not at his friend.

"For the playboy of the Western world, you're taking to this Christmas and Santa stuff pretty naturally," Jeff said, respecting his reluctance to speak of what had happened in Triglav.

Devon gave a bark of laughter. "That's what Michael said. Or words to that effect."

Jeff's face darkened momentarily, and Devon wished, as he so often did, that he'd never mentioned Jeff's half brother. Jeff was his best friend in Tyler, the first man of his own age who had accepted him as an equal, not as a jet-setting playboy with an Ivy League background and more money than he knew what to do with. Devon knew very well what to do with his money. He'd had an excellent teacher and role model to learn how to deal with it. Not his grandfather, the legendary Arthur Addison, but Edward Wocheck, Jeff's stepfather, and his.

Edward had come to like and respect Michael Kenton, as Devon did. Alyssa and both of Jeff's sisters had established relationships with Michael over the past year, but they were wary friendships that couldn't and wouldn't grow and strengthen as long as Jeff remained adamantly opposed to Michael's being accepted into the family.

"Yeah, I guess Michael would have kids on his mind now," Jeff said at length.

Devon looked at his friend from narrowed eyes. It wasn't much of an opening, but he took it. "Sarah hasn't been feeling well. Michael's worried about her. But I suppose Cece told you that already." Jeff's wife, Cece Scanlon Baron, had a mind of her own. She had been friends with Sarah Kenton since Sarah first arrived in Tyler. She still was. But Devon knew, because Alyssa had told him so, that Jeff's stubbornness had strained the two women's friendship to the limit.

"Cece did say something to that effect. She's been experiencing some fairly hard contractions and some slight spotting. Not good signs, but Hank Merton's keeping his eye on her. If there's any problem with the baby... Hank will be right on top of it."

Devon wondered if he'd just imagined the slight hesitation in Jeff's voice. Had his friend just realized he was talking about his own flesh and blood, his future niece or nephew, and not just expressing a vague worry about an acquaintance's about-to-be-born child?

"That's good to know." Devon swallowed the last of his beer, hiding the hint of a satisfied smile with the action. Jeff might not want to admit it, but he was more interested in the upcoming arrival of the Kenton child than he cared to let on. Otherwise why would he be discussing Sarah's pregnancy with Tyler's obstetrician, Hank Merton? Or with Devon himself, for that matter? It wasn't much, but at least Jeff was paying attention to what went on in his half brother's life.

"Well, buddy, I have to be heading home." Jeff dropped a bill on the table for a tip. "Early hours at the clinic tomorrow, like I said. Thanks for the beer."

"Anytime." They stood and began walking across the lobby just as the great double doors opened to admit Kathleen and the children along with a swirl of cold air.

"Hello, Kath," Jeff greeted her. "Hi, kids. Brrr. It must be getting colder by the minute out there."

"Hi," Andrej said. "Is very cold." Marta shivered, then smiled, but as always said nothing.

"Hi, Jeff. Andrej's right." Kathleen threaded her fingers through her windblown hair to tame the flyaway curls. "It's freezing out there."

"Hi, Kath." It was all Devon could manage. Her simple gesture had been natural and unstudied, but the inherent femininity of the action, the latent sexuality in her movement, struck a chord of response deep in his soul.

"Cece and I are looking forward to helping you celebrate Wednesday evening," Jeff said, ruffling Marta's hair. "Thanks for including us."

"We're happy to have you." Kathleen smiled and managed to do a good job of it. Only someone who knew her as well as Devon did would notice the hesitancy behind the smile. The family gathering to be held at Timberlake Lodge after their wedding had been Anna's idea. Kathleen's mother simply refused to treat her daughter's wedding, even a simple exchange of vows in a judge's chambers, as anything but the joyous celebration it was meant to be.

"Well, I'd better be heading back to town. Cece will wonder what's become of me."

"Devon. Kathleen. Good, I'm glad I caught you." Edward strolled into the nearly deserted lobby from the direction of the family wing. "Hello, Jeff." He came forward to shake his stepson-in-law's hand. "I drove out to check on Dad and he said you'd just been in to see him."

"I was in Madison for a meeting and decided to stop in on my way back to Tyler," Jeff explained, dragging his gloves out of the pocket of his coat. "I was going to call you in the morning."

"How's Dad doing?"

"Fine." Jeff grinned. "He was as cross as two sticks tonight."

Edward chuckled. "Acting like his old self, eh?"

"Exactly."

"Good. Good. I'm glad to hear it. And these little rascals can claim most of the credit." He smiled fondly on Andrej and Marta, who were following his conversation with rapt attention. "Why don't you two go tell Grandpa Phil about your visit to the Kelseys'?" he suggested. "He just put some popcorn in the microwave for a snack."

"Popcorn," Andrej said, smacking his lips. "I am hungry."

"You just finished your dinner!" Kathleen exclaimed. She sounded a bit exasperated, but she was smiling again, a genuine, take-your-breath-away smile that did just that—took Devon's breath away. "You had two helpings of everything, including dessert."

"He's a growing boy," Jeff reminded her. When Marta reached out and tugged on his pant leg, Jeff hunkered down, bringing his eyes level with the little girl's. "And you are a growing girl. Do you like popcorn, Marta?"

She nodded and grabbed Andrej by the hand, pulling him off in the direction of the suite.

"Great kids," Jeff said, rising.

"We think so." Kathleen's smile was softer now, a mother's smile as she heard praise for her children. Her eyes caught Devon's, and when their gazes locked and held, the smile faltered and died. She looked away. "Good night, Jeff."

It was there again, that distance between them, that chasm, narrow but deep, that Devon could never seem to bridge. Their farewells followed Jeff out the door.

"I didn't know you were in the building, Edward," Devon said, moving behind Kathleen to help her with her coat and scarf. He schooled himself not to react to the nearness of her body, the scent of her perfume or the softness of her fingertips when they brushed against his.

"As I said, I just stopped out to say hello to Dad," the older man explained. "Amanda called while I was in the suite. She needs to talk to you." He looked from one to the other.

Devon was still holding Kathleen's coat. She hadn't moved; now she took a step away from him, toward his stepfather. "Did she say why she needed to talk to me...to us?" she amended quickly.

He tensed. Even though they were being married again in less than forty-eight hours, Kathleen still obviously considered the arrangement temporary, the responsibility for the children hers and hers alone. He'd do well to remember that or he had a suspicion he was going to get his heart broken in the process.

"She didn't say. Only that it is important and would you please call her this evening. Regardless of what time you get home."

"I—I'd better go," Kathleen said worriedly.

"I'll return Amanda's call."

"Devon..."

He didn't let himself react to her distress. He wasn't about to take no for an answer. He had to make her see that he was as involved in the children's well-being, in their lives, as she was. He'd stood back and watched from the sidelines too long already. "You go to Andrej and Marta. I'll call Amanda." Devon kept his attention focused solely on his wife, although he knew his stepfather was observing their exchange with interest and concern. "Whatever she wants to talk to us about is best done in private, not in the suite."

"Do you think something is wrong?" she murmured.

He nodded. "Possibly. But we don't know for sure. Kathleen, let me handle this."

"I . . ."

"Devon's right, Kathleen," Edward said firmly. "Whatever Amanda has to say will be better discussed when the children have gone to sleep."

She looked from one to the other of them. "You two are as alike as peas in a pod," she said. "And you're right. This time. I'll go stay with Marta and Andrej. You talk to Amanda, Devon."

An hour later, when he walked into the suite, there were dinosaur figures scattered on the hearth, a Barbie doll and a coloring book and crayons on the couch. In the past few days live plants had replaced the elaborate silk arrangements on the piano in the corner, framed photographs of the Kelseys and the kids adorned the end tables. All those things—Kathleen's knickknacks, the kids' toys, a quilted wall hanging made by Martha Bauer and her friends at Worthington House—had transformed what up until two weeks ago had been merely another hotel suite into a home.

Kathleen was standing with her back to the room, looking out the French doors into the darkness beyond the glass. The suite was quiet, Phil and the children already in their beds. A fire burned in the grate, threatening Andrej's discarded dinosaur models with meltdown. Devon scooped the endangered toys into a basket half-filled with pine cones and set it on the floor.

"What did Amanda have to say?" Kathleen turned away from the window, but kept her distance.

He debated for a moment the best way to tell her, then, as always with Kathleen, settled for the straight-out truth. "The cousins from Cleveland have contacted her. They had no idea there was family left in Triglav. They thought all their relatives had died in World War II."

Kathleen wrapped her arms around herself. "Of course. The war and then the Iron Curtain. How could they have known? We'll have to tell them all we know about Josef and Rujana. And we can send pictures of the children." She fell silent for a moment, then lifted her eyes to his. "That's not all they want, is it?"

Devon shook his head, trying not to let the unease he felt squeezing his gut make itself heard in his voice. "They want to meet the children. They want to come to Tyler. This weekend, if possible."

CHAPTER TEN

KATHLEEN SHIVERED as the night air rushed to meet her when she opened the French doors onto the terrace. It was quiet outside. There was bustle and activity at the lobby entrance but it seemed very far away. From where she was standing even the reflection from the lights on the veranda were nothing more than a scattering of fairy stars on the surface of the lake. The grass beyond the low stone wall bordering the private terrace was dusted with frost, and there was a sharp taste of winter in the air.

She took a deep breath, willing away the claustrophobia that had threatened to choke her in the overcrowded room. The panicky sensations came less and less frequently these days, but once in a while it flooded over her, the fear of being buried alive under tons of concrete and steel, that had plagued her so often in the dark confines of the Triglav hospital basement.

She couldn't stay away long, the others would notice. It was her wedding party. She should be inside with her family and friends. With her husband.

The sound of music came faintly through the thick log walls and insulated glass. It was an old Elvis song, a love song from the days when the singer was young and handsome, the way her parents and Alyssa and Edward remembered him best. She leaned her hip against the stone wall and looked back into the room. Anna and Johnny were dancing, her father's mouth moving to the words The King was crooning.

Johnny Kelsey was a little tipsy, relaxed, exuberant, very much his old self. Kathleen was glad. This past year had been hard on her dad and mom. Hard on the Ingallses. Hard on the town. But that time was in the past.

The fire that had destroyed the F and M had been an accident, after all. The teenager responsible had confessed everything to the authorities. The insurance company had paid off, and the plant was up and running at nearly full capacity again. Alyssa and Judson were even talking of having their annual Christmas party at the plant this year, an open house for all the town to come and celebrate the rebirth of Tyler's biggest employer. Kathleen liked the idea. She was glad she would be here to see it, and not sitting in some stuffy boardroom in London or Madrid.

The thought brought her up short. Was it only a few short months ago that she would have thought nothing of leaving the country on twenty-four hours notice to dig into the controversy surrounding the Addison Bangkok or one of Edward's far-flung DEVCHECK properties? She didn't feel that way anymore.

She wanted to stay home, in Tyler, with her children. A silent prayer came from her heart, directed to the heavens, to the unknown. *I do love them already, Rujana, as you knew I would. Thank you for entrusting their care to me.*

She looked back through the glass at Andrej and Marta. Dressed in new finery, they sat around the dining table with Jimmy and Megan, playing a game of some sort with Lee and Glenna. Devon leaned against the piano, handsome and aristocratic in the black wool blazer and charcoal slacks he'd worn for their marriage. As Kathleen watched, her husband shifted his attention from the children's game. He lifted his head, his storm-gray eyes meeting hers through the glass. Her heart squeezed tight, skipped a beat, then began to pound so hard that she raised a hand to her breast to slow its headlong pace.

She whirled around, staring out over the deserted grounds, past the black, icy waters of the lake. "Don't be silly," Kathleen whispered aloud to the bright, cold stars overhead. "It's dark as pitch out here. He couldn't see me watching him." *Wanting him. Needing him.* She bit down hard on her lower lip. She couldn't speak those words out loud, not even to the silent stars.

The door opened and someone came out onto the terrace. "I brought you something to put around your shoulders," Devon said, draping the homey cotton throw from the sofa around her. "I can't believe you came out here without a coat. It's nearly freezing."

"I wasn't planning to stay long. I just needed a breath of fresh air."

"Ah, I understand. The almost unbearable level of gaiety inside has you overheated," he said, staying close, but not touching.

Anxiety burned along Kathleen's nerve endings. She didn't want to be this close, didn't want to be this vulnerable to his warmth and caring. Today had been the hardest day of her life, living through a second wedding ceremony to a man who was marrying her only to keep faith with a promise.

She spun around, taking a step away as she did so. Her laugh sounded a little too bright, too forced. "Exactly." She gestured toward the warmly lit room. "It's all too much—cake and champagne and music and dancing."

Her mother and father were still dancing, to an early Beatles song now. Megan had coaxed Marta to dance, too, and Andrej and Jimmy were pestering them, hopping around the little girls like demented frogs until Edward signaled them to cease and desist. Phil was sitting near the fireplace talking to Alyssa. He was looking at his watch, Kathleen noticed. And Lee and Glenna were beginning to round up the children's things. It wasn't so very late in the evening, but tomorrow was Thanksgiving, a busy day that would start early in the Kelsey household. The same was true for Alyssa's family. The other guests had already left, attending to last-minute details for tomorrow's celebrations.

The Beatles song ended. Reluctantly Anna stepped out of her husband's embrace and moved toward Alyssa. The two friends spoke for a moment, both looking toward the remains of the wedding cake set out on the bar counter of the suite's tiny galley kitchen.

"I suppose I should go back inside and help Mom wrap the cake to take home with her. Even with all the food she's got planned for tomorrow, I imagine there will be enough people crowded around the dining-room table to make short work of it." Kathleen settled the folds of the heavy throw about her shoulders. The weight of it felt good, the warmth comforting, vastly different from the dangerous, alluring heat of a man's body—this man's body, close to her own.

"How many people is Anna expecting?" Devon asked, leaning one hand on the stone wall, sliding the other into the pocket of his slacks, oblivious of the effect his nearness had on her.

"Dozens, probably," Kathleen replied, rushing into speech to keep her mind off more dangerous thoughts. "All the family. Grandma Bauer. Brick and Karen. The boarders and any guests they might have visiting. Let's see, this year Michael and Sarah will be there. Hank Merton's insisting Sarah take it easy until the baby comes, so Mom wouldn't hear of her cooking Thanksgiving dinner, even for just the two of them. And, of course, Mom will invite anyone she meets at church or on the street who looks like they might be spending the day alone.''

"I have the feeling this is going to be a Thanksgiving unlike any I've spent before," Devon said thoughtfully.

Kathleen laughed. "Don't tell me it isn't the same way at Edward and Alyssa's house."

"I was teasing," he said, removing his hand from his pocket to reach out and smooth a strand of windblown hair from her cheek. "I'm looking forward to it."

"Are you, Devon?" She wanted to believe that. She wanted to believe that he truly did feel at home in Tyler, with her family, with her friends and relatives. But she couldn't forget the way he lived when he was away from this place, from these people. Like a prince. Like the multimillionaire, corporate executive that he was.

And she could never be a princess.

"I'm looking forward to everything the holidays in Tyler have to offer," he murmured, then waited in silence for her reply, his eyes holding hers.

Kathleen couldn't think of a single word to say. Her mind and her heart were in turmoil. It would be so easy to let herself believe him, so easy to fall under the spell of her own dreams of a Currier and Ives Thanksgiving, a Norman Rockwell Christmas. From there it was a small leap to imagining them together for the rest of their lives. A family, in their own home. Puppies and kittens tumbling about in the yard with Marta and Andrej. A toddler with Devon's blond hair and her blue eyes in Devon's arms. A new baby in her womb.

No, it wasn't possible. It was just a dream, a fantasy. Reality was a marriage of convenience. A business arrangement, nothing more.

There it was again, that sinking suffocating feeling that she dreaded, hated. Involuntarily her hand went to her throat as she fought to draw breath into her suddenly empty lungs. The throw drifted unheeded to the paving stones. Devon's gaze followed the movement of her hand. His eyes, thunderstorm gray in the faint light spilling out of the French doors, darkened to obsidian as they rested on her breast, then moved upward to her throat, to the place where her pulse beat a rapid tattoo against her skin.

"What's wrong, Kath?" he asked, his voice as gentle as moonlight on water.

"Nothing. Nothing. Really." She could tell him, she knew. He would understand. But she was afraid to let the words break free. Afraid she would be towed under by the old fear and the memories and that she would never find her way out of the darkness again.

His hand lifted slowly, as if of its own accord. "You're wearing the ring," he said softly, his finger hooking around the fine gold chain that held the intricately chased gold and silver band he'd given her earlier that afternoon.

The terrible constriction eased off, dissipated in the heat of his touch. She could think again, speak again. "It was a lovely gesture." Kathleen hadn't thought to warn Ethan Trask they wouldn't be exchanging rings. But when Amanda's husband came to that part of the ceremony, Devon had produced a jeweler's box from his coat pocket and removed the wedding band and a delicate gold chain obviously meant to wear it on. He took her left hand in his, as Ethan instructed, but instead of slipping the ring on her finger, Devon turned her hand over and placed the ring and chain in her palm. "It's a friendship ring," he had whispered, with just a hint of a smile. He folded her cold fingers around the metal, already warmed by the heat of his hand. "There is a chain. But no other strings attached."

The band caressed her skin now as he pulled it from beneath her clothing. He moved closer, still holding the chain, his knuckles grazing her breast. She swayed toward him, held prisoner by the necklace as completely as if the links had been made of solid iron, and not gossamer-thin gold.

"I wasn't sure you'd accept it," he said, his mouth only inches from hers. "I was certain you wouldn't wear it."

Kathleen closed her eyes. "I shouldn't. We don't have a real marriage. It makes a mockery of the vows for me to wear your ring."

"We could have a real marriage, Kathleen," he said. He still held the chain. Still held her in bondage, though she wouldn't have moved away from him if she could have.

"Oh, Devon, please." She didn't know if she meant to tell him to stop speaking her dreams aloud, or not to stop, to go on saying all the things she wanted to hear—even though he didn't mean them. At least not in the way she wanted him to. He would tell her the affection they had for each other, the friendship they shared, the sexual attraction that sizzled between them was enough to base a relationship on. And she supposed for him, for the way he had been brought up, it might be.

But not for her. Never for her.

"You're thinking too much again, Kathleen, analyzing your feelings to death. I can see it in your eyes." With his free hand Devon pulled her close, let her feel how much he wanted her. She tried to draw air into her lungs. Tried to still her racing heart so that she could hear herself think over the roar of blood in her veins.

She managed a breathless laugh. "I'm not thinking," she lied. "I can't think when you're this close." It was a dangerous admission to make, but she couldn't stop herself.

"Good. You think too much. I want you to feel. Let's send everybody home," he whispered against her mouth. "Let's put the kids to bed. Let's spend some time together. Just you and me, alone. It will be the way it used to be for us."

"Don't tempt me," she said, and she meant it. He was temptation, carnal lust, the threat of eternal damnation—not for her soul, but for her heart and peace of mind.

"I've married you twice," Devon said, brushing his lips across hers softly, sweetly, with tantalizing gentleness. But he did not release the chain, and his body was hard and urgent against hers. "Doesn't that tell you something?"

"It tells me you are as committed to the children's welfare as I am." She closed her eyes against his sensual assault on her reason, her senses.

He groaned, lifting his hands to frame her face, hold her steady for his words and his kiss. "God, Kathleen. That's not what it means at all. It means—"

The French doors opened. Alyssa stood framed in the light spilling from the room beyond. Devon dropped his hands and Kathleen's eyes flew open. They turned to face the older woman, although at first Kathleen could scarcely comprehend what she was saying.

"I'm sorry to interrupt you two," Alyssa murmured. Her expression was hidden by the shadows, but there was real regret in her voice, and something more—a slight edge to her words that drew Devon's eyebrows together in a frown.

"What's the matter, Lyssa?" he asked.

"You've got company."

"Company?" Kathleen tried to look past Alyssa's shoulder to see who the newcomers were, but Devon chose that moment to move forward, blocking her view. Kathleen knelt to retrieve the throw, folding it over her arm, to cover her confusion and order her thoughts. "Is it Michael and Sarah? She said they might drive out for a few minutes after the community Thanksgiving service was over."

"No, it's not Michael and Sarah."

Devon's voice was hard. "Let me guess. It's my mother."

"Nicole?" Kathleen's heart sank.

"Yes, it's Nicole," Alyssa informed them.

"I thought she was in Switzerland," Devon said.

"She's here. And she's not alone." Alyssa took a step away from the door, indicating that he should precede her into the suite.

"My God," Devon muttered, glancing into the living room. He raked a hand through his hair. "She's brought a bloody army with her."

Kathleen stayed where she was. She wasn't certain her rubbery legs would carry her if she moved away from the support of the terrace wall. She sat down with a thump, her mind in such turmoil she scarcely noticed the shock of the cold, damp stones against her silk-clad bottom. She knew her confusion and her desire for her husband were written plainly on her face. She knew that Nicole would see it. "I can't go in there, Alyssa. I can't face that woman," she said, as Devon moved through the doors and into the now crowded room.

Alyssa sat down next to her, reaching out to take Kathleen's cold hand in her two warm ones. "Yes, you can. And you will." She nodded toward the ring around Kathleen's neck. "But I don't think she needs to see your wedding ring tonight."

"No," Kathleen said numbly, tucking the chain back inside the neck of her shell. "I don't want her to see it. Thank you for reminding me."

"That was a very romantic gesture, Devon giving you a ring. You weren't expecting it, were you?" Alyssa asked, her smile barely visible in the near darkness.

"No, I wasn't expecting it." Through the glass, Kathleen watched Devon greet his mother. Nicole Holmes held out her hands to her tall son, reached up on tiptoe to brush a kiss across his cheek as he bent to accommodate her. Kathleen turned to the older woman. "I'm so confused. Alyssa—"

"There you are." Nicole Holmes swept through the French doors like a small whirlwind. She stopped short, shivering delicately. "Hello, Kathleen."

"Hello, Nicole."

"Congratulations on your marriage." Even in the fitful light Kathleen thought she detected a gleam of malice in Nicole's eyes. "Again."

"Hello, Nicole. Welcome back to Timberlake Lodge," Alyssa said, breaking the awkward silence that followed Nicole's words. She moved forward, but didn't offer her cheek for the breezy kiss that was Nicole's preferred greeting. "We weren't expecting you this weekend."

"Hello, Alyssa." Nicole made a face, a pretty pout. "Surely you didn't expect me to miss Devon and Kathleen's wedding, even if no one had the courtesy to inform me it was taking place until forty-eight hours ago. We had the most ghastly experience trying to get here on time. And all that effort went for naught." Her tone was bright, but the words were as sharp-edged as broken crystal.

"Until forty-eight hours ago we didn't know when Ethan could fit us into his schedule, Mother. I told you that," Devon said, blocking most of the light to the terrace when he reappeared in the doorway. "Come inside. Phil's beginning to complain of the chill from the open doors. And you've neglected to introduce us to your guests."

Nicole whirled around, taking Devon's arm. "How gauche of me. And you're right. It's absolutely frigid out here." She gave her son a brilliant smile. "Such a tedious climate, don't you think? Either too hot or too cold, too dry or too wet. And when it does snow there isn't a ski slope in sight."

"Shut the door," Phil hollered from his seat by the fireplace.

"I don't know why that bothersome old man isn't in a nursing facility," Nicole said, just loudly enough for Alyssa and Kathleen to overhear. "He's embarrassing my guests."

The unkind words galvanized Kathleen. She took a step forward, but Alyssa held out her hand. "Don't bother. It's just her way. Believe me, my father-in-law is a worthy match for her."

Kathleen managed a smile, though her heart and mind were still in turmoil. She was falling in love with Devon all over again; she couldn't hide from the certainty of it any longer. *God, what was she to do?* She stepped through the doorway into the crowded living room of the suite. Her steps faltered, and if it hadn't been for Alyssa's buoying presence at her back, she might have turned tail and run.

"Heavens," Alyssa whispered, so quietly that only Kathleen could hear. "Where are we going to put all these people?"

Kathleen glanced around, bewildered. Marta had been sitting on Phil's lap, but jumped down and hurried to her side. Kathleen bent down and scooped the little girl up against her, comforted by the trusting arms that wound around her neck, the red-gold curls that tickled her cheek when Marta laid her head on her shoulder to observe the strangers from the haven of Kathleen's embrace.

Nicole clapped her hands and whirled in a circle. "Everyone, let me introduce my dear, dear friends who came with me to celebrate my son's marriage and a real, down-home American Thanksgiving. May I present Lady Amelia Claremont. And her brother, Randall Gateway."

The elderly gentleman in tweeds bowed from the waist without spilling a drop of the drink Edward had handed him—quite a feat, Kathleen thought, for someone who was already obviously tipsy. "Charmed, all," he said, turning back to the bar.

Nicole dismissed him with a wave of her hand. "Lady Amelia and Randall are the brother and sister of the late earl of Wycliffe." She giggled prettily. "Or should I say the aunt and uncle of the present earl?"

Lady Amelia was as thin as her brother was stout, with wiry red hair peppered with gray, and a commanding beak of a nose. Her mouth was pinched, her close-set eyes slightly narrowed, as though that nose had just sniffed something unpleasant. She wore her designer suit and handmade Italian shoes with the complete lack of style and grace that Kathleen had come to believe only the English aristocracy could manage. "Good evening." Lady Amelia addressed the room in general, and no one in particular.

"And these are Amelia's children, Samantha and Gregory Claremont," Nicole continued.

Kathleen studied the younger Claremont woman for a moment. Unlike her mother, she wasn't lacking in the fashion department. Her watered-silk pantsuit, a becoming forest green, the same color as her eyes, was beautifully made and gracefully fitted. Gregory, too, was very well turned out, his navy blue blazer and dark pants a perfect fit, his button-collar shirt obviously handmade.

"Hello," Samantha said, smiling at everyone, and most particularly at Devon. "Hello, Devon," she said softly. "It has been a long time."

"Two years, Sam," Devon responded, without moving closer to the young woman. "How have you been? And you, Greg?"

"Couldn't be better." Gregory headed for the bar to join his uncle.

"And of course, you all know Wellman," Nicole concluded. The long-suffering butler bowed with far more grace than the uncle of the earl had.

Nicole squeezed Devon's arm. "Now, I'm going to let Devon do the honors of introducing all of you." She gave her son a pretty, pleading smile. "I just know I will forget somebody's name if I do it myself."

"Of course," Devon said, but he didn't smile back. He removed his mother's arm from his jacket sleeve and turned to Kathleen. "This is my wife, Kathleen," he said, still not smiling. "And these are our children, Marta and Andrej."

Devon smoothly moved the introductions on around the room. But when he came to Phil, the old man motioned for Andrej to bring him his walker, then stood up slowly, leaning his weight on the bars. "It is late. I am very tired. I will meet you all again tomorrow when I can remember your names without cracking my skull. I am going to bed."

Nicole danced over to place a kiss on his cheek, and Phil held still reluctantly. "Good night, Father Wocheck," she caroled.

"Humph. I will have a good night," Phil returned, heading for his room. "But will you? This place is full to the rafters. Where will you sleep, Lady Holmes?" He smiled wolfishly, pleased to have the last word.

"Full?" Nicole's hand flew to her mouth. "What does he mean, full? Devon? Edward?"

"It's Thanksgiving weekend, Nicole," Edward said, as he came out from behind the bar. "The hotel is fully booked."

"Oh no." Quick tears filled her eyes. "That's impossible. We have been traveling the entire day. There were delays in London and New York. Our car was late at O'Hare. Our luggage is piled in the middle of the lobby. I simply refuse to believe that there is no place for us."

"Let me talk to Sheila," Kathleen said, shifting Marta's slight weight as she reached for the telephone. "She's still on duty. I'll see what we can do."

"No," Devon said, forestalling her. "I'll talk to Sheila. I'm sure she'll find a place for all of you."

"We'll wait here," Nicole said.

"No, Mother. Why don't you wait in the bar?" He took her arm and steered her firmly toward the door. "You'll all be more comfortable there."

Nicole dislodged his hand with a graceful shrug. "Don't be silly! We'll stay here."

"I imagine Kathleen wants to get the kiddies to bed," Samantha Claremont said, bestowing a vague smile in the general direction of Kathleen and the children before turning the full effect on Nicole. "Why don't you show us around this charming old place while Devon sees to our rooms, Lady Holmes?"

Samantha motioned for Wellman to open the double doors. "You know it was rather naughty of us to just drop in on them this way." She lowered her voice to a conspiratorial whisper as she whisked a reluctant Nicole out into the hall. Then, turning slightly, she slid Devon a quick look from beneath lowered lashes, her ash-blond hair drifting into a curve along her cheekbone, her smile turning slightly mischievous. "After all, my dear, it is his wedding night."

CHAPTER ELEVEN

DEVON LET HIMSELF into the suite and shut the door behind him. He carried his shaving kit and a change of clothes. The room was dark, everyone asleep in their beds. No wonder, he thought, glancing at his watch. It was after midnight, and it had been a long day.

"Damn," he said under his breath, leaning back against the door. He hadn't expected Kathleen to wait up for him. But somewhere deep inside he'd hoped that she would.

Tonight was their wedding night. His second wedding night, and this one promised to be as unsatisfying and uncomfortable as the first.

His eyes strayed to the French doors and the dark, cold terrace beyond. Ten more minutes alone with Kathleen out there and he would have had her convinced. Before his mother's unexpected arrival he'd come so close to breaking through Kathleen's defenses. She had been within heartbeats of trusting him, of giving herself to him. He didn't want to think that magical moment had passed, perhaps never to come again. That there wouldn't be another chance for him to make her understand how deeply he felt, how deeply he was committed to their marriage. But as matters stood, when they met over the breakfast table in the morning, he would be back to square one.

Damn. Would the timing ever be right? he wondered. He dropped the shaving kit on a chair, laid his clothes over the back and headed for the bar.

"Devon, is that you?" Kathleen's voice came from the shadows of Andrej's bedroom doorway.

"Yes. I'm sorry. Did I wake you?"

"No. I was just checking on Andrej. I was afraid he might be having bad dreams tonight. There's been so much excitement and he's nervous about meeting these cousins from Cleveland. Frankly, so am I."

Devon moved toward her. She shut the door quietly behind her, but came no closer. "We can't deny the kids a chance to know their relatives," he reminded her.

"I know. But I wish...I wish we didn't have to deal with them so soon. The children are still so uncertain—"

"They'll do fine. I doubt we'll ever see their relatives again after Sunday."

"You're probably right."

"That's me. Infallible Addison. Is Andrej okay?"

"He's sound asleep." She appeared out of the shadows. His eyes had adjusted to the gloom of the big room, and he saw that she was wearing the shabby old blue robe he'd seen her in that first morning. But with each step she took the robe parted, and beneath it her nightgown was soft and silky, shades of white and silver, light against the darkness.

"Does he have nightmares often?"

"No. Thank goodness, no."

"What about you, Kathleen?"

"Me?" Her head turned toward the French doors. Her hand went to her throat. It was the reaction he'd expected. He'd noticed it often these past few days, her need to be near a window, to be able to see out into the daylight, or even the darkness.

"Yes, you. What dreams do you have of Triglav?"

"None. I'm fine." Her voice had risen slightly.

"No, Kath. Don't lie to me. You're not fine." He moved closer. Her eyes were wide and dark in her white face. She took a step backward.

"I'm fine, Devon. Please. I don't want to talk about Triglav and what happened there. I—"

"All right, Kath." Paul Chambers, Jeff, Alyssa—they all told him not to push the children, not to make them remember what was too awful for them to contemplate. Surely that applied to Kathleen as well? *But God, it hurt to know she didn't trust him enough to tell him of the terrors she kept locked away inside.*

"I—I didn't expect you back here tonight," she said.

"It's a long story. How about a nightcap? It will help you sleep."

"No..." Once more her hand went to her throat. Just above the V of her robe, where the soft swell of her breasts shaded into darkness, the faint warm gleam of gold caught his eye. Devon pretended not to see her fingers close over the fine gold chain, the small frown that momentarily furrowed her brow. "All right. Just a small one. Perhaps it will help me to sleep..."

"One glass of champagne coming up." Once more he pretended not to notice how abruptly she'd lapsed into silence.

Pulling himself together, Devon pulled a bottle of champagne out of the small refrigerator behind the bar and worked the cork out of the neck of the bottle. It came loose with a tiny pop and a sigh of bubbles. "You're very good at that," Kathleen said, taking the glass he offered, careful not to let their fingers touch.

"Only amateurs let the cork fly halfway across the room." He set the bottle down before she could see that his hands were shaking.

"Who told you that?"

"The head barman at the Addison Mayfair. I learned bartending from him. My grandfather apprenticed me to Edward the summer after I graduated from Harvard. Didn't I tell you all this before?"

She shook her head, avoiding his eyes. "If you did I— I've forgotten." A faint hint of color rose to her cheeks.

"You're right," he said. "We've never wasted much time talking about ourselves, have we? When we were together in Paris there were too many other, more pleasant activities to indulge in."

"Devon." There was a warning note in her voice.

He heeded it. Their past was off-limits. They weren't going to solve anything tonight. And perhaps that was for the best. The small, quiet hours of the night were made for moonlight and shadows and love, not acrimony and debate. He turned the conversation back to his unconventional and very thorough education in hotel management, relieved to find his voice sounded normal. He had himself under control again. If she didn't move, didn't bend forward so that her robe gaped open, exposing the silky white lace of her nightgown so that he could imagine he saw the faintest hint of a darker shading on the tip of her breast, he could get through this. . . .

"For the next two years Edward turned me over to the best Addison employee in each and every department, one after another." He ticked the points off on his fingers, enjoying her attention, enjoying the play of firelight on her expressive features, the scent of her skin—flowers and spice and woman. "He sent me to the Addison Mark in San Francisco to work the front desk. The next spring I went to the Addison Marquis in New York for six months to learn the food-service side of the business from the bottom up. And I mean the bottom. I waited tables for three months in the Grill Room before I ever got inside the corporate offices. Shall I keep going?"

Kathleen smiled and shook her head. She was relaxing slightly; the nightmare memories had faded from her sapphire eyes. "I get the picture. Was that your grandfather's idea all along? Is that why you studied finance at Harvard, and not hotel management?"

"Exactly. You don't go to an Ivy League school to learn the family trade. At least not if you're Arthur Addison's grandson. You learn the hotel business from working in the hotel business."

"And it didn't cost the old reprobate another dime in tuition costs," she said, smiling up at him.

Again his breath stuck in his throat. He had to make a conscious effort to draw it down into his lungs. "Precisely. No wonder the old man liked you. You're a woman after his own heart."

Kathleen looked pleased and a little flustered by his words. "I'm surprised he even knew who I was. We only met two or three times before his health got bad."

"He knew who you were, don't think he didn't. He was a shrewd old bastard, but a great judge of character. And one hell of a hotel man." He lifted his glass in a toast. Their gazes caught and held. Kathleen's smile faltered. She looked away.

"Did you get your mother and her friends settled?"

"Yes." He might as well get this over with. Kathleen was going to have to know sooner or later that he was here to stay. "After a fashion. Lady Amelia and her family are settled into a junior suite on the second floor that was vacant because of a noisy heating unit. Her ladyship isn't too pleased, but Samantha's a good egg."

"Samantha. Have you known her a long time?" Kathleen's expression was noncommittal, but she refused to meet his eyes.

"She's a good friend." Kathleen raised her gaze from her glass. Devon met the look head-on. "Once, after Paris, I tried to talk myself into believing she could be much more. It didn't work."

"Devon... that's none of my—"

"Yes, it is. Sam and I are friends. Nothing more."

Kathleen inclined her head in a gracious little nod. "I believe you."

He steered the subject back to safer waters. He didn't want to think of those lonely, bitter months after she'd broken off their affair any more than she did. "The Honorable Randall and Gregory are sharing the sleeper sofa in the living room," he revealed with some satisfaction.

"I see." Kathleen ventured a small smile. "I do hope they're comfortable."

"If you ask me, they're both too drunk to care. The Gateways are notorious tipplers."

"And your mother?"

"Mother's in the hidden-staircase room."

"My goodness, we must be overbooked," Kathleen said, her eyes wide with surprise. The room he had mentioned was the one Margaret Ingalls had died in so many years before. It was seldom rented, not because there were rumors it might be haunted, but because the staircase behind the wall leading to the vast attic above the original building was a liability no hotel would willingly incur. She twirled her glass between her hands. "What about Wellman?"

"Ah," Devon said in the English public-school accent he mimicked so well. "Just like an American to worry about the lower orders."

Kathleen made a face, indicating she didn't appreciate the joke. "What does that mean?"

"It means I don't have a place to sleep." Devon took a swallow of champagne, then grimaced. He hated champagne. "Wellman is in my room."

"You gave him your room?"

Devon shrugged. "Kathleen, it's after midnight. I couldn't very well send the old fellow off to the Green Woods Motel, could I?" he asked, naming the shabby fifties-era motel on the edge of town. He poured the rest of his champagne in the bar sink.

"Where are you going to sleep?"

"I planned to bunk down on the couch, if you don't mind."

"Of course I don't mind," she said too quickly. "I'll— I'll get you some sheets. And a blanket. The room is getting chilly." She stood and walked to the French doors, wrapping her arms around herself. "The fire is almost out."

"Don't bother about the sheets." He followed Kathleen across the room.

"It's no bother, really," she said, whirling around when she heard him approach. "You'll be more comfortable."

"I'll manage."

"No. I insist." Her glance skipped past him, as though she was looking for an escape route. He stopped just short of touching her. He was afraid if he did reach out, take her in his arms, she would bolt for the safety of her bedroom, shutting him out, shutting herself away.

"It's been one hell of a wedding day, hasn't it, Kath."

She didn't smile, didn't frown. "Shouldn't you say it's been one hell of a wedding day *again?*"

"Maybe I should."

"I'm not complaining." She shook her head and a faint glimmer of firelight touched the gold chain around her neck, once more drawing his eyes to the shadowed V. "It was a very nice wedding day—"

"Until my mother showed up with her sprigs of the aristocracy?"

"Don't tease me, Devon."

"Oh hell, Kathleen." He was never going to break through that invisible, diamond-hard wall of resistance she'd erected around herself. He would never convince her that he wasn't like his mother's friends, that he could handle the privilege and the responsibilities of his inheritance. *But God, didn't she know him well enough to see that for herself?*

Maybe he'd have another drink, after all. Maybe he'd polish off the whole bottle and pass out on the couch. That way, at least, he wouldn't spend the night tossing and turning, dreaming of Kathleen in his arms, of what was so close, so nearly his, yet wasn't his at all. He turned away, sick at heart.

Kathleen reached out and laid her hand on his sleeve. "Don't go, Devon. I'm sorry. Please..." Her eyes were as dark as indigo, bright with unshed tears, sparkling with firelight. "Can't we go back..." She lifted her hand to her throat, to the gold chain around her neck.

"Back to what, Kathleen?" He touched the gold chain, traced its path, felt her shudder and sway toward him. He took her in his arms then. She was trembling. So was he.

This was what he'd been waiting for—the taste and touch and scent of Kathleen. This was what no other woman had been able to give him, not before Paris, not after. Loving Kathleen was what made him whole, complete. She filled an emptiness inside him that all the power and wealth in the world couldn't erase. He had tried to tell her that so many times, but she wouldn't listen. He had never been able to reach past her prejudices with words, only with his touch.

But tonight words would have to do. Tonight he'd put his vaunted negotiating skills to the test. Tonight he would try and make a bargain with Kathleen.

"You're still wearing your wedding ring," he said, his voice gruff, filled with longing and desire. It sounded unfamiliar to him.

"I . . . yes. It was a lovely gesture."

"I'm glad you like it." He kissed her then. For a moment she resisted, her body stiffening as he pulled her close in the circle of his arms. But only for a moment. Then her mouth flowered open beneath his. Her arms slipped around his neck. Her fingers threaded through his hair, sending shock waves of live current up and down his spine.

"Oh Devon." He didn't know if she spoke his name in encouragement or despair. He didn't care. He only knew that having Kathleen, his wife, in his arms was what he had hungered for almost since the day she had left him four years ago. He nuzzled her neck, pushed the gossamer fabric of her gown from her shoulder. She gasped as the cool air touched her, as his lips touched her. "Devon, don't." Her hands moved to frame his face. "Please, don't ask this of me. It's a mistake. You know it is."

"No, it's not." He covered her softness with his hand. "It's not a mistake. Kathleen, we're married. We've got something special between us. Remember Paris."

"No. I don't want to remember Paris," she said, but her lips grazed his, her breath mingled with his. She swayed toward him ever so slightly.

He let his lips brush across her cheek, down over her throat to where the gold chain lay warm against her skin.

"We're good together, Kathleen. We belong together like this."

"But we're not in love, Devon."

He lifted his head. "Do we have to be?" He held his breath, waiting, wondering, caught between hope and dread at what she would answer.

"I..."

"We can make this marriage work, Kathleen. But not if we're constantly at each other's throats, always afraid we'll say the wrong thing, make the wrong move. Not as long as all we can think about is Paris. And you do think about Paris, don't you?"

"Yes," she said, tears glistening like diamond chips in her eyes. "I do think of Paris."

"Then let me stay, Kathleen. Let me be your husband. I'll be the best husband I know how. I'll be as faithful as the day is long."

"But without love—"

Devon wanted to tell her he loved her, but he knew to his sorrow she wouldn't believe him. "We're a hell of a team working together, Kathleen. We can do this. One day at a time. For the children's sake. For our own peace of mind." He didn't really know what he was saying. What he was asking. He only felt, in his gut, in his heart, that if he could make her his, body and soul, somehow, some way, he could make her learn to love him again.

"A real marriage of convenience. A business partnership." Her voice was infinitely sad.

"A stable family, a real family, for Marta and Andrej."

"Can we make it work?" she asked.

"I give you my word I'll never knowingly do anything to make you unhappy, Kathleen. What more do you want me to promise?"

"Nothing," she said, lifting her arms once more to encircle his neck. He lowered his head to kiss her again and tasted the saltiness of tears on her mouth. "And I promise you the same."

KATHLEEN AWOKE, chilled and frightened. She strained her ears, listening for the sounds of the people around her—all the others forced underground, to live their lives like moles in the airless, windowless hospital basement.

She held her breath. Nothing. Silence. Had they left her there alone to die when the shells eventually, inevitably, found their target? She tried to force her eyes open, but she knew that would be even more frightening—to be blind and alone in the dark.

Alone. She reached out. Nothing. *Where were the children? She had to find the children. They were her responsibility. Their safety, their very lives depended on her.*

"Andrej! Marta!" She knew the moment she spoke the names aloud that she had been dreaming again. She sat up in bed, clutching the sheet to her breasts, her mind a whirling mass of dream fragments and memories.

"Shh, Kath. Marta's fine. Everything's fine." Devon whispered, shutting the door of Marta's room behind him. "I thought I heard her cry out. I must have been dreaming myself. She's sound asleep." He was wearing nothing but his slacks. His chest and arms were lightly muscled, limned in gold and copper by the faint glow of the security lights beyond the window. *The window, large, uncurtained, her lifeline to sunlight, moonlight and sanity.*

"Devon?" Old nightmares mixed with bits and pieces of newer, heated images of the hours just past. "I—I was dreaming of Triglav, of Rujana and the shelling." She shuddered.

"It will pass, Kathleen. The nightmares will fade away soon. I promise."

"Will they?"

"Yes. And then you'll be able to look out a window only because you want to see if it's raining, or if the tulips you planted last fall are getting ready to bloom."

"How did you know? I try so hard not to let anyone know, but sometimes I remember how dark it was and I can feel the weight of that whole building pressing down on me.... I can't breathe.... I don't want the others to know, to worry about me."

Devon put one knee on the bed. His long, strong fingers closed around her wrist. "Shh, Kath. It's all over. You'll never be alone in the dark again, I promise. And when you're ready to talk about it the people who love you will be ready to listen."

"We would never have made it out of there without you." Devon slid out of his pants, lay down beside her and pulled her against him, tangling her leg with his. The gold band on its chain pushed into her skin where her chest lay against his.

"Yes, you would, Kath—you'd have made it somehow. I'd bet every last dime I have on it."

The remnants of nightmare were fading. It was very different being in the dark with Devon. Kathleen could face the memories with him beside her, holding her. She could look at the nightmares, remember and face them down, diffuse them, banish them from her heart.

"That's a lot of dimes," she said.

"Kathleen," he said warningly, but she could feel him smile where his lips touched the soft skin of her temple.

"I'm sorry."

"It's okay. Feeling better now?"

"Mmm. No more nightmares." She snuggled against him. "It's gone, the band around my chest I didn't even know was there. I can breathe again."

"I'm glad. Remember, Kathleen, I'll always be here to keep the nightmares away." He wove his fingers through her hair, tugged gently until she raised her head for his kiss. Kathleen's thoughts turned to liquid fire, melted away. She was no longer a functioning, rational human being. She was only woman.

She rose above him, offering herself, reaffirming herself. Devon groaned, tightening his embrace, his breathing as short and rapid as her own. He rolled her onto her back, kissing her eyelids, her cheek, nibbling the lobe of her ear. She lowered her hand to touch him intimately.

Kathleen drew in a long, shaky breath, as much amazed now as she had been four years earlier that he should want her this badly, that she had the power to move him this way. She knew that such a response was wondrous and rare, because she had learned to her sorrow, in other relationships, that it was not always like this between a man and a woman.

She continued the rhythmic stroking of her hand, feeling the silkiness of his skin sheathing the pulsing heat beneath. There were no barriers between them, and she ached to feel him inside her again. It had been so long, and she had wanted him so much, yearned for him, and thought never to be one with him again.

Life was precious and rare. It could be snatched away at a moment's notice, snuffed out in a heartbeat. She wanted to feel she was alive, and Devon sensed that as well, gave her access to his body, held nothing back.

Time and reality fell away. Not a word was spoken as Devon's mouth settled on her breast and he began to suckle. His kisses became deeper, more demanding, his caresses more intimate. Still he didn't speak, not even to whisper love words in her ear. He only used his hands, his lips, the rhythm of his body to give her what she wanted, what she needed. Heat. Passion. Life. Continuity. Wordlessly he offered; wordlessly she took and gave back. Warmth and moisture welled up inside her, making her ready for him, heating her blood to the boiling point.

She tugged him closer, but Devon didn't immediately enter her. Once more he lowered his head, kissing her breasts again, teasing the engorged nipples, grazing her stomach with his beard, stringing a line of kisses over her hipbone to the soft skin of her inner thighs. His mouth and tongue teased her intimately, and she writhed in passion, bit down on her lower lip to keep from crying aloud in need, and in want.

But she didn't want to journey alone to that place beyond the stars where he was taking her. She tugged him upward until their mouths fused once again, and she tasted her own passion on his lips, as he must taste his on hers. It was an intimacy they had never shared before. The power of it was beyond description. She moved sensuously beneath him until she was open and wet and waiting. She urged him closer with each instinctive, erotic movement of her hips, inviting him to enter the very center of her, to claim her as his for the rest of time.

His. For the rest of time. For a moment she faltered, lost her focus. But Devon was there with her, slowing his movements to match hers, kissing her again, stilling her doubts, refusing to let her instinctive worries about their future, about the foolishness of believing in dreams, spoil the enchantment, the completeness she felt in his arms.

"Don't think, Kathleen," he whispered in her ear, breaking his silence, his breath searing her skin. "Don't mourn the past. Don't worry about the future." His voice was dark, seductive, demanding obedience. "Don't think, just feel. Feel us together. Feel me in you. Admit how good and right it is. That's all I ask. Just feel."

She pushed her doubts aside as she was caught up in the whirlwind. She moved with him, sighed with pleasure when he buried himself completely within her, held her so close their hearts beat as one, their breath came as one. Together she climbed with him to the heights; together they spiraled toward the stars, together they came to earth again and slept the sleep of oblivion.

Much later Kathleen awoke to a cold gray dawn. Her eyes didn't go immediately to the window, as they had every morning since she returned from Triglav. Instead she focused on the man beside her—her husband, in deed as well as by the laws of God and state. Devon had offered her a straightforward partnership, a marriage based on devotion to orphaned children, with the added bonus of terrific sex thrown in, but nothing more. He had held her and comforted her and banished her most terrifying nightmares with the touch of his hands and the sound of his voice. He had offered her the promise of great happiness, but she could not forget that he had already caused her great pain.

CHAPTER TWELVE

"THERE, THE DISHES are done. Now we can have a nice visit before you leave," Anna Kelsey said with a smile as she neatly folded the dish towel over the edge of the sink.

The words *nice little visit* might have struck panic into Kathleen's heart if she and her mother were alone, but they were not, so she relaxed and kept on about her task. She knew her parents and her brother and sisters were worried about her. She knew they wanted and needed to know what had happened to her and the children in Triglav, and someday soon, Kathleen thought, she would find the courage to speak of it. But not today, not just yet.

She replaced the last of her mother's shining copper pots and pans on the rack above the restaurant-style range and started wiping off the work island in the center of the room. The dishwasher hummed in the background, and the kitchen was warm and steamy, still redolent with the smells of turkey and corn bread, spiced cider and pumpkin pie.

Kathleen looked around the big homey room with fond eyes. How many evenings had she sat with friends at the round oak table doing her homework, talking about boys and what they wanted to do when they left Tyler High? She used to dream of bright lights and big cities. Now when she sat at that same table she dreamed of different goals, of a different life, of coming home each night to her own family, to her own kitchen in her own home.

"I'd like that, Anna. A nice long chat." Sarah Kenton seconded her mother's suggestion in her light, clear voice, bringing Kathleen back to the here and now.

Sarah was sitting at the table drying Anna's good crystal wine goblets by hand. She placed the last one on the tray and turned expectantly but laboriously in Kathleen's direction, her advanced state of pregnancy making any sudden moves impossible. She indicated the empty seat beside her. "I want to hear all about the wedding."

Kathleen stretched her lips into a smile. The wedding she could handle. It was her wedding night she'd didn't want to talk about, or even think about, right now.

"It was very simple," she began, sitting down across the table from Sarah, taking up an extra towel to help polish the delicate glassware.

"But very nice," Anna inserted, joining the younger women. "Kathleen wore her ivory silk suit with the lilac shell, and her Grandmother Bauer's amethyst earrings for something old and borrowed."

"What did you have that was new and blue?" Sarah asked, leaning forward, her chin on her fist, her plain gold wedding band gleaming dully on the third finger of her left hand.

"Her underwear," Glenna chimed in, choosing that inappropriate moment to enter through the swinging doors from the dining room and overhearing Sarah's question. "Everyone in there is either snoring on the couch or watching football," she explained, jerking a thumb over her shoulder toward the living room. "I thought I'd see what's going on out here."

"Kathleen's underwear was what she wore that was new and blue?" Sarah's hazel eyes rounded in surprise. "You're not serious, Glenna?"

"Totally."

"A gift from the groom?" Sarah asked Kathleen mischievously, feeling enough at home in the Kelsey family circle to put aside her rather formal "Reverend Sarah" persona and be herself.

Kathleen was appalled to feel herself blush.

Glenna laughed. "No. The fancy undies came from Patrick."

"Patrick?"

"Pam was mortified when she found out," Anna revealed.

"It's very nice lingerie," Kathleen informed them, finding her tongue at last. "It was very...thoughtful of him."

"He dreamed it up with Grandma Bauer when she told him she was going to loan Kath her amethyst earrings," Glenna explained to Sarah. "He picked them out himself at Gates. A teddy with lace cups and tap pants. Really hot." She laughed as Kathleen made a strangled noise in her throat. "Although I'll bet you a quarter Nora Forrester was in on it. I doubt Patrick would have got the size right, otherwise."

"I expect she was," Anna said, patting Kathleen's hand soothingly. "Nora always was one for a good joke."

"I remembered to get flowers for everyone," Glenna said. "So all the proprieties were observed."

"The bouquet was beautiful," Kathleen said. "Thank you for thinking of it."

"That's what sisters are for," Glenna said breezily, but her blue Kelsey eyes shone with pleasure. "And admit it. You *were* glad to have something to do with your hands."

Kathleen laughed. "I admit it."

"We had a very nice dinner at Timberlake, Sarah. I'm sorry you and Michael couldn't join us. Timberlake's chef provided a beautiful cake," Anna said.

"We were having a very nice party in the suite until that insufferable Lady Holmes—" Glenna clamped her hand over her mouth. "Oops." She looked at Kathleen and rolled her eyes. "Sorry, Kath. I forgot she's your mother-in-law."

"It's all right, Glenna. Nicole is...a bit much," she finished lamely.

"I'll say." Glenna was in high gear. "She waltzed into the suite with half a dozen people in tow. Not to mention that snotty English butler of hers. What's his name—Mellman?"

"Wellman," Kathleen corrected her.

"Whatever. And I swear that Samantha Claremont would snatch Devon away from you in a minute if she got the chance."

"Glenna," Anna cautioned.

"It's all right, Mom," Kathleen intervened. "Samantha's an old friend of Devon's, that's all."

"Well, maybe she is and maybe she isn't. Anyway, Sarah, there they are, standing looking down their aristocratic noses at all us common folk." Glenna pushed her nose up in the air with the tip of her finger. "While *Lady Holmes* demanded rooms for all of them. At once. And the inn booked to the rafters." She spread her arms in an expansive gesture. "It was quite a performance."

"What did you do with all those extra people?" Sarah asked, clearly enjoying Glenna's performance.

"I don't know. The kids were acting like little monsters and Lee and I had to take them home before everything got settled. Where did you end up putting everyone, Kath?"

I ended up with my husband in my bed.

Luckily she caught herself before she said the words aloud. There was so much more to it than that. So much she hadn't come to terms with yet herself. "We—we managed," she said through stiff lips. "Devon put his mother in Margaret Ingalls's room."

"He didn't," Sarah said, looking shocked.

"Good for him," Glenna chortled.

"She likes it there," Kathleen revealed. "She told Devon this morning that she's going to stay there for her entire visit." He had had early-morning coffee with his mother while Kathleen got the children ready for Mass.

"How long is that going to be?" Anna asked, a frown between her dark eyebrows. "Do you think she'll still be here on the fifth of December?"

"I don't know, Mom. Nicole pleases no one but herself."

"What's going on the fifth of December?" Glenna asked, pouring herself a glass of iced tea before joining them at the table.

"Well..." Anna shrugged. "I was thinking. If it's all right with Kathleen...and Devon...of course, maybe we could do something special for the children that day."

"Like what?" Glenna inquired.

"Well, a little party or something."

"December sixth is St. Nicholas Day, isn't it?" Sarah said, rubbing a tiny spot from one of the crystal goblets she'd been drying with the corner of the dish towel.

"Yes," Anna replied. "In Triglav they celebrate the night before, on St. Nicholas Eve. The children put their shoes on the windowsill, and when they wake up there's always a present from St. Nicholas inside."

"What a nice custom," Sarah said. "I'm sure it will help Marta and Andrej feel less homesick to keep their Christmas celebration as familiar as possible."

"And it will be good for the other children to learn there are different Christmas customs around the world. Although I doubt that Jimmy will be pleased to learn that in

Triglav a child's presents are usually small enough to fit in a shoe," Anna said with a chuckle.

As if on cue a herd of small boys erupted into the kitchen through the swinging doors. "Mom and Dad are taking Grandma Bauer back to Worthington House," bellowed Timmy, Kathleen's second-oldest nephew, as he raced through the room toward the back door.

"Brick and Karen are going along to visit with Mr. Phelps. Mom wants to know if you want to go with them." Peter, Laura's firstborn, swung to a halt behind Anna's chair as the others pelted by, Andrej among them, red faced and laughing.

"Goodness, what time is it?" Anna glanced at the clock above the sink. "Almost four. Mother must be wanting her nap. I think I will go if the rest of you don't mind," she said, shooing the gangly, red-haired preteen along after the others. "And shut the door. It's freezing outside."

"Okay, Grandma."

"Anna, I'd really like to help plan the St. Nicholas party for Marta and Andrej," Sarah said, as Michael entered the kitchen. Devon, carrying the sleepy-looking Marta, followed on his heels.

"What's this about a party?" Michael stepped forward and rested his hands on his wife's shoulders. "I thought you were going to take it easy until the baby gets here." There was a slight frown between his dark brows, but when Sarah turned her head to look up at him and smiled, the frown vanished, replaced by a look of love and concern.

"Planning a children's party isn't work," she said softly. "I'll be careful, Michael. Truly, I feel better if I have something to occupy my time. I dread the thought of lying around on the couch for another four weeks."

"We won't let her overdo, Michael," Anna promised, grabbing a jacket from the antique oak hall tree by the back door. "He has our word on that, right, Kathleen?"

"Of course." Kathleen smiled at Michael. "We'll be very careful with her."

Michael studied his wife's face for a long moment, then smiled in turn. "It's a deal. She never listens to me anyway, but she might behave herself for you."

"Michael!" Sarah slapped playfully at his hands. "I'm pregnant, not an invalid. But I will be careful, I promise."

"What party are we talking about, may I ask?" Devon interrupted, shifting his weight so that Marta could reach the counter and snag a chocolate chip cookie from the dessert tray. He was wearing a gray-and-black patterned sweater and an open-neck shirt and casual slacks. He looked comfortable and at ease with his surroundings, one of the family. Kathleen glanced down at her hands. Of course he looked at ease. He had impeccable manners. He looked at home and at ease anywhere in the world. Again a small arrow of doubt and distress jolted through her nervous system. *What had she done last night? What had she agreed to—a loveless marriage, a business deal with a man who desired her, but didn't love her... ?*

"For the children," Anna said, patting Marta's cheek, then smiling up at her tall new son-in-law. "On St. Nicholas Day Eve. We don't want them to forget their roots."

Marta seemed to be listening intently. She tilted her head, smiled at Anna through a mouthful of cookie. Anna smiled back. "Would you like a party, sweetheart?" she asked.

Marta kept her silence.

"Well, I didn't expect an answer," Kathleen's mother said cheerfully. "But soon. I think it will be soon. And when this young lady does decide to start talking, I think we had all better watch out. Right, Marta?''

Marta laughed out loud, the first time she had done so. Kathleen's eyes flew to the child's happy face. Two days before, Phil had reported that he had heard Marta humming along with the Seven Dwarfs as they ''heigh-ho'd'' their way from their diamond mine back to their cottage in the forest. Was this the beginning of the return of her speech? Kathleen would have to call Paul Chambers the first thing in the morning and ask his opinion.

Devon was watching the little girl, too, a bemused look of wonder on his face. *He loves her,* Kathleen realized, her heart beating even harder. *He loves both these children as much as I do.* But was that enough of a bond, along with the undeniable physical attraction between them, to base a marriage on, a real marriage? Was she strong enough to accept Devon as he was? Was she strong enough to hold her own, to be true to herself, in his world?

''I think the party is a good idea, Anna,'' Devon said. ''Andrej has been worried about St. Nicholas finding his way to Tyler. But why not have it at Timberlake? Since the fifth is a weekday it would be more convenient. And the children can work off some of their excess energy in the activities room.''

''Great,'' Anna said. ''But I insist on making all the arrangements. With Sarah's help, of course.'' She waved goodbye.

''Good, that's settled,'' Sarah said, rising from the table with some difficulty. ''Give me a call and we'll work on the guest list.'' She was very big, Kathleen noticed, and beautiful in her pregnancy. As Sarah shifted position, the baby inside her shifted, also. Kathleen stared in fascination as movement rippled across Sarah's swollen belly, causing her to laugh and place a hand on her side. ''Ouch, that hurt.

This baby has the sharpest heels and elbows in the known universe.''

What if she herself were pregnant? The thought had not entered Kathleen's mind until this very moment. Their lovemaking had been entirely unexpected, unplanned. She and Devon had not used any method of birth control the night before. What if she already carried his child nestled inside her body?

''Athletic. Must be a boy,'' Michael said, but his proud comment barely registered.

A baby. Devon's baby and hers. The landslide of longing inside Kathleen's heart was even stronger than it had been when the idea first occurred to her days before. *It couldn't be. It mustn't be.* Perhaps it was a sin to wish that she wasn't pregnant, but a baby was a complication she could not afford in her life right now.

''You don't know if it's a boy or girl yet?'' Glenna asked, her interest piqued by the subject of a new baby.

''The sonogram was inconclusive,'' Sarah related. ''But Michael's convinced we're having a boy. Some days I think that he'll refuse delivery of a little girl.''

''Not if she looks like you.'' Michael wound his long arm around her shoulders. ''I think we should be going,'' he said gently. ''You still have visits to make at Tyler General this afternoon.''

''Yes, you're right.'' She smiled at them all. ''Goodbye. And once again, Kathleen and Devon, our congratulations and heartfelt wishes for much happiness.''

''Thank you,'' Devon said easily.

''Thank you.'' Kathleen knew her voice was shaky and off key. She hoped none of the others noticed, Devon especially. She dragged her eyes away from Sarah's gravid belly and smiled a tremulous goodbye.

"Is MARTA ASLEEP?" Kathleen asked. It was getting late. The inn was quiet, the guests sleeping off their Thanksgiving excesses, the old building settling down for the night.

Devon paused as he entered the living room. His wife was busy picking up toys from in front of the fireplace, her breasts outlined by the thin, ivory silk of her blouse, the lush curve of her hips covered by the soft, worn denim of her jeans.

"Out like a light," he said, leaving the bedroom door slightly ajar.

"Andrej, too. I just checked."

Devon chuckled. "And Phil. I can hear him snoring from here." He bent over and picked up one of the small action figures that had been dropped near the sofa. "Hey, this isn't a dinosaur. It's Luke Skywalker. Have we moved out of the Jurassic period? Don't tell me Glenna's getting these kids hooked on those old *Star Wars* movies?"

Kathleen laughed, the throaty, rich laugh that had been one of the first things that attracted him to her, but there was still a slight shadow in her eyes. "I'm surprised you remember I told you she was a science-fiction buff."

I remember everything. "I suppose *Star Trek* will be next."

"Undoubtedly. But the original series first. Glenna's a purist."

"I'm an Indiana Jones fan myself."

"Harrison Ford," Kathleen said with a smile. "I've had a crush on him for years. I'll watch any movie he's in."

"I walked right into that one."

She smiled, but still the shadow in her eyes remained. "You did," she agreed.

He tossed the figure of the valiant Jedi knight into the basket where Andrej kept his toys. Devon wanted to keep

Kathleen talking, perhaps find out what had brought that slight frown to her eyes, the tremor to her hands. He thought back over the eventful day, enjoying the intimacy, the domesticity of the quiet, firelit room, and the rare opportunity for them to be alone, man and wife, talking of children and family, of little everyday pleasantries and disappointments. "Andrej's adapting fast. Maybe too damned fast." He gave a rueful laugh. "The other day we were walking past Gates and he insisted I check out these shoes."

"Not the ones that cost $115!" Kathleen straightened from adding one of Marta's dolls and a box of crayons to the basket.

"The same. And Andrej informed me—confidentially, of course—that he thinks they will make him jump as high as Michael Jordan, and also impress the girls."

"Girls? What girls? He's much too young to be thinking about girls."

"I think Timmy put the idea into his head."

"Timmy?" Kathleen's expression was horrified. "He isn't even ten."

Devon laughed. "You don't know much about boys, do you? They're always thinking about girls. But at that age males are only out to impress the opposite sex, then pester the life out of them when they've got their attention."

"You didn't tell him he could have the shoes."

"I said perhaps he could ask Santa Claus to bring them. I didn't pull out a wad of bills big enough to choke a horse and buy him a pair in every size and color they carried. And while we're at it Kathleen, I know how much Edward pays you. Even if I disappeared off the face of the earth right this moment you could well afford to buy Andrej those shoes on your own." He'd done it again, made mention of money—his money, their money, the forbidden subject. He regretted the words the moment they were spoken, but he'd felt her pulling away from him by degrees all day, and he didn't know how to stop it.

She looked for a moment as if she might cry, then lifted her chin a fraction of an inch, straightened her shoulders. "I want him to learn the value of money."

"So do I, Kathleen." He held up a hand in a gesture of surrender and reconciliation. "Let's not fight. I'll leave the decision about the shoes up to you."

"I think they would make a very good Christmas present."

He nodded wearily. "Whatever you say."

"Devon, I don't want to fight, either." Her eyes flickered to the French doors, but returned to his almost immediately. She touched the fine gold chain at her throat. "Did you make my apologies to your mother for not joining her for a nightcap?"

Devon accepted the change of subject. "Yes, I did."

"Did you explain that Marta's not feeling well?"

"I explained."

"I'm not avoiding her, truly, Devon. Marta just overindulged today. I forget sometimes how deprived these kids were, especially this last year. We should have monitored what she ate more closely. I was afraid she was going to be sick—"

"She's fine. And, yes, we should have watched what she ate a little more closely, but she's not in danger. She has a tummy ache. You gave her Pepto-Bismol and you read her a story and rocked her to sleep. That's the perfect treatment, according to both your mother and mine."

"Nicole?"

"Does that surprise you?"

"Frankly, it does."

"Perhaps it wouldn't be such a surprise if you spent a little more time getting to know her." He waited for the storm to break over his head, but Kathleen remained thoughtfully silent.

"Maybe it wouldn't," she said at last. "Was Nicole a good mother, Devon?"

"Yes. In her own, unique way she was. I had a good childhood. And she was married to Edward most of the years I was growing up. He was a great stabilizing influence on my life." Devon stretched his arm along the back of the couch. Physically Kathleen was very close, but emotionally she still maintained a distance between them. They had consummated their marriage. *They had made love.* But now their wedding night was past, the magic between them muted. Coward that he was, ordinary lamplight made it too difficult to speak what was in his heart. He had been the one to suggest their marriage could survive and prosper as a business deal, as a partnership based on shared responsibility and devotion to Marta and Andrej, not love. He had dug the pit he was tumbling into. He had no one to blame but himself.

Kathleen rested her head against the back of the couch, her neck arched, her eyes closed. Her dark eyelashes lay against her cheeks, where purple smudges of fatigue marred the pale cream of her skin. A stray tendril of dark, curling hair lay within inches of his fingertips. He balled his hand into a fist, fighting the temptation to touch her. He sat quietly, watching the fire, waiting for her to speak.

"You haven't mentioned the Bangkok property for three days," Kathleen said, when the silence became too much to bear. She kept her eyes closed. Her feelings, confused, chaotic, were too close to the surface, too easy for this familiar stranger to read. "That's not like you."

"No, I suppose it isn't," he replied thoughtfully. "I might mention that you haven't asked me about the problems with the Bangkok property for as long."

"That's not like me," she whispered, turning her head, daring herself to look at him. He was staring at the fire, little more than embers now.

"No, it's not."

"Why do you suppose that is?"

"I imagine it's because we've had other things on our minds. The kids. The wedding. The cousins from Cleveland coming."

"That might account for it."

"I trust Liam Hardesty implicitly. If he needs me, he's as close as the fax machine."

"That's true, also."

Devon leaned forward. Kathleen steeled herself for his touch, but none came. "But those aren't the primary reasons, Kathleen. You know that as well as I do."

"I—I don't know what you're trying to say." His expression was unreadable. Did he regret the agreement they had struck last night as much as she did? Did it weigh as heavily on his heart and soul as it did on hers? Did she dare ask?

"I'm trying to say that we haven't discussed the Bangkok property because we've been doing what thousands of other married couples do all the time. We're trying to leave business at the office."

"Do you think that's possible for us?"

"I don't see why not." He waited for her answer, his expression carefully neutral.

"I—I never considered combining a career and a family before—before Triglav."

"It's a decision women make every day."

"It's not a decision I make every day."

"You'll have my complete cooperation whether you decide to stay with Edward, stay home with the children, or any combination of the two."

As per our agreement. Quick tears stung the back of Kathleen's throat. "Instant parenthood." Her voice broke on the words. She bit her lip, wishing she could take them back.

This time he did touch her, his knuckles brushing her cheek in a fleeting caress. "What's wrong, Kath?"

"We shouldn't have made love last night, Devon. We were unprepared."

"Do you regret it?"

"Yes."

"I see. Are you afraid you might be pregnant?"

She had never heard his voice so cold, so controlled. They might be sitting at opposite ends of the imposing, solid mahogany conference table in the Addison boardroom in London, instead of being separated by a handsbreadth, a heartbeat.

"No. At least I don't think I can be." She colored slightly. It was harder to talk about than she had supposed. *She couldn't go on like this.* "I checked the calendar. Last night was safe. But I don't think we should make...sleep together again."

"You didn't feel that way last night."

Last night she had felt the old magic, it was true. Last night he had helped her free herself from her nightmares of Triglav, but their lovemaking had stirred memories even older, equally as painful.

"I feel that way today." She lifted her eyes to his, made herself look at him with steady regard, though her heart was beating frantically against the walls of her chest. "You told me we would take this marriage one day at a time."

"Give us—"

"It's not a decision I make every day."

She shook her head. "No, Devon, let me finish." She'd spent the day with her parents, people who loved each other, who cared for each other more than life itself. They had made and kept vows to support and cherish and honor each other, not to take their marriage one day at a time, to be faithful as long as it was convenient to both of them, to go their separate ways when the children were grown and on their own. Kathleen could accept no less for herself. "We were wrong to consummate this marriage. We were wrong to take the chance of bringing a child into the world without love. I can't and won't sleep with you again."

CHAPTER THIRTEEN

KATHLEEN WOKE late Friday morning. The nightmares had not returned, for she had barely closed her eyes all night. She pulled herself out of bed feeling both restless and unrested, an enervating combination. On top of everything else that preyed on her mind, the children's long-lost relatives were due to arrive sometime today or tomorrow.

Devon had spoken to the cousin, William Drakik, on the telephone. Drakik was the Anglicized version of Drakulic. William's father was Josef Drakulic's uncle, there was no doubt of that. Devon had had a private investigator check the man out.

The elder Drakik, it seemed, had been a prisoner of the Germans in World War II, and when the war was over he was unable to return to his family because of the Communist takeover of Triglav. He'd made his way to America, had married and raised a family. He died never knowing that Josef's father, his youngest brother, had survived the war, the only other member of the family to do so.

Now William and his wife were on their way to Tyler and there was nothing Kathleen could do to stop them. Andrej, already worried about Mrs. Parker's home visit next week, was also uneasy about meeting these relatives he'd never known about. And Marta. Marta was still silent. Kathleen had no idea what she felt.

She went through the doorway into Marta's little room. The child's bed was empty. Her pajamas were tossed on the foot of the bed and clothes were hanging out of the drawers of her wardrobe. Obviously, Marta had awakened, dressed herself and left the bedroom without Kathleen hearing a sound.

She opened the door and peeked into the living room, relieved to find it occupied by the children and Phil. She waved to the trio, engaged in watching a pre-Christmas parade in some balmy, southern city on the TV, and hurried into the shower.

Fifteen minutes later she was back in the living room. "Where's the parade?" she asked with false brightness.

"Miami," Andrej shouted. "In Florida. Where Disney World is."

"No, I think this is Houston, Texas," Phil corrected him, then he shrugged. "Or maybe I am wrong. Maybe this is Dallas? Someplace where there isn't three inches of snow on the ground."

"Goodness, did it snow that much last night?" Kathleen glanced out the French doors. It had snowed enough during the night to cover the grass and to frost the branches of the trees. "I guess winter is here," she told Marta, who was looking out the window, too. Marta nodded, her face still pale from her stomach upset of the night before, but as always, a smile on her thin little face. "How pretty you look this morning, sweetheart."

The little girl was wearing a cotton turtleneck decorated with a multitude of stars in bright primary colors, and a pair of bib overalls with ticking stripes in green and white—an enchanting combination, in Kathleen's opinion. More than once she'd been impressed by Marta's inborn fashion sense. She had never expected so small a child to be conscious of what she wore.

Someone had even brushed her hair. Phil, she suspected, and as she had so many times already, said a little prayer of thanks that God had given the old man and the orphaned children a place in each other's hearts.

"Do you want to go outside and play in the snow, Marta?" she asked, kneeling down and pointing at the snow piling up outside.

Marta nodded vehemently, her smile growing even wider.

"Good. Me, too. What about you, Andrej?"

"Later," he said, engrossed in the colorful floats and marching bands filling the screen. "Santa Claus is coming soon. I want to see him."

"Okay. That will give me time for breakfast. I'm starved. Have you eaten yet?"

Phil looked away from the TV and growled. "It is already ten-thirty in the morning. Of course we have eaten breakfast."

"Well, I haven't. Does anyone want to come with me to the restaurant?"

Marta reached out and took her hand.

"Would you like to have a glass of juice there?" Kathleen waited for a moment, hoping for a reply. Marta's laughter yesterday, Phil's revelation that he had heard her humming a tune gave Kathleen hope that her silence was about to end. But the child started tugging her toward the door, still without speaking. Kathleen swallowed the tiny lump of disappointment that had formed in her throat and let herself be led away.

The lobby was busy with post-holiday travelers checking out. A few hardy souls were heading out to the cross-country ski trails for the first time in the season, and one or two late-risers like herself were having coffee and croissants in front of the huge, fieldstone fireplace.

But despite all the movement and activity, one slight figure dominated the big, open space. Nicole Holmes stood by the polished walnut table in the middle of the room, pulling on her gloves. She was wearing a full-length fur coat with a hat to match, glossy and glorious, and undeniably the real thing. Since her boots had three-inch heels, Nicole obviously didn't plan on doing a lot of walking today. "She's lucky the antifur people aren't well organized in this part of the county," Kathleen whispered to Marta.

The little girl looked up at her and nodded wisely. Her grip on Kathleen's fingers tightened when Nicole looked over and spotted them coming her way. "Good morning, Kathleen. Good morning, Marta," she said with a nod.

"Good morning, Nicole." Kathleen managed a smile, but of all the people on earth, her mother-in-law was the last one she wanted to see right now. "Marta and I are going to have breakfast and then play in the snow."

"Do you like snow, Marta?" Nicole's smile became genuine, warming and softening the finely chiseled lines of her mouth and lips. Marta pressed herself close to Kathleen's side and dropped her gaze to the jewel-toned hues of the Oriental rug beneath their feet. Nicole's smile vanished. For a moment Kathleen thought she detected real hurt in her mother-in-law's gray-green eyes.

She rushed in to cover the awkward silence, not sure why she did so. Certainly Nicole had shown little-enough interest in the children thus far in her visit. "I'm not sure how often Marta's ever played in the snow. It seldom snows in Triglav, only higher up in the mountains. Would you like to join us outside later, Nicole?"

Her mother-in-law's laughter trilled across the lobby like wind chimes in a summer breeze. Heads turned toward them. Nicole smoothed her butter-soft leather gloves over her hands, her gaze flickering over Kathleen's faded jeans and Northwestern University sweatshirt. "No, thank you, dear. I'm not dressed for playing in the snow. At least not the way you mean."

Kathleen bit her tongue to keep from voicing a sarcastic retort. Then found herself surprised again when Nicole knelt gracefully to bring herself to eye level with Marta. "But I am going shopping. Which is far more fun than playing in the snow. Would you like to come with me sometime, Marta? There are a couple of very nice shops in Lake Geneva where they have lovely dolls."

Marta didn't reply, of course, but she wasn't pressed as tightly against Kathleen's leg as she had been moments before.

"Do you know the word for 'doll' in the child's native language?" Nicole asked, still facing Marta and tucking a stray red-gold curl behind her ear with one gloved finger.

"No, I'm afraid I don't. We could ask Phil to translate, if you like."

"I'm afraid I haven't time for that." Lady Holmes rose gracefully. "The others will be here momentarily."

"Others?"

"Yes, my guests. We're all going shopping. Isn't that what everyone does on the day after Thanksgiving? Go shopping for early Christmas bargains?" She gave a slight, delicate shudder. "Or watch sports on TV?"

"Yes, I suppose it is."

"Well, that's what I promised my guests, you know. A one hundred percent American Thanksgiving. After lunch we're coming back here to watch a football game." Her voice was tinged with such horror that Kathleen couldn't help chuckling.

"Truly going above the call of duty to one's friends," she said dryly.

Nicole gave her a sharp look from beneath carefully arched eyebrows, then smiled unexpectedly, a dazzling smile, the feminine equivalent of Devon's devastatingly sexy grin. "Exactly. Perhaps you and Devon will join us and translate for Samantha and Gregory. They do know the rudiments of the sport, I believe. But for Amelia and Randall and myself, it will be a hopeless cause. I'm certain by Monday they'll be begging me to go on to Aspen with them."

"Most likely. But thank you for the invitation. We'll join you if we can." She glanced down at Marta, who was no longer paying attention to the conversation, but was eyeing the bowl of hard candies by the centerpiece on the table. "All our plans have to be contingent on the arrival of the children's cousins."

"When are you expecting them?"

"Today or tomorrow. They're driving in from Cleveland. There's no set time."

Nicole was watching the big double doors. "Good. Here come Devon and Samantha. Don't they make a handsome couple?" Implicit in her comment was another exchange of information, as clearly understood as if Nicole had spoken the words aloud. *This is the woman, or one very like her, that my son should have married. His match in looks and breeding, lineage and wealth.*

Kathleen's heart did an uncomfortable flip-flop into her throat. Devon and Samantha did make a handsome couple, arm in arm as they were, her head tilted slightly toward him, attentive to his every word. Kathleen refused to acknowledge a sharp jolt of something that felt very like jealousy streaking like an electric current along her nerve endings.

The perfect match for him. Samantha Claremont was nearly as tall as Devon, willowy slim, elegant and beautifully made-up. Her coat wasn't fur, but an excellently tailored, all-weather affair belted at the waist. A designer scarf covered her ash-blond hair and framed her fine-boned face. Her gloves and shoes and bag all matched.

Kathleen suddenly regretted leaving the suite so casually dressed. It occurred to her that women like Nicole and Samantha dressed the way they did precisely to put other women at a disadvantage, and this morning, at least in her case, the tactic was working quite well.

"Did you find Gregory?" Nicole called out in her cultured, chiming voice. She turned to Kathleen, her gray-green eyes bright with interest, and more than a hint of malice. "I sent Samantha out to the car barn to find Devon and her brother," she explained. "They disappeared in that direction more than an hour ago." She sighed. "Men and their toys."

"I heard that, Mother," Devon said smoothly, coming toward them, still with Samantha attached to his arm. "But just to set the record straight, those cars were Grandfather's toys, not mine."

Nicole laughed, lifting her face for Devon's greeting. Samantha let go of his arm and he brushed Nicole's cheek with a light kiss. "So true. What are you going to do with all those noisy monstrosities? Except for the Rolls, of course. I do adore the Rolls."

"I haven't the slightest idea, Mother. Those cars are the least of my worries at the moment." He stepped forward and hunkered down on the balls of his feet. "Hi, sweetie. Is your tummy feeling better this morning?"

Marta threw her arms around his neck and hugged him tight. Devon rose with her in his arms. "I take it that is a yes."

"She's feeling much better," Kathleen told him, not quite able to meet his eyes.

"Good morning, Kathleen," Samantha said, as she lowered her scarf and shook her sleek, shining cap of blond hair free of snowflakes.

The Englishwoman's smile was cool, refined, but it reached all the way to her eyes. *Just a friend,* Devon had told Kathleen. *She's just a friend.* "Good morning, Samantha."

"Good morning, Kathleen," Devon said in turn. His voice had dropped a note or two, sounding husky and intimate, too intimate for their surroundings. Her eyes flew to his. His very presence short-circuited her mental defenses, leaving her aching and vulnerable. Tiny shivers of desire and longing curled along the back of her neck and raced down her spine.

"Good morning, Devon," she replied. He had left her without a word last night, without a backward glance. She didn't know where he had slept, if he had slept or if he had tossed and turned all night as she had.

"I trust you slept well." He reached out and brushed a fingertip along her cheekbone.

Kathleen felt herself flush. She knew there were dark circles under her eyes attesting to her restless night. "No," she said truthfully. "I didn't sleep very well. It... I must have eaten too much yesterday."

Nicole was watching her every move, watching the reaction to his touch she couldn't completely hide. Devon dropped his hand, but didn't look away. "I'm sorry—"

"Devon!" The sound of his name sliced the connection between them like a knife. Kathleen turned her head. Nicole had a look of horror on her face. "Don't tell me."

"Don't tell you what, Mother?" Devon blinked and shifted his gaze to his parent. For a moment, the space of a heartbeat, he looked as off balance as Kathleen felt.

"Don't tell me you two are... sleeping together?"

Devon's expression hardened, his shoulders tensed. Marta wiggled to be free and he set her down. She ran to Kathleen and pressed her face against Kathleen's hip. "Mother, you're out of line," Devon warned.

Nicole, always a creature of impulse, wasn't about to be restrained by her son's obvious displeasure. "Devon, how could you be so imprudent?"

"Mother, don't pursue this."

Over his shoulder Kathleen saw Samantha's face, her dark blond brows drawn together in a slight frown.

"Oh God, I'm right."

"Nicole, please," Kathleen begged. "Not here."

"You've consummated this marriage, haven't you? Devon, tell me it's not so." Nicole reached out, clutched the sleeve of his coat. "You assured me you married Kathleen only for the children's sake. You said this was to be a marriage of convenience. A way to assure the children's future, nothing more. Think of the consequences. Why, the financial complications alone—"

"That is enough, Mother." Devon didn't raise his voice, but Nicole's face paled. Her gray-green eyes filled with tears. She twisted her head, looking first at Kathleen and then back to her son. "Oh God, Kathleen, you're in love with him, aren't you?"

"Mother, drop the subject," Devon commanded.

"Nicole. This subject would better be discussed in private," Samantha said quietly.

Nicole shook off the younger woman's restraining hand, returning her scrutiny to Devon's thundercloud-dark face. She lifted her arm, pressed her gloved fingers to her lips. "Oh Devon, don't tell me you've made the mistake of falling in love with her?"

"Samantha, would you see my mother to her room?"

"Of course. Nicole, please. Let Devon and Kathleen sort this out on their own."

Without saying a word, Kathleen scooped Marta up into her arms, whirled around and raced from the lobby as if all the demons of hell were at her heels. She heard Devon's determined footsteps behind her but didn't slow her headlong flight. She kept on walking. Her breath was coming in quick, hard gasps, partly from emotion, partly because Marta had gained weight in the month they'd been living at Timberlake.

"Kathleen. Stop. I want to talk to you."

She put Marta down, opened the door to the suite and gave her a little push. "Go inside, honey. I have to talk to Devon." Marta looked at her white face and Devon's dark one, then scuttled inside.

Using every ounce of self-control she could muster, Kathleen lifted her eyes to his face. "I'd rather not talk to you right now," she said through clenched teeth. A flare of self-preserving anger had ignited inside her as she ran down the hallway. She wasn't about to be discussed like an errant serving girl in front of milady's guests. She concentrated on the heat of her anger, drew strength from it and was able to hold the tears at bay.

"Kath, I'm sorry. She was way the hell out of line."

"She was," Kathleen agreed. "But totally in character." A muscle jumped along the line of his jaw, but he didn't contradict her. "Please, Devon. Let's just forget about it." Holding on to the anger wasn't working. She wanted to cry. She wanted him to say he loved her. Even if he didn't mean it.

"I can't forget it. She hurt you."

Kathleen sighed. "And she embarrassed you. It's a draw."

"Kathleen, I—"

"Please, Devon. I don't want to fight with you." *I don't want to care about you. I don't want to love you.* But it was too late. She had created her own hell and she must live in it, survive in it. Arguing with him wouldn't make the pain go away, and it would frighten the children. From this moment forward they would be her only concern. For her soul's sake, for her sanity's sake, there could be no other way. "I have to go. I—I promised the kids I'd take them out to play in the snow."

"I'll come, too."

"No." She opened the door and stepped over the threshold, then turned back. "Please, Devon. I don't want you to come along. Not now. Go make peace with your mother."

"I'll make peace with my mother," he said darkly, "but first I'm going to give her a piece of my mind."

"Tell her not to worry. Tell her I'm not in love with you." Kathleen took a deep breath. "Monday I think it will be best if the children and I start to look for a place of our own." Then, very softly, she shut the door in his face.

"AH, DEVON. Here you are." His stepfather was standing in the doorway of the small office where he'd been using the fax machine. "So this is where you've been hiding."

"I'm not hiding. I'm waiting for Liam Hardesty to reply to my last fax."

Edward's gaze flickered to the clock on the wall. "Making a long day of it for him, aren't you? And a long week. You don't usually ask your people to work through the weekend."

"He's being well paid."

"Another problem with the Bangkok property?"

"No. I've just been out of touch over the holiday. Time to get back to the grind."

"It's Sunday in Bangkok," Edward reminded him.

"I'm aware of that." He couldn't quite meet the older man's knowing gaze. He could talk to Edward if he wanted to, but he wasn't ready. Edward would know that and accept it. He wouldn't press. Devon was grateful for that.

"Ice storm coming," Edward said, changing the subject. He jerked his thumb toward the window and waited for Devon's reply.

His stepfather had been the greatest single stabilizing influence on his life when he was young. Sometimes Devon thought he might have saved his life, giving him his love and guidance, instilling in him his rock-solid Midwestern values. Hell, Devon knew that was what had happened when he considered the fate of many of his contemporaries—the drugs, the booze and suicides. A lot of tragedies, the result of growing up with too much money and too little supervision.

He looked over his shoulder. The afternoon was dark and dreary; a cold wind whirled through the bare branches of the trees along the service road. It would be dark in a few minutes. It was raining—cold drops that pelted the window and froze on the pane, glazing the snow with a hard sheen of ice.

"Getting nasty. Has Mother returned from the city?"

He had had his talk with Nicole. He'd smoothed her ruffled feathers and done his best to dissuade her from the notion he'd fallen in love with Kathleen, but had let her know in no uncertain terms that if she couldn't treat his wife with the respect and consideration she deserved, she would no longer be welcome in his home. Nicole had been defiant and tearful by turns, but he'd refused to back down. After a few more tears she'd apologized prettily and agreed to be on her best behavior.

Privately he'd asked Samantha to keep her occupied and out of Kathleen's way, and his old friend had obliged. Friday's shopping expedition to Lake Geneva had been succeeded by a trip to Chicago for a visit to the Art Institute and yet more shopping, and dinner at the Heidelberg.

"Not that I know of," Edward replied.

"Wellman's a good driver and the Rolls is like an armored vehicle, but he's not used to this kind of weather."

"Did you try to talk her into staying here today?"

"I didn't know she was going. She left a note."

"I'll have the front desk let you know when she returns."

"Thanks, Dad. I'm not sure I want to talk to her right away, though."

"Difference of opinion?" Edward asked dryly.

"You could say that." Too bad Devon hadn't inherited his mother's theatrical flair. If he had, he would have just swept Kathleen up in his arms, run off with her to some deserted tropical island, and kept her there until she was as much in love with him as he was with her. He took one more look out the window. "Never fails, does it? Holiday weekend. People traveling, so the weather gets bad."

"Lake effect," Edward said with a native's acceptance of a capricious climate. "Lake Michigan has a way of affecting everything going on around it."

"Do you ever regret coming back here?" Devon didn't know what made him ask that question. From time to time he'd thought about making Tyler his home, or at least as close to Tyler as he could manage. Chicago, probably.

"No. It was the best decision of my life."

Devon nodded, wanting to ask advice of the older man, yet not knowing exactly how to go about it. If anyone knew the full circumstances behind his sudden marriage, it was Edward. Or at least most of them. Edward didn't know about Paris.

"Kathleen's trying to locate you," the older man said now. From the slight frown between his eyebrows, Devon realized it wasn't the first time he'd relayed the information.

He looked up from staring at his shoe. "Is something wrong?"

"Bad weather or not, the Drakiks have arrived. She would like you to join them in the suite."

Devon stood up, straightened his collar. He wondered if he should have put on a tie and worn a suit, intimidated the hell out of these people so they wouldn't think of putting forward any claim to the children. He'd do the latter if he thought he had to, would hound them to the ends of the earth if they so much as hinted at formalizing their relationship with his kids.

"Let's go," he said.

"Why do you need me?" Edward asked, not moving.

"Firepower," Devon retorted. "I want the Cleveland cousins to know from the word *go* just who it is they're dealing with."

"Devon, I don't—"

"Please, Dad. I need the backup."

Edward nodded, still frowning. "I'll come. But you know there's an old saying around these parts, a bit homespun but appropriate. You might do well to remember you can catch more flies with honey than with vinegar."

"ANDREJ, WOULD YOU like to show your cousins the game room?" Kathleen asked in a last-ditch attempt to stave off a total breakdown in communications.

Andrej looked from her to the kind, middle-aged face of the man who had been introduced to him forty minutes ago as his cousin, William Drakik, and gave him a tentative smile. He nodded shyly. "Yes," he said.

"I'd like that, too, Andrej." His cousin had the family looks, with the same red-gold hair as Marta's and the same laughing, warm brown eyes that had given Josef's rather homely face such appeal. Marta and Andrej had recognized the resemblance immediately.

So had Devon. Kathleen could only assume that was what made him realize beyond any doubt that the Drakiks' connection to the children was legitimate, and possibly strong enough to supersede their own. There was no other explanation for the way Devon was acting. None at all.

"Okay." Andrej gave a stiff little bow, and Kathleen hoped somewhere in heaven Rujana saw and approved of his remembering the manners she'd taught him in better days. "Do you want to go see our fun play?" he asked William's wife, Karla.

Kathleen bit her lip. Andrej was so nervous, so flustered by the tension in the room that his English seemed to have deserted him. Marta sat on Karla's lap, looking more like a life-size child mannequin than a living, breathing little girl.

"Would you like to show me where you play on nasty days like this?" the woman asked Marta very gently. The child stared back for a moment, then slid off her lap, looking to Andrej for guidance.

"I'd be honored to show you around Timberlake Lodge before I leave," Edward interjected smoothly, before the silence in the room became too deafening.

"I'd hoped you and Alyssa would join us all for dinner," Kathleen said quickly. It was cowardly of her to put Edward on the spot like that, but she was desperate.

"I'm afraid my wife and I have a previous commitment." The commitment was dinner with her parents, Kathleen was aware—an engagement that could be broken at a moment's notice. Obviously, Edward intended to distance himself from this situation. His action spoke more clearly than words. She and Devon were on their own, and floundering badly. Edward went on speaking to the Drakiks. "But I hope you will be our guests for dinner on your next visit to Tyler."

"We don't want to impose." William glanced at Devon's set face out of the corner of his eye.

"You're not imposing," Kathleen said forcefully. She hadn't wanted to like these people, but dammit, she did. They were good, solid, hardworking folks like her parents, like most of the people she had grown up with and met on the streets of Tyler every day. It would be good for the children to know them. "Our chef has won several regional awards. I'm sure you'll enjoy the food." From the uncertain look on the couple's faces, she knew she couldn't say the same for the company.

"Please, join us," Devon said stiffly. "You won't be disappointed."

If Devon thought the grudging invitation was going to undo all the damage of the past hour, he was sadly mistaken. But it was a start. Kathleen smiled. "Please stay."

William Drakik looked at his wife. "Well . . ."

"We'd be glad to join you." Karla smiled back at Kathleen. She was a plump, sweet-tempered woman of about forty.

"Good." Edward offered her his arm. "I can't join you for dinner, but I can still give you the four-star tour. Would you like to see the lodge?"

"Thank you," Karla answered for both of them.

"Excellent. We'll meet you in the lounge for drinks in, say, an hour, Kathleen?"

"Yes. An hour will be fine."

Edward indicated the door with an expansive sweep of his arm. "Now we're off to see the eighth wonder of the world, the children's activity room at Timberlake Lodge, Tyler, Wisconsin. Andrej, would you like to lead the way?"

Andrej managed a bigger smile this time. "Yes, sir. I will go first."

The door had barely shut behind them all when Kathleen whirled on her husband. "What was that all about?" she demanded as he headed for the bar.

Devon turned to face her. "What was what all about?"

"Don't play dumb with me, Devon Addison. And lower your voice. You'll wake Phil from his nap." She took three angry strides toward him. "Those poor people had barely introduced themselves before you were grilling them about their motives for wanting to come and meet the children."

"Up until an hour ago, you were ready to do the same thing. What changed your mind?"

"I—I was mistaken. They're fine people." She didn't want to admit that she'd been as suspicious of the Drakiks' motives as Devon was. She didn't want to even begin to remember that when he had first entered the room, proud and aristocratic, she had been pleased to see the recognition of his power and authority in the other couple's eyes.

Devon wasn't about to back down that easily. "They are Marta and Andrej's blood relatives, Kathleen. Their claim to them is every bit as good as ours. Have you thought of that? We may have physical custody, but that's all. We have no proof Rujana wanted us to have the children. Nothing in her handwriting. The best we can do is an adoption certificate in a language damn near no one in the country can read."

"William and Karla never said they wanted to take the children. They only want to have them visit." Kathleen had been taken aback by that suggestion herself, but had tried not to show it. She thought of the hungry, haunted look on Karla Drakik's face as she'd held Marta in her arms, and felt her pain, her loss, as deeply as if it was her own. "Their only child was killed by a drunk driver, Devon. Finding they have Andrej and Marta to help fill the emptiness must seem like a miracle to them."

"Enough of a miracle for them to start thinking of putting up a fight for them, maybe?"

"No." Even as she denied it, Kathleen knew he might be right. But she still couldn't condone his high-handed tactics with the Drakiks. "You didn't have to throw the threat of the entire Addison legal department at them."

"I'm not so certain."

"They assured us they wouldn't challenge our right to the children," she reminded him.

"Today they feel that way. But what about tomorrow? Or the week after that?" He planted himself directly in front of her. "I saw their faces. They fell in love with those kids at first sight, just like you did. Just like I did. They're dangerous as far as I'm concerned. I don't intend to roll over and play friendly puppy for them like you did, just because they're your kind of people."

"And I don't intend to treat them like child stealers for the same reason. You underestimate the lower orders," she said bitingly, fighting back with words because that was the only way she could keep from breaking down in tears over what they had come to. She wrapped her arms around herself. "Threats just make us serfs and chattels more determined to see a fight through to the end, no matter what the cost."

He grabbed her by the shoulders. "Get this straight, Kathleen Kelsey Addison. This is one place where your damned Midwestern, middle-class, salt-of-the-earth superiority is dead wrong. We vain and idle upper-class snobs are just as stubborn, just as determined to fight for what is ours. And if you'd just admit it, you're damned glad to have all that dirty old money to back you up."

"I am not," she said through clenched teeth. "I am not." But she was, although she couldn't admit it, not now, maybe never. She *had* been glad the Drakiks' had been awed by their surroundings, had realized that Kathleen and Devon, as a couple, had nearly unlimited resources and professional expertise at their command. She was glad, and she despised herself for it, because with no difficulty at all she could also picture herself in the Drakiks' position.

"Kathleen?" Their heads turned in unison toward the door. Devon dropped his hold on her arms.

"Yes, Andrej?" Kathleen tried to smile. Devon walked over to the piano.

The little boy looked from one to the other, smiling a little, but Kathleen was too upset to notice the fear and confusion beneath the smile, and Devon was too far away. "We want to play in game room. Mr. Edward says to tell you we stay there."

"Don't you want to show the hotel to William and Karla?"

"Me and Marta we see it already," Andrej explained, his eyes darting from one face to the other.

"Go play, Andrej," Devon said. The residue of anger in his voice was apparent to Kathleen. She hoped that Andrej was not as perceptive.

"Okay."

"We'll have dinner in one hour. I'll come for you."

"Dinner with all of us? Whole kit and caboodle?"

Kathleen managed a smile, hearing her mother's influence in Andrej's choice of words.

"Yes," Devon said, not looking at Kathleen, not really looking at the little boy. "One big happy family."

"What?" Andrej looked confused. His smile disappeared.

"Devon..." Kathleen stopped herself from renewing their argument in front of the child. "Go play, Andrej. Take care of Marta and have fun."

"Okay." He shut the door. They were alone again.

Devon came to stand in front of her. "I'm sorry I made you angry, Kathleen. But I'm not sorry I behaved as I did. What's mine I fight for with every weapon I can get my hands on."

She swallowed a sob. "We can't go on like this." This was how it had been when they'd left Paris—the difference between fantasy and cold, hard reality; the chasm between his world and hers. Only this time it was worse, a thousand times worse, and it would take her a thousand times longer to heal—if she ever did.

He nodded, his face grim, his expression guarded. "I know that. But for now we don't have a choice. I'll meet you in the dining room in an hour."

CHAPTER FOURTEEN

KATHLEEN WALKED through the lobby without a clear-cut destination, or even a reason for being there. It was too early to meet Edward and the Drakiks in the lounge for a drink. It was too late to try and talk to Devon, to mend the damage their argument had caused.

It was too late to say she was sorry.

"Kathleen, hello." Sarah's voice came from the depths of a fur-trimmed parka as a gust of cold wet wind heralded the entrance of the Kentons.

She managed a smile. "Hello, Sarah. Hi, Michael. What are you doing out on a night like this?"

"I'm making sure that she's away from the parsonage this evening," Michael explained, helping Sarah out of her coat. "The push is on. The TylerTots Christmas bazaar is next week. My wife thinks they can't manage without her. She's made fifteen trips up and down those steps today. I decided there wasn't going be a sixteenth. So here we are."

"I told him it was much more dangerous to be driving in this weather," Sarah teased, a low, rumbling clap of thunder and flash of lightning adding credence to her words. "Did you ever see such a storm?" She frowned at the snow coming down beyond the veranda. "Thunder and lightning and snow all at the same time. It's unnatural."

"It's not unnatural," Michael said. "It's unusual but not unnatural. Sarah's right, though. It's going to be terrible driving by morning." He qualified his last remark. "But it's not too bad now. We'll have dinner and be back home safe and sound in two hours."

"Can you and Devon join us for coffee in the lounge?" Sarah asked. "We could discuss plans for the children's party if you have time."

"I...I'd love to, Sarah," Kathleen said. Under ordinary circumstances she would have welcomed the opportunity to become better acquainted with Sarah Kenton. "But the children's cousins have arrived."

"What are they like?" Sarah's hazel eyes searched her face. An intuitive woman, it seemed she had no trouble at all discerning the pain that shadowed Kathleen's heart.

"They're very nice people."

"I'm glad." Sarah gave her a tiny private smile. "Although it might have been easier for you if they weren't."

"Exactly." She shrugged. "Edward's showing them around the lodge. I'm on my way to the activities room to collect Marta and Andrej. We're going to have dinner together."

"Then we'll talk about the party some other time."

"Yes. But soon. I promise."

"Our table will be ready in ten minutes," Michael announced as he returned from checking their coats. "Want to go into the lounge or sit here by the fire?"

"By the fire," Sarah said. "I'm chilled to the bone." She did look chilled, and Kathleen detected a faint tremor in her hands. Her face was pale, there were dark circles under her eyes, but her smile was beautiful and serene. "I'll call you tomorrow after services," Sarah promised, giving Kathleen's hand a squeeze.

"We'll talk tomorrow." Tomorrow she would have herself under control. Tomorrow she would have had the night to consider what she must do next, what choices to make for the children's sake, for her heart's sake.

She hurried on down the short corridor to the activities room. It was situated in the new addition to Timberlake, but there was a shortcut through the oldest part of the building, an intersecting hallway that took her past Margaret Ingalls's room, where Nicole Holmes was now established.

One of the maids was pushing a linen cart along the hallway, clean towels in her arms. She knocked and entered the unoccupied room as Kathleen passed. It was a nightly ritual. Each evening, while their guests were at dinner, Timberlake's staff turned down the beds, replaced dirty glasses and soiled linens and left small gifts of chocolate or fresh flowers on the pillows. Such conscientious and gracious attention to detail kept people returning to Timberlake over and over again.

Kathleen rounded the corner and entered the new wing. She could hear the bells and whistles of a pinball machine and the laughter of children playing as she came up to the doorway. But when she looked inside the log-paneled, high-ceilinged room, she saw neither Andrej nor Marta. The tumbling mats where Andrej liked to practice his cartwheels and back flips were empty. The game tables, where Marta colored and played with her dolls, were deserted. A teenage girl was watching a video in the corner. There were two older boys playing the pinball machines along one wall and a little girl, steadied by her father, teetering along the rope bridge of the elaborate wooden jungle gym.

"Excuse me." Kathleen paused to catch her breath. "Have you seen a boy, about eight, with brown hair, and a little redheaded girl playing here? She's about four."

The man shook his head. "We've been here half an hour. The girl watching TV was the only one in the room when we arrived. Maybe she saw them."

Kathleen hurried to the carpeted TV corner and asked the same questions. The teenager looked up a bit sheepishly. "Sorry. I fell asleep. I only woke up when those guys started playing the pinball machines. I never saw your kids."

"She didn't see them either, huh?" The toddler's father guessed when Kathleen returned.

"No. She was sleeping."

"They probably just went back to your room. The weather's too miserable for them to have headed outside."

"Yes. I imagine that's what happened. Thanks," Kathleen said.

"Kids," the man said, grabbing his little one by the seat of her jeans to keep her steady on the swaying walkway. "They sure know how to push our buttons, don't they?"

"They sure do." Stretching her face into a reasonable imitation of a smile, Kathleen thanked him.

"Sorry I couldn't be more help," he called out as she left.

Back in the lobby Kathleen ran into Edward, standing by the fireplace talking to Sarah and Michael.

"Where are the Drakiks?" she asked.

"They stopped off at their room to pick up some photographs of their home in Cleveland for the children to see."

A terrible suspicion stirred. Kathleen pushed it away, unable to face the scenario her imagination had produced. "When did you leave them? How long ago?"

"About twenty minutes. I had a message from Nicole. She called from the car, said they'd be back in an hour or so. The roads are getting bad, but she didn't want Devon to worry. Then I stopped in my office to call Alyssa and tell her I was going to be delayed a bit, to go on ahead to your parents' house. Why?'' His eyes narrowed. "What's wrong?''

"I'm not sure. Andrej and Marta aren't in the play-room. I thought perhaps they were with you,'' she finished lamely.

Sarah and Michael were sitting together on a love seat at right angles to the huge fieldstone fireplace. They said nothing, but Kathleen could feel their eyes on her.

"The last time I saw them they were heading for the suite to ask your permission to go play,'' Edward said.

"That's where they must be. In the suite. Excuse me.''

She made herself walk at a reasonable pace. The children would be in the suite with Devon, or at least Phil, who would be up from his nap and waiting for his supper. There was nothing unusual about them not being in the activities room, except that Andrej was such a conscientious child. He never wandered away; he never asked permission to do one thing and then went off and did something else.

She pushed open the door of the suite, blinking in the sudden brightness. Phil was indeed sitting at the table, inspecting his recently arrived dinner. Devon was standing at the French doors watching the unsettling spectacle of lightning and snow. "Are the children here?'' she asked, swiveling her head to take in the farthest corners of the big room.

Phil looked up from his meal and shook his head. Devon stepped away from the window. "No,'' he said. "They're in the activities room.''

"No, they're not,'' Kathleen whispered. "They're not there. I checked.''

"Maybe they decided to stay with Edward and the Drakiks."

Kathleen shook her head, unable to trust her voice. She swallowed hard, then took herself in hand. "I just spoke to Edward. He hasn't seen them for nearly an hour. And Devon...Devon, I'm worried. The Drakiks weren't with him, either."

Edward was still talking to Michael and Sarah when they reached the lobby. The children were nowhere in sight. Neither were the Drakiks. "Kathleen says the children are missing," Devon said without preamble.

"They didn't return to the suite?"

Kathleen shook her head. "No." A swirl of panic clouded her vision. She blinked, pushing it away.

"Where are the Drakiks?" Devon demanded.

Edward's gaze narrowed. "In their room. I'll give them a call."

"Edward." Kathleen put out a restraining hand. "Do you think..." She hesitated, but couldn't stop herself from asking the question. "Is it possible they left with the children?"

Horribly, he didn't contradict her. "Anything's possible, Kathleen. But that's a pretty long leap. I don't see how they could walk out of here without someone noticing."

He moved toward the desk, but at that moment the Drakiks came down the stairway from the second floor. Karla was carrying a small photo album. They looked a little grave, slightly worried, but their expressions and body language were not those of a couple with something to hide. They didn't look or act like kidnappers.

Kathleen hurried toward them, already ashamed of her unfounded suspicions. "Have you seen Marta and Andrej?" she asked.

"Aren't they playing in the game room?" William questioned in return.

"No. They...we can't find them. They've disappeared."

"You mean they've run away?" Karla clutched the photo album to her breast. "In this awful weather?"

"We don't know where they are, Mrs. Drakik," Devon interjected. "But they aren't where they said they'd be. Did anything unusual happen while you were with them?"

William looked at his wife, a frown between his eyes. "I can't think of anything we said that would have upset them."

"We talked a little more of them coming for a visit," Karla related, continuing to the bottom of the wide oak staircase. "We want to take them to Cedar Point—it's a wonderful amusement park on Lake Erie. Perhaps take them to Jacobs Field to see an Indians game. Or the zoo. The usual things." She bit her lip. "I... Andrej seemed excited by the idea."

"He was awfully quiet, honey," William observed, frowning harder. "Maybe he wasn't excited. Maybe he was frightened of taking such a long trip. I—I never thought..."

"I didn't, either. We would never, ever, do anything to frighten or upset those children." Karla's hand came up to cover her mouth. Tears pooled in her eyes. "You must believe that."

Devon spoke before Kathleen could. "We believe you, Mrs. Drakik. We all want what is best for Marta and Andrej. Kathleen and I are as much to blame as anyone. We were arguing when Andrej came looking for us."

"Our being here was the cause of that argument, wasn't it."

Devon nodded. "Yes," he said, "I'm afraid it was."

"I'm sorry."

"No more than I am," Devon said quietly. "I'd like to apologize for my behavior earlier. I—"

She shook her head. "Never apologize for caring enough to fight for what you want."

"They've run away," Kathleen whispered, the awful certainty searing her brain, stealing her breath. Blindly she reached for Devon's hand. She forgot how angry she had been with him just minutes before. She refused to think of all the differences that still remained to be settled between them. She only wanted to have him near, to give her strength to face the unthinkable. "They've run away because Andrej heard us arguing, and he was afraid that we would send them away with the Drakiks."

Devon touched her cheek, very lightly. "We don't know that for certain, Kath. They may be playing hide-and-seek—"

"No. It's nothing like that. They wouldn't play tricks on us. They're scared and alone. We have to find them, Devon. Hurry. Get our coats."

"Slow down, Kathleen." It was Edward's voice that penetrated the fog of panic that thickened and swirled at the corners of her vision. "We need to decide who will search where so nothing gets overlooked."

Devon nodded. "Okay, Dad. What do you suggest?"

Edward motioned to the desk clerks to join them. "We'll split up. I'll take the Drakiks with me and search the service wing. Marie?" He turned to the tall young woman in a gray blazer who answered his summons. "Andrej and Marta have come up missing. Round up whomever you can spare and have them check the public rooms and the attics. Call valet parking and see if anyone noticed them leaving the building. And get maintenance on the line. We need flashlights and a couple of walkie-talkies. If the kids don't turn up by then, we'll institute a room-by-room search."

"Dad, would you give the Tyler police a call?" Devon's face was as grim as his words. "I don't want to take any chances on a night like this if they did leave the hotel. We'll need all the manpower we can muster if we have to widen the search beyond the grounds."

"You're right. Marie, get the station on the line, please."

"I'll check the car barn," Michael offered, as the young woman hurried off to do Edward's bidding. "Andrej loves the cars. Maybe he thought he could figure out the keypad and get inside."

"Good call," Devon said. "I'll go with you. Hang on while I get our coats." He turned and headed toward the suite with long, distance-eating strides.

"I'll check the shore path," Kathleen said. "We've walked that way several times, to meet Liza and Margaret Alyssa and feed the geese on the lake." She fought panic again when a picture of the dark, ice-rimmed waters of the lake flashed across her inner eye.

"I'll go with you." Sarah rose awkwardly from her seat by the fire.

"No, you won't," Michael objected.

She looked at him, her pretty face set and uncompromising. "I will. I can still walk."

"Sarah, is that wise?"

"I'm not sitting here biting my nails while the rest of you are out searching." The look she gave Kathleen was no less determined than the one she'd bestowed on her husband.

"I'll have Marie call Cliff and Liza," Edward suggested. "Cliff can meet you at the property line. That will save time, and Sarah won't have to negotiate any of the bluff path."

"There. It's settled." Sarah reached up and touched her husband's cheek, smoothing the deep crease that ran from nose to mouth. "I'll be careful, my love."

"And I'll be careful of her," Kathleen promised. Secretly she was relieved to have Sarah's company. Sharing the cold walk would help keep her thoughts off the terrifying possibilities of what she might find.

Devon returned with their coats and the information that Phil would keep vigil in the suite in case the children were just hiding somewhere and showed up there. Thirty seconds later a maintenance man appeared with flashlights and walkie-talkies.

"Stay in touch," Edward reminded them as they headed for the doors. "And good luck."

There was no moonlight. The night was dark, the combined rain and snow still coming down from a leaden sky. Thunder rumbled off in the distance. The lightning flashes were fewer and farther between, but still disturbing, distorting the snowy landscape.

They walked in silence, splitting up almost immediately as Devon and Michael headed toward the service road and the building that housed the Addison auto collection. Their flashlight beams, playing over the ice-glazed snow as the men searched for small footprints, grew fainter and fainter until they disappeared.

Kathleen scanned the ground with her flashlight as well, but Sarah, in deference to her condition, kept hers trained steadily at their feet. The two women walked in silence, their breath condensing in smoky wreaths around their heads. There were no footprints, no small shadows flitting ahead of them on the path. The lake was an eerie, silent expanse of gray and silver. Kathleen forced herself to play the light beam over the surface, praying that she wouldn't see a double trail of small footprints leading to a darker area, where jagged edges and open water would indicate too much weight had been placed on the thin, new ice.

Finally, she could stand the silence no longer. "I should never have sent Andrej off after he heard us quarreling," she said, her voice shaky and breathless from the cold and fear. "I should have gone after him, explained why Devon and I were angry with each other."

"Do you want to tell me what caused the disagreement?"

"Devon's behavior toward the Drakiks," Kathleen related. "He was overbearing and totally out of line. Devon Addison, President of Addison Hotels, the heir to the Addison millions. Not the man I love." There, she had said it aloud. The genie was out of the bottle.

"We often behave badly when we're afraid of losing something precious to us," Sarah said, her breathing even more ragged and uneven than Kathleen's. Automatically, Kathleen slowed her pace so that the pregnant woman could more easily keep up.

"Karla Drakik said the same thing."

"Would you have acted differently if you were in Devon's position?"

Maybe it was the darkness, so like a confessional. Maybe it was Sarah's knowledge and acceptance of human nature. "I did feel the same way," Kathleen confessed. "I was glad he was rich and powerful enough to frighten those poor people into leaving Tyler and never trying to see the children again. And then I remembered. The Drakiks are like you and me."

"And we are not like Devon?"

"Devon was born to power and wealth."

"And you can't learn to live with that?" Sarah asked.

"No, I don't think I can."

"Because it's too tempting? Or too much responsibility?"

Kathleen sighed. "Both."

Sarah laughed and reached out to pat her gloved hand. "I'm sorry, but I can't picture anyone less likely than you to be led into a life of idleness and dissolution. I don't know Devon very well, but I think I'm safe in saying he doesn't fit that mold, either."

Devon fit a mold? Kathleen almost smiled. No. Devon Charles Addison was definitely his own man. Had she been trying to fit him into a mold? A middle-class, just-another-regular-guy persona that fit him no better than the lord-of-the-manor, sword-and-helmet kind of thing?

"Think of all that money as a challenge, not a burden. Think of all the good you can do. Together."

A challenge. Why hadn't she been able to see Devon's money in that light before? Work. Business. Not their *life*. They had always worked well together....

"Kathleen? Hallo! Is that you?" Cliff Forrester's voice came from somewhere on the bluff path above them.

"We're down here, Cliff. Have you seen any sign of the children?"

"Nothing up here," he called back. First his flashlight beam, then his tall, shadowy form appeared around a bend in the path. Liza's husband opened the gate and passed through, shutting it behind him. The wrought iron was heavy, the hinges balky in the cold. Cliff played his flashlight beam over the ground around the gate. The snow was pristine, disturbed only by their own boot prints.

"As far as I can tell they haven't been this way. I'm sorry, Kathleen."

"We'd better get back to the lodge," she replied, hiding her dismay, doing battle with the panic demons that with every passing moment increased their efforts to be let free.

"Hello, Reverend Sarah," Cliff said, identifying her when a stray beam of light played across her face.

"Hello, Cliff." She turned to acknowledge his greeting and abruptly, without warning, crumpled to her knees.

Kathleen was at her side instantly. "Sarah, are you all right? What happened? Did you slip on some ice? Twist your ankle?"

Sarah remained on her hands and knees for several seconds, then took Kathleen's outstretched hand to help her rise. Cliff assisted on the other side. "I'm fine," she said breathlessly. "I got a cramp and stumbled, that's all. I'm fine. Let's keep looking."

"Sarah, I'm not so sure."

"Really, Kathleen..." A groan escaped her. She clutched at her swollen stomach. "I'm fine, really."

"No, you're not," Cliff said, his deep voice brooking no argument as he swept her up into his arms. "You're in labor."

"No. It's just a cramp," Sarah moaned. "I can't be in labor. The baby's not due for three weeks yet."

"Babies don't read calendars," Cliff said, and started toward the lodge so quickly that Kathleen could barely keep up, let alone use the walkie-talkie to radio the others that they were coming.

They rounded a corner of the building and the main entrance came into view just as two Tyler police cruisers pulled up, red-and-blue emergency lights flashing out across the snow, followed by a black, late-model sedan that Kathleen thought she recognized as Jeff Baron's. She was relieved to see her cousin, Brick Bauer, Tyler's police captain, and even more relieved when Jeff Baron emerged from his car.

"Brick! Jeff!" she called, hurrying ahead of Cliff. "I'm so glad you're here. Hurry, we need help. It's Sarah Kenton. She may have gone into labor." Kathleen shoved her worry and fear for her lost children into a corner of her mind. For the moment, Sarah's predicament was top priority.

"I'll radio the EMS unit to get out here," Brick said, his heavy police parka giving him the look and shape of a huge black bear. He glanced over her shoulder at Cliff and the pale, tight-lipped woman in his arms as he reached into the patrol car's open window for the radio.

"Jeff, thank God you're here. But how did you know?" Kathleen asked, giving his arm a squeeze.

"I was at the hospital when Edward's call came over the scanner. Any sign of the kids yet?"

Kathleen shook her head, not trusting her voice.

"We'll find 'em safe and sound, Kath," he assured her. "Don't worry."

"I'm trying not to."

"Where's Michael?" Sarah asked.

"Searching the car barn," Edward answered for her, coming out the doors onto the covered porch. "Jeff." A brief smile touched his mouth. "Glad you're here. Bring Sarah inside, Cliff. I'll get Michael and Devon back at once." He turned around, already speaking into the walkie-talkie.

"I'll get my bag," Jeff said. "Be right with you."

Kathleen held the door for Cliff and Sarah. Devon and Michael must have already been on their way from the car barn, because they arrived before Kathleen had even had time to ask the bellman to fetch a blanket for Sarah.

Michael's face was whiter than his wife's. He knelt by the edge of the sofa where Cliff had laid her. "I told you not to go out there, Sarah," he said brokenly, watching as Jeff sat down beside her, checking her pulse, running his long, strong-fingered hands over the swollen mound of her belly, timing the strength and duration of the contraction.

"You are definitely in labor," Jeff announced. "And I have the sneaking suspicion you're going to try to break my sister Liza's record time for a first delivery, if that contraction was any indication."

"It was a doozy," Sarah admitted, grasping Michael's hand so tightly he winced.

"Where's the damn ambulance?" he asked, his eyes meeting Jeff's for the first time. "She's in pain, can't you see that?"

"She's doing fine, Michael. I can't say the same for you."

"What kind of crack was that?" Two sets of midnight-blue eyes locked and held.

"I mean, it won't do Sarah any good if her labor coach falls apart." Jeff looked down at Sarah and smiled.

"I'm not going to fall apart," Michael said.

Kathleen held her breath. The two men hadn't spoken face-to-face in months, as far as she knew. She could feel Devon tense behind her, ready to step forward and intervene if necessary. She reached back, put her hand on his chest to halt him.

A ghost of a smile still twitched at the corner of Jeff's mouth as he looked at his half brother once more. "I didn't think you would. We Baron men are tough in the clinch."

"Here comes another one," Sarah said. "Dear heaven."

"Breathe, Sarah. Breathe," Michael urged, coaching her through a contraction that made Kathleen's insides roil in sympathy.

"Hang on, Sarah. You'll make it." Jeff rested his hands on his patient's belly, talking softly, soothingly. "C'mon, little one, slow down. Uncle Jeff wants you safely at Tyler

General so Hank Merton can coax you into this big old, cold world."

Uncle Jeff. Kathleen turned her face up to Devon's and saw him smile. Maybe there was hope for the two brothers yet.

They'd drawn a small but interested crowd in the lobby. At a signal from Edward, Marie, the night manager, began to herd the curious into the lounge with an offer of drinks on the house. The group around the sofa paid little attention to the exodus, their concentration focused on Brick Bauer, as he came through the big double doors.

He leaned over the back of the couch and patted Sarah's shoulder. "The emergency unit is already on a run to Tyler General. Some guy out on Lake Shore Road slammed his snowmobile into a telephone pole. It'll be at least thirty, maybe forty minutes before they can get rolling again."

"What about the Belton unit?"

"Same time for them to get here. They've got more ice over that way. We'll have to transport her in one of the patrol cars."

"I don't know," Jeff began.

The main doors banged open once more, and Nicole Holmes and her entourage sailed into the lobby. "Edward," she called, spotting her ex-husband across the room. "What's going on here? We've just endured the most ghastly drive up from the city and now there are police cars blocking the driveway. Wellman can't park the Rolls." Her gaze swiveled to the small group gathered around Sarah. "Good Lord, has there been an accident?"

"Not an accident. A baby." Devon stepped forward as Edward deftly steered Lady Amelia and her family out of the way. "Sarah Kenton's gone into labor and it's urgent that we get her to the hospital."

Nicole's gray-green eyes narrowed. "A baby?" She looked at Sarah, then back to her son. "That's not all, is it? I can see by your eyes that something else is terribly wrong."

"The children are missing, Mother."

Her mouth dropped open. "Oh, dear God, missing? How? Why?"

"We're not sure. I'll explain later," he said hastily, as Sarah stifled another moan.

"Yes. Please. I must know everything. Those poor little ones. But first things first." Nicole turned her attention to Brick. "There is no ambulance among the vehicles in the driveway."

"It's being used to transport another patient to the hospital. Sarah's going to have to be taken to Tyler General in one of the patrol cars."

A look of dismay crossed Nicole's fine-boned features. "No, she isn't." She stepped forward, stripping off her gloves as she talked. "Dr. Baron."

"Yes, Lady Holmes?" Jeff said, replacing his stethoscope in his bag as he spoke.

"My car and driver are at your disposal."

"What?" Brick was shocked out of his professional calm by the announcement, while Kathleen could only look on in astonishment at this sudden display of Nicole's organizational talents.

Devon's mother raised a haughty eyebrow and gave the astonished chief of police look for look. "I said, my car and driver are at Mrs. Kenton's disposal. Surely transporting a laboring woman in a Rolls-Royce is far superior to bundling her into the back of a police cruiser."

"I—"

"Wellman is an excellent driver and the Rolls corners like it's on rails. Wellman!"

"Yes, your ladyship."

"Be very careful with Mrs. Kenton."

"Of course, madam." Wellman, every inch the perfect English butler, bowed slightly, as if his employer's demand was no more unusual than a directive for a Sunday drive in the country. "This way, Dr. Baron, Mr. Kenton. Captain Bauer, if I may be so bold. While I have every confidence in the Rolls, a police escort would be most appreciated."

Outnumbered and outmaneuvered, Brick gave in gracefully. "You've got it, Mr. Wellman."

"Just Wellman, sir."

"Okay, Wellman, let's hit the road." Brick stepped around the sofa and took Kathleen's hand. "I'm leaving two officers here to help search the grounds. I've already contacted the county search-and-rescue patrol. If the children aren't found by morning they'll be out at first light."

"Thanks, Brick." She reached up and gave him a quick kiss on the cheek, and he caught her up in a bear hug.

"Don't worry, cuz. It'll all work out."

She blinked back tears, determined not to break down. "Of course. Now go. Take care of Sarah." She turned as Michael swept his wife up in his arms.

"Wait, Michael. Kathleen."

"Yes, Sarah?" Kathleen took the woman's cold hand between her own. Devon had returned to stand by her. The warmth of his body helped hold the cold terror at bay a little longer.

"I'll pray for the children."

"I'll say a prayer for you," Kathleen whispered.

Sarah shook her head, reaching up to touch her husband's strong, handsome face. "You don't need to worry about me." She turned her head and held out her hand to Jeff. Her hazel eyes were bruised with pain, but her smile was screne. "The Lord knows I'm in excellent hands."

CHAPTER FIFTEEN

"YOU REALLY SHOULD TRY to get some rest, Kathleen."

"Yes. It's only a little after midnight. Hours till dawn."

"I couldn't sleep." Kathleen stirred the embers of the fire with the poker, watching the flames quicken and leap, before turning to smile at Alyssa and Nicole, uneasy allies united in their concern for her lost children. "I'm fine, really."

"Would you like another cup of coffee?" Alyssa asked. Kathleen shook her head. "Nicole?"

"Thanks, no. I'm awash." Devon's mother leaned her head against the back of the sofa. "I do so hate not being able to *do* something."

"The entire hotel has been searched from top to bottom," Alyssa reminded the other woman. She had arrived about ten o'clock, along with Anna and Johnny. Anna was now in the hotel kitchen, helping the chef make sandwiches for the weary searchers. Johnny, Edward and Devon were in the lobby, working with Brick Bauer to prepare a search plan for first light. Phil had finally been persuaded to give up his vigil by the fireside and go to bed. The Drakiks had retired to their room after having been assured they would be told immediately if the children were found.

Half the world was asleep, but Kathleen thought she might never be able to close her eyes again. Every time she did, she saw what the lake would look like at first light, imagined the jagged hole in the ice the flashlight beams had not detected in the darkness, the place where two frightened, lost children had tumbled through to their deaths.

"I think I will have that cup of coffee, Alyssa," she said, to banish the waking nightmare. She wrapped her arms around her waist and leaned toward the fire's warmth, but no amount of heat seemed able to thaw the icy tendrils of worry and fear that chilled her heart and slowed her blood in her veins, making her feel thickheaded and sluggish, unable to think or to act, only to feel.

"The coffeepot is empty," Alyssa observed, returning to the fireside. "I'm going to the kitchen to get some fresh."

"Okay." Kathleen tried to smile her thanks and failed utterly.

"Are you sure you'll be all right?"

"I'll stay with her," Nicole said.

Alyssa looked at Kathleen, who nodded. "It's all right. Please check on my mother, see that she's not working too hard."

Someone knocked at the door. Alyssa, who was closest, opened it, and Wellman stepped across the threshold. "Good evening," he said formally.

"Wellman. I thought I told you to stay at the hospital as long as Dr. Baron needed you."

"I did, Madam," the butler informed Nicole with a small bow. "I am the bearer of good news."

"The baby," Alyssa breathed. "Is it here?"

"Yes, Mrs. Wocheck. Dr. Baron has asked me to tell you all that he is an uncle again."

"An uncle again?" Alyssa's eye caught Kathleen's for a moment. Kathleen lifted her shoulders in a shrug.

"Yes, madam. Mrs. Kenton was safely delivered of a son one hour ago."

"A boy," Alyssa said, laughing aloud. "How wonderful. A boy. Michael will be so pleased."

"I myself have seen the infant. Quite small, of course, but all in all a most remarkable child."

"And Sarah?"

"Mrs. Kenton is naturally fatigued, but she is recovering."

"Thank goodness. A boy. And my son has proclaimed himself a proud uncle?"

"His very words, madam." Wellman bowed again.

Alyssa laughed, delighted. "Thank you, Wellman."

"My pleasure, madam."

"The pleasure is all mine." Alyssa reached up on tiptoe and gave him a kiss on the cheek.

"Why, thank you, madam," he said, looking flustered, but only for a moment. "Now, if you ladies will excuse me, I'll return to the lobby and offer my services in the search for the two missing youngsters."

"You must be very tired, Wellman," Kathleen said, appreciating the butler's offer.

"I couldn't sleep, Mrs. Addison. Is there anything else you require of me before I go, Lady Holmes?"

"No, of course not, Wellman. Thank you for all your help," Nicole said.

"Then I'll be off to join the others."

"Good night."

"I'll walk with you, Wellman. I think I should go to the hospital. Kathleen, do you mind?" Alyssa looked torn.

"Of course not."

"Then I will drive you, madam. The roads are still quite treacherous."

"Thank you, Wellman."

She came over and gave Kathleen a hug and kiss. "My prayers are here. Call the hospital if there is any news. Any news at all."

"I will."

The door closed behind the pair and the silence grew heavy once more. The wind had picked up, Kathleen noticed. It was much colder than it had been earlier. The unusual thunderstorm had moved off to the south, the icy rain had turned back to snow and now had stopped.

"Devon was born on a stormy night like this," Nicole said. "Little boys and stormy nights. What is it about them that seems to go together?"

"His birthday is in February, isn't it?" Kathleen drew her knees up to her chest and rested her chin on them. Nicole seemed inclined to talk, and even though the scene in the lobby was still fresh in her mind, it seemed of little importance in the light of what had happened in the past few hours.

"Yes."

"Where was he born?"

"New York. My father insisted on it. London was his home for forty years, but he never gave up his U.S. citizenship."

"Your mother was English, wasn't she? What did she think of having her grandchild born so far from home?"

"She died the year before. Devon never knew her. Never really knew any of his English relatives, actually. The family disowned Mother. They didn't approve of my father. Too common by half." She laughed aloud. "I've shocked you, haven't I?"

Kathleen shook her head. "Yes, I guess you have. Arthur Addison always seemed to me to be the epitome of the perfect English gentleman."

"He tried very hard to be. The truth is Arthur was born and raised in Pittsburgh, Pennsylvania. He was a self-made man in every sense of the word."

"I . . . I never knew."

"Very few people did. My father was a man of extraordinary drive and ambition. He set out to make himself a millionaire and an English gentlemen. He succeeded admirably in both endeavors. Except, of course, the English aristocracy have very long memories. My mother's family always treated my father with polite contempt. Although his money and power saw to it that that never happened to Devon or me." She tilted her head slightly, regarding Kathleen from assessing gray-green eyes. "You're thinking I take after my mother's family, aren't you? That I'm as snobbish and insular as my friends."

"I never thought that," Kathleen said, too hurriedly.

Nicole laughed. "Yes, you did. You do." She leaned forward.

"You've never given me reason to believe otherwise." Kathleen was too tired to mind her tongue.

"You don't like me, do you?"

"I don't know you, Nicole."

"I could make your life miserable." Her mother-in-law's voice hardened. Her lips were a thin scarlet slash across her face, but there was fear in her eyes.

Kathleen sat up a little straighter. "Why would you do that?"

"Because you're taking my son away from me."

"I'm not taking Devon away from you. I—I don't know if our marriage will survive the night." There, she had said the words aloud, made her doubts and fears concrete, animate.

"It will survive." Nicole raised her chin. "He loves you. He loves you more than anything else on earth."

If only that were true. If only she could believe it. "He's never told me so."

"Have you given him the chance?"

"Nicole, please. That's not important now."

"My son's happiness will always be of the utmost importance to me," Nicole said, all her old haughtiness back. She stood up, moved to the piano, agitation evident in every move, her skirt swirling around her slim legs. She picked up a silver picture frame, a photograph of Kathleen and Devon and the children, taken a few weeks before.

"Devon's happiness is important to me, too, Nicole."

"If you break his heart I will never, ever forgive you. Not as long as I live." Her posture was defiant but there was a slight break in her voice.

Kathleen had never thought of Nicole Holmes as a lonely woman. Now she realized she had been mistaken in that assumption. Nicole feared growing old, unwanted and unneeded. Kathleen could understand that fear. Every woman could. "I don't want to take Devon away from you, Nicole. You're his mother."

"Perhaps you wouldn't try to keep us apart," Nicole said grudgingly. "But how can it be otherwise with him buried here in this miserable place for the rest of his life?"

"Devon and I have never discussed where—"

She whirled around. "You know I wanted him to marry Samantha Claremont, don't you," Nicole interrupted without a qualm.

Kathleen swallowed her anger, and the unexpected pain of the blunt words. "Yes."

"Do you know why?" Nicole answered her own question. "It's not because of her background or breeding, but because my son would never have fallen so deeply in love with her that there would be no room left for me in his life.''

"Devon doesn't love me that way, either, Nicole." *He couldn't love me or he wouldn't have offered me a marriage of convenience, a partnership, a business deal.*

"You're very wrong. He does. And there's nothing *I* can do about it.''

"There's nothing you have to do about it, Nicole.''

"Good heavens." Her mother-in-law's laugh was brittle, but Kathleen heard the uncertainty beneath the chiming sound. "You aren't suggesting that we become friends, are you?''

Kathleen smiled. "No, Nicole. Not close friends. But not enemies.''

A thin smile curved the corners of Nicole's mouth. She tilted her head, gauging Kathleen's sincerity, then she held out a tiny beringed hand. "Perhaps—" The door opened and Devon came into the room.

Kathleen was on her feet in an instant. But she didn't move toward him, even though she wanted nothing more than for him to take her in his arms and hold her tight. *But that could never be, not anymore.* As soon as the children were found, were safe, she would have to tell Devon that she couldn't stay married to him, regardless of how seriously it might complicate their already complicated legal situation. "What is it, Devon? Is there news?''

"Sorry, Kath. We haven't found them." He looked drawn and tired. There were two deep lines carved from nose to chin. He hadn't shaved and the dark blond stubble of his beard shadowed his face. He ran his hands through his hair, fingers splayed. "I came to ask you to help me choose some articles of the children's clothing.''

"What for?''

"When the search team gets here at dawn they'll have a pair of dogs with them. We need something to give them with the children's scent on it."

"Dogs." Kathleen clenched her hands into fists.

"Dogs," Nicole echoed.

"They're search-and-rescue animals, Kath. This isn't going to be a manhunt."

"I know." She held on to the shreds of her control with all the willpower she could muster. "It's just that Marta—the soldiers . . ." She couldn't go on. The look on Devon's face told her he understood what she was worried about.

"Kath, they aren't going to chase the children down with a pack of baying hounds. These are trained animals and handlers." He came forward, held out his hands. She let him draw her into his arms. She could feel the tension in his body, knew it echoed her own.

"No," she said, letting her cheek rest against his heart, to renew her strength from his just for a moment, for one last time. "That would be too cruel. It would make them feel as if they're back in Triglav, hiding from the soldiers."

Devon stiffened, held her away from him. "What did you say?"

"Hiding from the soldiers." She closed her eyes, looking back in time, remembering. "When the shelling was very bad Andrej would tell me the plans Rujana had made for them to hide if soldiers ever came for them. There was a closet or a big cupboard, something like that, in the basement of their apartment building, hidden behind a tangle of wires and pipes. Almost no one knew about it. They were to go there. And be very quiet."

Not say a word. Not make a sound. Dear God, was tiny, sweet Marta still trying to keep quiet, be still and not bring the soldiers down on them? Did she not trust her new parents enough to break her silence?

Kathleen's eyes flew open. "Devon, last night. The Drakiks arrival, our arguing. The thunder and lightning." She grabbed his hand with both of hers, held on so tightly he winced. "Devon, do you think they're *hiding* from us?"

His expression told her his thoughts had followed the same tortuous path as her own. "They could be. But where? There's no basement here at Timberlake. We've searched every room in the place. The car barn, the boathouse..."

"What about the attic?" Kathleen had only been in the echoing attic above the original building once in all the time she'd worked for Edward Wocheck. It was filled with odds and ends the Ingalls family had not claimed when they sold the property—cast-off summer-house furniture, scarred and broken chairs and cocktail tables, boxes and chests, as well as air-conditioning ducts, wire conduits. Lots of places for two frightened children to conceal themselves. But surely the attic had already been searched?

"I sent a couple of the maintenance staff up there as soon as we began looking," Devon assured her. "They checked it. Even though both the original and the new entrances were closed and locked from the outside, as usual."

Kathleen's heart sank. Of course the entrances were locked. The hotel's insurance carriers would never have allowed otherwise. "I—I just thought perhaps—"

"Wait!" Nicole pressed her hands against her lips as though in prayer. "There is another way into the attic."

Devon nodded. "The hidden stairway in your room. But the children don't know about it."

"Yes, they do."

"What?"

"I—I told Andrej. Just yesterday." She looked from one to the other, lifting her shoulders in a graceful apology. "They were walking down the hall when I came out of my room. Andrej stopped. He asked me if my room was really haunted."

"Where did he hear that story?" Devon asked.

Kathleen's mind was whirling. "Peter or Jimmy? They both must have heard it by now. It's a Tyler myth—Margaret Ingalls's ghost haunting Timberlake. When we were kids we all tried to sneak into the lodge and find the room. Go on, Nicole."

"I don't know where he heard the story. He didn't say. He appeared disappointed when I told him I had heard and seen nothing unusual. I thought... I thought, perhaps, if I showed them the staircase it would be exciting enough to make them forget their disappointment. I showed them how the latch works...." She broke off, lifting her hands as though to ask for their understanding. "I hoped they might begin to like me. I'm to be their grandmother, aren't I?" she finished in a defiant rush.

"How could they have gotten into your room, Mother? You left the hotel hours before they disappeared."

Nicole's face fell. "Of course, how stupid of me."

"Wait! Nicole's right." Kathleen was already moving toward the door as she spoke. "The maid. The maid was in Margaret's old room when I went looking for the children. If they were very quiet..."

"And she was in the bathroom..." Devon's gray eyes flared with new hope. "It's worth another look."

Kathleen's hand was already on the doorknob. She heard Nicole and Devon behind her as she hurried down the hallway. In the lobby, a fire still burned in the big fireplace. A clerk stood behind the desk, talking quietly to Brick Bauer and one of his men. Edward and Kathleen's father were seated nearby. The Drakiks were there, too. Anna Kelsey was nowhere to be seen.

"We couldn't sleep," William said, taking Karla's hand in his. "We came down to see if there was any news."

"Kathleen, Devon. What's happened?" Edward asked, rising to his feet along with Johnny Kelsey. Brick broke off his conversation and came toward them.

"The children. It's possible, just possible they're in the attic," Kathleen replied in a rush.

"The attic has been searched."

"Nicole showed them the hidden staircase," Devon explained.

"The maid was straightening the room about the time they disappeared." Kathleen could barely stand still. She had to hurry. The attic was vast and unheated, a death-trap almost as surely as the thin ice on the lake....

Edward motioned to the desk clerk. "Bring the passkey and turn on the lights up there from the master switch."

"Yes, the key," Nicole whispered breathlessly. "I left my bag in the suite."

"We'll come, too," William said.

It was Nicole who stepped forward, who took charge. "No. I think it's best if most of us stay here. The children are frightened. It will terrify them if we are all tramping around up there like a herd of elephants." She took Karla Drakik's hand and led her back to the couch. "We'll wait together." She turned her head. "Go with Devon, Kathleen."

"Hurry," Kathleen urged, stepping back so the clerk could precede her down the narrow hallway. "Hurry."

When they entered the room that had once been Margaret Ingalls's, and years earlier, Judson's before her, Devon went immediately to the far side of the fireplace and touched a place on the paneled wall. A small door swung outward, revealing a stairway Judson Ingalls's father had built to satisfy a little boy's dream of playing knights and dragons in the vast, empty space above. Brick stepped forward with a large flashlight. Devon paused, his hand on the knob that could be used to push the door open from the inside—if you knew where the release catch was and could find it in the dark.

"Sorry, Brick, but my mother's right. If they're up there, they're scared and hiding from loud noises and loud voices and men in uniforms. It might be better if we go up alone."

Brick nodded and handed him the torch. "You'll need this."

Devon held out his free hand to Kathleen. "Ready, Kath? Let's go look for our kids."

There was no convenient layer of dust on the risers to indicate that two small children had climbed ahead of them. Kathleen swallowed her disappointment and followed Devon up the steep, narrow staircase into the big, echoing space beyond. The row of utility bulbs affixed to the main beam shed only enough light to banish the shadows from directly beneath them.

Kathleen found herself silently repeating every prayer she'd learned since childhood. The attic was terribly cold, and she shivered uncontrollably. "Andrej! Marta! It's Kathleen. Are you here?" she called, her voice echoing oddly among the flotsam and jetsam of years and lifetimes.

The answering silence was awful and complete. There was no sound of small bodies stirring, not even the sound of wind in the eaves. Nothing.

"Andrej. Marta." Devon didn't raise his voice, only called to them, as if they were in the activities room and he had come to fetch them. "C'mon, kids. It's getting late.

You missed dinner. If you want a pizza you'd better come out now. The kitchen is about to close down for the night."

He half turned, giving Kathleen a rueful smile and holding out his hand once more. "Andrej never turns down a chance for pizza," he whispered. *A small thing to know, a loving thing.* Kathleen choked back a sob, taking the hand he offered as they started forward down the length of the big room. Devon shone the flashlight back and forth. Kathleen hardly dared breathe for fear she would miss something, some sound or movement.

They went all the way to the small gable window, a trip that took only minutes, but to Kathleen's overwrought nerves seemed to last for hours. Then they turned and started back. Kathleen was aware of every footfall, every breath they took. They walked past trunks and old dressers, a wicker rocking chair that creaked slightly as they passed. Kathleen swiveled her head, her eyes straining into the darkness, but the chair was empty, with no small body curled up on the wide seat. Panic assailed her, forced its way into her throat. She bit back a sob.

Something moved back near the eaves. A whisper, a clunk, as though a small shoe had kicked a box or trunk. They froze where they stood.

"Andrej? Marta? Come out, kids," Devon called, his voice wonderfully normal, unconcerned, his hand as cold as ice in hers. "C'mon. It's Devon and Kathleen. It's all right. C'mon to Devon."

And then they heard it—a small voice, high-pitched, uncertain, calling their names. "Devon. Kathleen."

"Marta?" Devon's voice cracked on the word. He shook his head, as though getting his emotions under control. "Marta?"

"Devon!"

"Yes, sweetie." Devon played the flashlight over a pile of boxes and trunks pushed up against the eaves. Marta's small white face peered over one of them.

"Andrej sleep." She turned and pointed into the darkness. "Here."

"Devon! She's speaking English." Kathleen's legs refused to hold her. *When she's ready she'll start talking.* She sank to her knees on the plank floor and held out her arms. "Marta. Sweetheart, come to Kathleen."

Devon lifted Marta from behind the trunk and set her in Kathleen's lap. He played the flashlight over the little girl. Her face was dirty. There were cobwebs in her hair. She was wrapped in some kind of shawl, a horrible, gaudy thing in shades of green and gold, which smelled of dust and mothballs and made Kathleen sneeze. None of it mattered. She pulled Marta close against her and kissed her. "Oh darling, I'm so glad to see you."

"Hi," Marta said, and snuggled against her.

"Devon." Kathleen was laughing, crying as she rocked Marta in her arms. "She's speaking English! I wonder how many words she knows? How did she learn?"

"Heigh-ho," Devon said, with a shrug and a grin. He hunkered down and shone the flashlight into the darkness. "Andrej," he called softly. "Wake up. C'mon, old buddy. There's nothing to be scared of here. Not at Timberlake. Not with Kathleen and me to look after you. C'mon out." Moments later the little boy emerged from the dark nest, wrapped in an old overcoat he had probably found in the same trunk as Marta's shawl, and threw himself into Devon's waiting arms.

"Andrej, baby, why did you run away?" Kathleen reached out a free hand. Her children. *Their children.*

Andrej rubbed a grimy fist in his eye. "Too many people. Too much yelling. And the guns. Gunfire," he said, sniffing back a tear.

"That wasn't gunfire, buddy." Devon pulled a clean white handkerchief out of his pocket." His hands were shaking, Kathleen noticed. He was shaking all over, but he wiped the tearstains and dust smudges from Andrej's face with sure, gentle strokes. "It was only thunder and lightning. You don't have to be scared of gunfire ever again."

He loved these children. Loved them more than life itself.

And she loved him. Had always loved him. Would always love him. The certainty of it was complete and absolute and hit her with the intensity of a sunburst.

And she loved him for all the right reasons, although she'd been too stubborn and too foolish to see past her own self-righteous prejudice. Devon's authority, his air of command didn't come from privilege and a vast fortune. It came from within, from hard-earned experience and integrity. She was the one who was afraid of what money could do. She was the one who feared that she wasn't strong enough, or good enough, to withstand the temptation of power and wealth.

"No guns. No bad men. Not again. Promise." Andrej threw his arms around Devon's neck, squeezed tight against him. "And no more fights."

"No more fights. I promise, son." Devon was no longer smiling. His expression was guarded, grim. "Kathleen and I will never fight again."

"Devon?"

"Let's get them back downstairs, Kathleen." He looked straight through her. "They've been up here for hours. They're tired and they're scared and hungry."

"Yes, of course." She could hear footsteps on the stairs, voices coming closer. "Then we'll talk—"

"Yes, Kathleen," he said wearily. "We'll talk."

He stood up, Andrej still in his arms, and held out his hand to help her rise. But it was as if she no longer existed for him, as though they were already miles apart, a chasm between them.

It was over. He was going to leave her. There was nothing she could say or do to change his mind, and the inevitability of it cleaved her heart like a knife.

KATHLEEN SAT on the edge of her bed and watched her children sleep. Dawn light filled the room, pushing back the shadows of the long, terrifying night just past. The last of the searchers had left less than an hour ago. The suite was quiet. The hotel was quiet, at least for a little while, until the hustle and bustle of a new day began.

The little girl hadn't spoken again, not until they were back in the suite with platters of sandwiches and cookies spread out on the table, and then she had demanded pancakes, and with only a little prompting from Andrej, maple syrup to go with them. Ten minutes later the head chef herself had delivered the requested delicacies, received Marta's "thank you very much," and, beaming with pride, set the seal on the celebration that followed.

But the children were bewildered by the number of people crowded into the suite, the hugs and kisses and tears of joy and thanksgiving. They ate too much and drank too much and refused to go to sleep in their own beds. They wanted to know where Devon was, and were only somewhat mollified when Kathleen explained that he was with Brick Bauer, taking care of the paperwork their little adventure had generated, and would be back soon. Assurances she couldn't be certain weren't an out-and-out lie.

Finally Kathleen had tucked Andrej up in her bed, then sat down beside him holding Marta in her arms and rocked her to sleep, humming a lullaby under her breath.

Anxiety set razor-sharp claws in her heart. *Where was Devon?* Surely he hadn't left the hotel without telling her. He had promised he would stay with them, promised to always be there for her. But that had been yesterday, a lifetime ago.

She reached out to brush a wisp of red-gold hair from Marta's forehead, but before her fingers touched the sleeping child a breath of air stirred the gossamer strands, settling them into place. *A breath of air? Or angel wings?*

"Rujana?" she whispered. "Help me. Help me get Devon back so we can be the family you wanted us to be."

"Kathleen?" She hadn't heard the outer door open or close, hadn't heard him come into the quiet suite.

"I'm here, Devon." She hoped because she was whispering that he wouldn't hear the catch in her voice. He appeared in the doorway of her bedroom, a dark silhouette against the light. "I—I was afraid you might already have left the hotel."

"I almost did. But something stopped me."

"You couldn't leave without saying goodbye to the children."

"No," he said. "I couldn't leave without saying goodbye. But I am leaving Tyler, Kath. I'm going as soon as the children wake up. I want—"

Fear was like a living thing inside her. Dread threatened to choke off her words. Then once more Kathleen felt a faint stirring of air currents, the brush of wings against her cheek. Her panic fled. She had to get control of herself. She had to be strong, sure of herself. She had to get past the hurt and anger she heard threaded through his words, and fight her hardest to get him back. She stood, took a step toward him. "No, Devon, please don't leave us."

Anguish twisted his mouth, darkened his eyes to charcoal. "God, Kathleen. Don't do this to me."

"Devon, you promised we'd take this marriage one day at a time."

"It was a mistake," he said, his voice a low rasping growl. "I can't do it. I'm not made of stone."

Kathleen called on all her strength, all her reserves of willpower and determination. She had to make him understand. She had to make him realize how much she loved him. How much she wanted him. "Our bargain *was* a mistake, Devon," she said, seeing him absorb the words as though each and every one was an arrow through his body. She held out her hands, took his between them. He resisted slightly, as though her touch were fire, but she drew them to her heart. "It was a terrible mistake to try and make a business deal out of the most sacred compact two human beings can enter into. I don't want to renegotiate our marriage every day, Devon."

"Kathleen? What are you getting at?" He didn't pull away from her embrace, but neither did he return it. She ruthlessly ignored the almost overpowering desire to throw herself into his arms, pull his wide, chiseled mouth down to hers and kiss him until everything that stood between them was consumed in the inferno of her love. But that would be the easy way out, and in the long run, when the heat of their passion had melted away, the questions and uncertainties would still remain.

She lifted her face to his, met his onyx gaze head-on, unflinching, letting him look deep into her soul. "I'm saying I love you, Devon Addison. I've always loved you, and if you don't love me back I have no one to blame but myself."

"Kathleen, nothing's changed since yesterday. I'm still the same man I was twenty-four hours ago, when you thought you couldn't spend another night under the same roof with me."

His hands were like ice between hers. Doubts flared inside her again, searing her heart, sapping her courage, but she beat back the darkness. "I know you haven't changed, Devon. But I have."

He was very still. She could hear him breathing, see the steady beat of his pulse where the collar of his shirt lay unbuttoned at his throat, feel the echo of her own heartbeat against his fingertips. "What do you mean?"

"I'm not the same woman I was four years ago. I didn't want to admit that to myself at first, but I am. I didn't want to admit that my life wasn't going to be exactly like my parents', with the same joys and sorrows, the same challenges and struggles. I didn't want to admit that I wanted all the good things that money and power and prestige could bring to my life." She took a deep breath, lifted her chin a fraction of an inch. "I didn't have faith in myself, in my values and principles. I didn't have faith in you."

"I want the same things you do, Kathleen. I always have."

"I know." She couldn't stop the tears that had been blurring his face as she blinked to hold them back. She stopped fighting the upwelling of emotion, let them fall. "A home. A family. Love. I do love you, Devon Addison. With all my heart and with all my soul. No strings attached."

He watched her for a long time, searching her soul, and she let him. Then he smiled, and Kathleen's heart jumped up into her throat, beating so hard she could feel the blood rush through every inch of her body. Devon shifted his grip, brought her hands to his lips. "I've waited a long time to hear you say that."

"I love you," she repeated, so that there would be no mistaking. "I'll love you until the earth falls into the sun and beyond. And I need you, Devon. I'll go on needing you every day for the rest of my life. But most of all I want you. I want you as the father of all my children, as my lover, my friend."

"No, Kathleen," he said, very quietly.

"No? Devon—"

He hushed her with a finger to her lips. He lifted the fine gold chain from her breast, snapping the delicate links so that the heavy gold wedding band lay free in the hollow of his palm. He looked down at the ring and then back into Kathleen's eyes. "The first time Rujana asked me to marry you in the middle of a war. The second time *you* asked me to marry you in a lawyer's office. Both times we did the right thing for the wrong reasons. We couldn't get past the problems, see past the barricades we'd both thrown up to protect ourselves from any more heartache. This time is going to be different. This time I'm doing the asking. And for one reason and one reason alone."

He took the heavy gold band and slipped it onto the third finger of her left hand. Kathleen held her breath, didn't dare look up, didn't dare look away. "I love you, Kathleen Kelsey Addison, with all my heart and all my soul. I want you. I need you. Stay with me for all our lives and beyond. Say yes, Kathleen. Say you'll marry me, and we'll keep each other focused on what's true and certain so that nothing will ever come between us again. Be my wife, my lover and the mother of all our children.'' He leaned close, brushed his lips across hers, sealing the vow. And then she felt him smile again before his mouth claimed hers for a kiss that she would remember all her life long. ''After all, don't they say the third time's the charm?''

EPILOGUE

"QUITE A TURNOUT, wouldn't you say?" Edward Wocheck observed, coming to stand beside his stepson on the catwalk outside Alyssa's office at Ingalls F and M.

Devon rested both hands on the waist-high railing and gazed onto the factory floor below. He grinned. "Looks like the whole town is here tonight."

"Why not? Judson lays on a good feed, as they used to say in these parts."

"Alyssa's idea of having the Christmas party here this year to celebrate the grand reopening of the F and M was a masterstroke."

"I'll tell her you said that."

"I already have told her."

Devon rested one hip against the black iron railing and they both looked down on the festivities below. The huge machinery was buffed and polished to high sheen, the floors immaculate. People wandered up and down the aisles, dressed in their holiday best as they toured the facility. Judson and Alyssa had decided to incorporate every latest technological advance as they rebuilt, and the F and M manufacturing process was now state of the art, a model of precision and efficiency. Tonight the factory was idle, on show, but come Monday morning it would be back to work for everyone. Orders were pouring in. It was going to be a good year.

At one end of the facility a hearty buffet was displayed beneath a canopy decorated with evergreens and poinsettias and a myriad of tiny twinkling lights. A second canopy showcased a local dance band providing Judson and Alyssa's guests with musical entertainment. In the middle of the large open space, in reality the factory loading area, a twelve-foot Christmas tree held pride of place, its lower branches hidden by the enormous pile of gaily wrapped presents destined for the children of Tyler's less fortunate families.

Chairs and tables were grouped in concentric circles around the huge tree, candles flickering from red and green and gold tinsel centerpieces. People were eating, dancing, laughing, talking. Outside it was snowing, big white flakes that coated the ground and stuck to the bare branches of the trees like sugar sparkles. "Christmas-card perfect," Nicole had said earlier, with only the faintest touch of irony in her voice. "Small-town America at its best."

Mother, you don't know how right you are, Devon thought with a grin.

"It's been a hell of a year," Edward said, handing the younger man a glass of punch before copying Devon's relaxed stance.

"Amen to that." Devon took a swallow, looked down at the glass of red liquid and then at the older man. "This is no ordinary punch," he said, taking another, bigger swallow.

"I borrowed some of Judson's private stock from his office," Edward admitted. "I thought it needed a little kick."

"A definite improvement." Devon lifted his glass in a salute. "To the New Year."

"To your new family," Edward added.

"I'll drink to that." Devon drained his glass, then returned his attention to the milling throng below. He spotted Liza and Cliff Forrester heading for the buffet with Sheila and Douglas Wagner. One table seemed filled with members of the Tyler Quilting Circle, the ladies in flowered dresses and snowy-white sweaters squired by a band of elderly gentlemen, including Phil Wocheck and newlywed Clarence Stirling. Flashbulbs were going off here and there as representatives from the area papers snapped photos of the event. Rob Friedman himself was covering the occasion for the *Tyler Citizen*.

Devon saw Judson and Alyssa moving through the crowd welcoming newcomers, accepting congratulations on the reopening of the F and M, making one and all welcome for the evening. Alyssa, regal in black and gold, had even talked her father into donning a tuxedo for the speeches that would come later at the ribbon-cutting ceremony.

Devon scanned the assembly. He was looking for Kathleen and the children, but so far he hadn't seen them. Then his gaze dropped to a table almost directly below him. There, surrounded by an admiring group of well-wishers, sat Reverend Sarah Kenton, the proud mother of Tyler's newest citizen. And there, also, he saw his wife, her dark hair pulled into a soft knot on top of her head, her emerald-green dress the perfect foil for her creamy skin. She lifted her hand to touch the top of the baby's head and her wedding band gleamed golden in the candlelight.

Cece Baron was holding Damian Baron Kenton, laughing and tickling him under the chin. Something had happened between Jeff and Michael Kenton the night Damian was born. Devon suspected it was the fact that they both saw something of each other in the little boy, a continuation of the blood they shared, an affirmation of life and love, and hopes and dreams for the future. If he couldn't yet say the two men were friends, they were at least coming to terms with being brothers. It was a beginning.

As Devon watched, Cece handed Damian to Kathleen, who bent toward the small bundle, her hair shining in the candlelight, her head turned just enough that Devon could see the curve of her mouth as she smiled at the little one. Something tightened inside him, a ripple of wonder and anticipation that lanced through his heart like an arrow. He sucked in his breath, amazed as always when he realized that Kathleen was his, heart and soul, truly and forever. In a few weeks, when they completed the religious counseling that Father Hennesey and the Church required, they would be married for the third and last time in the church where generations of Kathleen's relatives had been married and baptized and sung to rest.

And soon after that, he hoped, they would have a child of their own. At first Devon had resisted the idea of having a baby right away. But then he'd looked at his wife and realized that if anyone could do it all, be wife and mother and businesswoman, it was his Kathleen.

Marta and Annie and Belle Baron ran up to admire the baby. They leaned against Kathleen's knees, oohing and aahing over Damian's tiny fingers and nose. Andrej and Laura's boys were somewhere back among the machinery, getting the cook's tour with Johnny Kelsey. Margaret Alyssa ran up, whispered in the little girls' ears and they all raced away from the table, Marta laughing at the top of her voice.

Devon closed his eyes briefly against another thrust of happiness so sharp it almost hurt. Marta, silent so long, had turned into the world's biggest chatterbox. She was learning English so quickly her tutor could barely keep up with her. And both children were slowly but surely putting the horror and sadness of their past behind them, growing into the strong, happy children Rujana and Josef had so wanted them to be. They were doing so well that plans were in the works for them to travel to Cleveland to visit the Drakiks before the end of summer. Meanwhile the adoption would be final in a few weeks. To Kathleen and Devon's great joy, the children were all theirs.

"There's your mother," Edward said, nudging his arm. "I understand she's planning to stay on in Tyler until after Christmas."

"Yes," Devon said, watching as his mother, a vision in a plum velvet minidress with a jacket heavily embroidered in jet beads, paused to admire the little one. "And then she's going to Aspen to ski. But she says she'll be back in the spring."

"House hunting?" Edward asked, producing a slim silver flask from his inside coat pocket and proceeding to top up their drinks.

"Yes." Devon's grin was rueful this time. "But not here, thank God." He laughed. "I didn't mean that the way it sounds."

The look Edward gave him was sympathetic. "I know what you mean. I was married to the woman for eleven years."

"Actually, she's thinking of living in Washington."

"Ah. Then what Kathleen told me was true. Nicole has political aspirations for you."

"She can aspire all she wants," Devon said, amazed to see his mother take the Kenton infant into her arms. "I'm not running for office. Any kind of office. I've told her that."

"Good luck," Edward said, chuckling. "That only means she'll probably try to get you an ambassadorship."

Devon groaned. "Oh God, I never thought of that."

A movement below caught Edward's eye. "Alyssa's waving me down. Must be time for the ribbon cutting. Are you coming?"

"I'll be right behind you."

Edward paused a moment. "Seriously, now, are you comfortable with the choices you've made?"

"Do you mean planning to live here, in Tyler?"

"Yes."

"It doesn't seem to have done you any harm," Devon observed.

"I was born to it," Edward reminded him.

Devon glanced over the railing once more, saw Kathleen look around, then lift her face to his. She smiled, and he knew beyond any doubt that his choices had all been the right ones. "This is where I want to be. I've known that for a long time."

"It's not what you're used to. Quiet and off the beaten track."

"Oh, I don't know about that," Devon said, throwing his arm around his stepfather's shoulders. "I've come to the conclusion that if you take the time to look around Tyler, Wisconsin, you'll find there's almost always something interesting going on."

LOOK FOR OUR FOUR FABULOUS MEN!

Each month some of today's bestselling authors bring
four new fabulous men to Harlequin American Romance.
Whether they're rebel ranchers, millionaire power brokers
or sexy single dads, they're all gallant princes—and
they're all ready to sweep you into lighthearted fantasies
and contemporary fairy tales where anything is possible
and where all your dreams come true!

You don't even have to make a wish...Harlequin American
Romance will grant your every desire!

Look for Harlequin American Romance wherever Harlequin
books are sold!

SILHOUETTE®

Desire®

Do you want...

Dangerously handsome heroes

Evocative, everlasting love stories

Sizzling and tantalizing sensuality

Incredibly sexy miniseries like **MAN OF THE MONTH**

Red-hot romance

Enticing entertainment that can't be beat!

You'll find all of this, and much *more* each and every month in **SILHOUETTE DESIRE**. Don't miss these unforgettable love stories by some of romance's hottest authors. Silhouette Desire—where your fantasies will always come true....

DES-GEN

Harlequin Romance ®

Delightful

Affectionate

Romantic

Emotional

Tender

Original

Daring

Riveting

Enchanting

Adventurous

Moving

Harlequin Romance—the
series that has it all!

HROM-G

WAYS TO *UNEXPECTEDLY* MEET MR. RIGHT:

♡ Go out with the sexy-sounding stranger your daughter secretly set you up with through a personal ad.

♡ RSVP yes to a wedding invitation—soon it might be your turn to say "I do!"

♡ Receive a marriage proposal by mail— from a man you've never met....

These are just a few of the unexpected ways that written communication leads to love in Silhouette Yours Truly.

Each month, look for two fast-paced, fun and flirtatious Yours Truly novels (with entertaining treats and sneak previews in the back pages) by some of your favorite authors—and some who are sure to become favorites.

YOURS TRULY™:
Love—when you least expect it!

HARLEQUIN PRESENTS®

HARLEQUIN PRESENTS
men you won't be able to resist falling in love with...

HARLEQUIN PRESENTS
women who have feelings just like your own...

HARLEQUIN PRESENTS
powerful passion in exotic international settings...

HARLEQUIN PRESENTS
intense, dramatic stories that will keep you turning
to the very last page...

HARLEQUIN PRESENTS
The world's bestselling romance series!

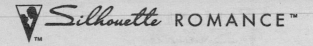

Silhouette ROMANCE™

What's a single dad to do when he needs a wife by next Thursday?

Who's a confirmed bachelor to call when he finds a baby on his doorstep?

How does a plain Jane in love with her gorgeous boss get him to notice her?

From classic love stories to romantic comedies to emotional heart tuggers, **Silhouette Romance** offers six irresistible novels every month by some of your favorite authors!
Such as...beloved bestsellers **Diana Palmer,**
Annette Broadrick, Suzanne Carey, Elizabeth August
and **Marie Ferrarella,** to name just a few—and some sure to become favorites!

Fabulous Fathers...Bundles of Joy...Miniseries...
Months of blushing brides and convenient weddings...
Holiday celebrations... You'll find all this and much more in
Silhouette Romance—always emotional, always enjoyable, always about love!

SR-GEN